A Stroke of Murder

A Stroke of Murder

The Shepherd Sisters Mysteries

Tracy Gardner

TULE
PUBLISHING

Dedication

For my seventh-grade English teacher, Mrs. Nancy Stoner

You created a writer

Carson, Michigan

Clinic

Village Offices

Law Office

Fancy Tails & Treats

Giuseppes

SCHOOL

Lickety Split Ice Cream

Kate's Yoga

Miss Priscilla's

Sweet Shop

Halle's Berries

Carson Mansion

Mitten Inn

Carson Ballroom and Theatre

Carson Park

Carson Marina

CLDesigns

Chapter One

S AVANNA SHEPHERD SHOT a quick glance across Main Street toward her sister's law office, but there was still no activity. She checked her watch, counting the minutes until she'd need to leave, possibly without seeing her fiancé. Her steaming mocha latte was a poor choice for the current unseasonably warm weather. December in Michigan usually meant snow. Each year, she looked forward to the cold, crisp weather, a freshly fallen blanket of snow bringing with it the extra sparkle of the season. But despite the wreaths and ribbons decorating each lamppost up and down Main Street and the fake snow in the window display at Fancy Tails and Treats, the spring-like temperatures lately made it nearly impossible to imagine the winter festival kickoff next week.

She'd convinced Carson City Council to greenlight funding for Frosty Fest, contracted with vendors for the weeklong event, and secured renowned ice sculptor Lars Anders and his team to create an evolving labyrinth of elaborate sculptures in Carson's lakefront park. Patrons would stroll through the entrance to the park near the towering Christmas tree, take in the ice sculpture exhibits, go for a spin on the ice-skating rink or visit with Santa Claus, and grab some hot cocoa and cookies while listening to live music. Savanna's friend and colleague Britt had connected her with the sculptor through their museum's curator.

The entire Shepherd family was involved in Frosty Fest in one way or another. Youngest sister Sydney's dog-centric bakery and grooming salon Fancy Tails and Treats was sponsoring a multi-category pet photo contest. Skylar and Travis were running the hot chocolate booth a few of the days. Uncle Max was supplying red and green carnation corsages from his flower shop across the street from the dog salon. Savanna had somehow convinced her friend Jack Carson to step into Santa's shoes and take toy requests from Carson's ten and under population. Most of the kids in town knew him as the elementary school librarian; she'd often cross the hall from her art classroom for lunch in the library with Jack and his girlfriend Elaina, a third-grade teacher. He'd worried one of the students might know it was him, but last week's test run with the Santa suit, beard and glasses, and a whole lot of padding around the middle made him unrecognizable.

This morning was the last day of school before winter break. Thank goodness it had only been a half day; the kids were all wildly squirrely and hyped up. Last week, when she'd scheduled today's meeting in the park with the ice sculptor, she'd envisioned talking through details while their words froze into opaque puffs suspended in the winter air. She'd also envisioned Aidan being part of their little group today since his clinic was one of the event's sponsors. But her fiancé had far bigger concerns than a festival.

Right now, Aidan Gallager was in a deposition with Jillian Black of Black, Jones, and Sydowski, doing everything possible to retain full custody of his seven-year-old daughter. Dr. Gallager was revered in the community, a noteworthy cardiothoracic surgeon who doubled as the primary care doctor most of Carson's residents trusted with their lives. Their little Lake Michigan town was lucky to have him. So were his daughter's grandparents—his late wife's parents— who were suing him.

Savanna placed a hand on her knee in an effort to still the nervous energy she'd had trouble controlling lately. Her jingle bells were driving her nuts; she'd worn the silver bell earrings with red bows her friend Yvonne gave her last Christmas, shooting for festive but not even thinking about the constant jingling in her ears with any kind of jostling. She'd tough it out until the Frosty Fest meeting was over and then these babies were being retired.

At the traffic light up the street, Britt Nash's car appeared. That was her cue. She slung her tote bag over one shoulder and stood at the curb, hailing them as if the little hybrid EV was a taxi. She'd walk back to her car up Main Street later. Britt came to a stop, leaning over the pretty woman in the passenger seat.

"Savanna. Didn't your parents ever teach you it's dangerous to hitchhike?" Britt gave her a mock stern look, her friend's close-cropped blond hair, tiny diamond earring, and stylish gray plaid suit lending them a young David Bowie vibe.

"Didn't your parents ever teach you not to pick up hitchhikers? How do you know I'm not a serial killer?" She smiled at Britt's girlfriend, also the Lansing Museum curator. "Hey Helene, how are you? Mind if I hop in?"

"I don't know. You might be a serial killer," Helene teased. A few years older than Britt, the curator was lovely, her porcelain beauty set off by her shiny black bob and signature red lips. In the few times they'd crossed paths while Savanna worked in the Lansing Museum of Fine Art this past summer, Helene Devereaux was always friendly and went out of her way to be helpful.

"We'll take our chances," Britt said. "You look harmless enough to me."

She climbed into the back seat. "They always do, you know. The perfectly polite neighbor or always helpful friend you'd never suspect of having bodies in their basement."

"True. It could be me, y'know," Britt said. "You could both be in danger."

"Pfft. As if," Savanna scoffed. "Have you met you?"

Helene shuddered. "Okay let's change the subject. You two are getting too creepy for me."

In the rearview mirror, Britt raised one eyebrow at Savanna. "Helene has a point. Probably not the best topic to joke about. Your little town seems to have an unusually high casualty rate. Wasn't the last murder just a couple months ago?"

"I don't think that counts. That happened way out in the woods south of the dunes. Sebastian's place isn't in Carson proper."

"A technicality. Carson's more than just your cute little downtown." The car turned into the parking area, the blue of the sky and Lake Michigan in the distance beyond.

Savanna laughed. "Well, cute or not, we may not even get to have the Frosty Fest we've spent this past month prepping for. Our famous, costly ice sculptor can't sculpt a thing unless the forecast changes." With wide-open spaces and winding walking trails devoid of a speck of snow, Carson Park offered ample space for the event, the entrance near the two-story high evergreen tree that awaited the tree-lighting ceremony next week.

The smaller evergreen that stood year-round near the statue of Jessamina Carson was already lit. In a phenomenon that had begun while Savanna was living across the lake in Chicago, the modestly sized tree transformed each December into The Gifting Tree. A hand-painted wooden sign declared the title and simple instructions. It appeared at the beginning of December along with a storage bin of paper hang tags on ribbon, pens, and an assortment of bows. She'd noticed it last year and asked her sister about it—shop owner Sydney normally knew all when it came to Carson happenings. But she'd simply shrugged, saying it was a mystery; no one knew who'd started the tradition years earlier or why.

Savanna scowled at the beautifully landscaped park and wished fervently for snow. Even a little would help. "I really hope this wasn't a colossal mistake," she murmured.

"Don't be so dramatic," Britt said, flashing a quick grin. "The weather will turn in a few days; it always does. This is just Mother Nature messing with you for a minute."

"I hope Lars Anders will believe that, after I've convinced him to drive hours from the snowy Upper Peninsula down here to the tropics for our ice festival."

"Lars doesn't mind driving," Helene said. "When Lansing acquired his initial works years ago, we drove the sculptures all the way down from Quebec—a twelve-hour drive one way. He lives much closer now."

"Quebec? His website says he emigrated here from Norway," Savanna said.

"Originally, yes. He's been in Marquette on Lake Superior for years though. He likes the U.P.—maybe he loves the cold weather up there. But he knows Michigan weather is unpredictable, don't worry."

As they crossed the park to the gazebo, Savanna pulled her ringing phone from the pocket of her holiday-themed dress. Her stomach made a nauseating little flip. The screen displayed the name *Rob Havemeyer*, her former fiancé. She hadn't spoken with Rob in two years, since he broke off their engagement to "find himself." Looking back, she cringed thinking of his "it's not you, it's me" speech. She hesitated, uncertain what to do, finger hovering over the green button to accept the call, until it stopped ringing and was presumably routed to voicemail. Relief washed over her at having dodged the call, just as anxiety set in at the thought of checking his message later to see what in the world he wanted. She turned her volume off.

An ancient camper van pulled into the parking lot. The driver slowly emerged, unfolding himself and straightening extra-long legs, making her wonder how he even fit behind the wheel. Or why he'd want to—she'd read online that Anders netted seven figures annually through his sculpting work. He could afford a much newer, nicer vehicle. He crossed the lawn quickly in long strides, joining their group. Up close, his ruddy cheeks and red hair and beard atop the red and black checkered flannel button-down made her think of the lumberjack show she'd seen with her little nephew Nolan last summer on their family trip up north into the U.P.

After introductions were made, Savanna jumped in. "Mr. Anders, we—"

"Lars please," the ice sculptor interrupted. His voice was low and held the hint of an accent.

She handed him a copy of the festival map Yvonne had created. "Lars, we appreciate you traveling all the way down here. This should give you a good idea of where we imagine your ice sculptures being. The inside walking path begins here, loops around the center, and ends at the ice-skating rink near the concessions." She pointed across the expanse of pale green grass to the cordoned off skating rink with no ice to speak of.

"We've ordered frigid temps and a solid foot of snow for the event, don't worry," Britt threw in, smiling.

"No worries," Helene said, "Lars never commits to something unless he's sure it'll work out."

Anders glanced at Helene, an odd look passing between them. Savanna felt guiltier than ever for dragging him down here to shorts and sandals weather to discuss ice.

She took another stab at kick-starting the conversation. "I really admire your work. It never occurred to me that there might be a transition between sculpting from standard materials to creating ice sculptures."

"Yes. Thank you. I'll need to take measurements for the ice."

Savanna followed him, Britt and Helene trailing behind. From the small black bag he carried, he drew a measuring wheel, assembling it and rolling it along the inside path to the far side of the area and then all the way back around to where they stood. He folded Savanna's map in half and scribbled some numbers on the back using a charcoal pencil. "Eight large sculptures, smaller displays in between, and the entrance piece you asked for. With pedestals, lighting, and the generator truck for the chainsaws and ice-cutting equipment, it'll come in close to what I quoted you. I'll schedule a trip back down here for about halfway through the two weeks, shortly after Christmas. But an exhibit of this size won't be possible if the weather doesn't turn." The large man's tone was apologetic. "Have you thought about rescheduling?"

"I—no. With the holiday just around the corner, I don't think we could."

"Perhaps it could be pushed back a week or so? Lars has a point," Helene said. "I'm sure you could get the word out in time if it had to be changed."

Savanna's mind raced. If they moved Frosty Fest out until after Christmas, her time would be consumed with managing the kickoff details, when she should be focusing on her New Year's Eve wedding. Waiting all the way into January wasn't a great alternative either, as so much of what she'd planned was holiday-themed.

Britt read her mind. "Delaying it isn't possible. It'll all turn out fine, I'm positive." Her friend's unwarranted confidence was inspiring.

"Let's play it by ear. I wouldn't say it's impossible," Savanna said. "I'll make it work if we have to reschedule; that is, if you and your team are available after Christmas?" she asked Lars.

He nodded. "I'll make it work," he echoed her.

"Great!" She cursed her inability to say no. Mother Nature really needed to come through for her.

After their little group had run through the rest of the Frosty Fest details, Lars departed. She hoped he was satisfied with the details of their arrangement. He'd been so deadpan and expressionless throughout their meeting, it was hard to tell for sure. She'd reserved a small block of rooms at nearby Mitten Inn for the sculptor and his crew, so they could get started this weekend, but she understood why he instead just headed back up north. There was no point in him staying in this balmy weather. Britt dropped her at her car. Before climbing out of the back seat of Britt's EV, she leaned into the front seat, giving Britt and Helene a quick one-armed hug. "Keep wishing for snow!"

"Oh!" Britt stopped her with a hand on her arm. "Your wedding invitation came yesterday. It's lovely! I mailed in the response card for Helene and myself, but you know we wouldn't miss it. The Carson Ballroom will make a beautiful reception venue."

Helene smiled, adding, "We'll have our dancing shoes on. I ordered the cutest dress to wear, and Britt has a gorgeous suit picked out already."

"Of course I do. I may take it for a test run at the gala Saturday. Are you getting excited? Are you mostly ready for the wedding and reception?" Britt asked her.

"It sort of doesn't seem real yet. We've got all the details confirmed, Uncle Max is doing the flowers, my final fitting is next Thursday... everything's going perfectly." They hadn't yet discussed where they'd live, which worried her. They'd made a plan to sit down and figure it out, but that meeting kept getting pushed in favor of more immediate issues.

"As it should," Britt said. "It will be perfect. You deserve it."

She smiled. "Thank you. Both."

Savanna's cell phone rang over her car's Bluetooth system as she drove past her sister's law office. Aidan's car was gone from the parking lot; he must be finished. She nearly answered the call on a reflex before seeing Rob's name again on her phone screen. She'd never changed his contact info in her phone when they got serious; not even after he'd proposed. Rob had no pet name or cute little heart next to his name, like her younger sister's new husband had. Why had she not noticed back then that they'd become more like business partners in the end than a couple in love? She took a deep breath and summoned her confidence.

"Hi Rob. How are you?"

"Savanna. Thank you for taking my call. I'm sorry to bother you. How are you?"

"I'm... good. What's going on?"

"I ah—this is awkward, I know—and maybe you can't help, but I have to ask. It's worth a try. It's Mother."

She waited, but he didn't continue. "What happened to your mother? What's worth trying?"

"She was attacked. It happened two nights ago. We had a break-in and a significant theft; Kenilworth's security system was breeched but we don't know how."

"Oh no—is your mom all right?" Savanna couldn't imagine how Kenilworth had been broken into either; the place was a fortress. But her concern over Faye Havemeyer outweighed any curiosity regarding what might have been taken. She and Rob's mother had been close, and that had taken some doing. Faye was an imposing, intimidating woman, commanding respect and difficult to impress. Earning her trust as an art authenticator at Kenilworth had taken months, and gaining acceptance as Faye's future daughter-in-law took much longer, but once she'd cleared those hurdles, Rob's mom had embraced her as part of the family. When Rob's father unceremoniously terminated her employment the same day Rob dumped her, Faye had argued, butting heads with the patriarch of the family. She'd followed Savanna out to her car, apologizing for the two Havemeyer men who'd just upended her life. The next day, a glowing letter of recommendation from Faye on Kenilworth letterhead was delivered to her by courier. In the end, she hadn't needed it, not to trade Chicago for her little hometown and Kenilworth for Carson Elementary, but she'd been floored by the gesture. "What happened? Is she badly hurt?" she repeated.

"She's in the ICU at Northwestern Memorial. They say she's critical but stable, whatever that means. She—" He paused, and when he spoke again his voice was thick. "Her arm is broken. And she has a periorbital fracture. The bone under her left eye is… it's shattered."

"My God," Savanna breathed. "Will she… do they expect her to be okay?"

"She had to stabilize enough before they could take her into surgery. The surgeon says she'll need pins or nails or something to fix the bones in her forearm. The swelling from the area around her eye has been the biggest problem. She looks—" Rob's voice cracked. He fell quiet.

Savanna realized she'd passed the turn for her street. Her mind was consumed with images of Faye. It all sounded horrible. "I'm so sorry. Who would do this? It sounds brutal. She must have been terrified."

"Security was there, but the surveillance video footage shows it happening so fast, there was no time for them to get to her and intervene. I'm—listen, I didn't call you to complain about what happened or get your sympathy, though I appreciate it. I didn't really expect you to take my call at all."

"Of course I'd take your call." She made a right turn into deserted Carson Marina, wanting to focus on the conversation. She parked in her usual spot near the dock that led to hers and Aidan's boat slip. The Catalina sailboat they shared was now on blocks nearby, shrink-wrapped and tucked in for the winter.

There was a beat of silence. "We've never really talked about what happened. That's my fault. I'm sorry, Savanna."

She was taken aback by his direct approach. She had no desire to rehash their breakup. "It's been over two years. I'm fine. We're fine—right? We can put the past behind us." For a split second, she imagined herself still in Chicago, married to Rob, working for his family; she shuddered. She hadn't realized until she came home how much she'd missed her sisters, her family, her little town and all that came with it. She'd never have met Aidan. She'd never have discovered how much she loved teaching, how self-sufficient she could be, or how easily a tiny girl like Mollie could infiltrate her heart.

"Yes. You're right," Rob said. Where she expected to hear the relief of absolution, his uncertain tone instead conflicted with his words. "I'm glad you're okay."

His arrogance needled her. As if she'd still be a mess, a completely decimated pile of mush on the floor because he'd left her. This was the Rob she remembered. She redirected the conversation. "Is there something in particular I can do to help with your mother? I was worried something was wrong when your number came up."

"Your intuition was right. Which is, I guess, why I'm calling you. It would be easier to explain in person."

She frowned, fighting against the concern that he might have ulterior motives. She'd been with him nearly seven years. Everything they'd been through didn't negate her regard for Faye Havemeyer. "I can come there, if you think I should. I feel awful for your mom; if I can help, I will. I'd love to see her."

"I'm sure she'd like that," he said. "But my flight lands in

Lansing this afternoon. Could we sit down and talk? Please. I won't take much of your time, I promise."

She was quiet simply due to surprise. There was no way she could leave the state if one of her parents was injured and awaiting surgery. "I can meet you. That way you'll be able to get back quickly. I'm sure it was difficult to leave her in that condition. We can grab a conference room to talk at the Lansing Museum of Fine Art, not far from the airport. I consult for them."

"I actually knew that," he said, his tone sheepish. "I've been following your career a little. The museum is perfect. I'd actually planned to try to get a meeting with your director and security team there before I fly back tonight; I left a message with your front of house person. Kenilworth's security has reason to believe your Lansing museum is one of the next targets."

Chapter Two

SAVANNA PULLED INTO her driveway to find Aidan waiting on her deck. The run-down fixer-upper home she'd bought was now, finally, finished with renovations, and the deck overlooking the dunes and Lake Michigan was her favorite part of the house. He'd used the key she'd given him to set her little dog free. Fonzie sprinted off the deck and met her in the driveway, the Boston Terrier's black-and-white body nearly vibrating with excitement as if he hadn't seen her in years, though she'd only been gone a couple hours.

"Okay, okay, I missed you too," she said, laughing. When the dog had received ample ear scratches, he ran back over to Aidan. She climbed the stairs to her deck, trying to read her fiancé's expression.

He encircled her in his arms, and she pressed her face briefly against his warm neck, breathing in his clean, enticing scent. She looked up, searching his gaze for some indication of how things had gone with the lawyers. The navy blue of his Brooks Brothers suit made his eyes seem an even lighter blue than usual. Before she could ask, he spoke. "My in-laws have agreed to a mediation. Jillian has a call scheduled with their lawyer, and they'll decide on a date."

"What does that mean? Is she optimistic this can be

worked out?" Jillian Black was excellent, according to Skylar. Aidan was in good hands.

"She's confident," he said. "The mediation means we'll sit down in a room with our lawyers and an impartial third party and hope to come to an agreement that will satisfy both parties. Jillian thinks she can get Tom and Jean to agree to a loose custody agreement granting them one weekend per month plus one additional overnight every other week."

She was flooded with relief. "That's good, right?"

"Definitely. I asked her to add in some verbiage that allows flexibility in scheduling. They have Mollie about that often now, or a little more. I don't want the Becketts to think I'm cutting back on their contact."

She pursed her lips. "I get that. But they're the ones who decided to sue without even speaking to you about their concerns."

"I know. Looking at it from their point of view, though, I can understand the fear of losing their only grandchild. Especially after losing their daughter."

She could understand where he was coming from, but Mollie's grandparents taking legal action before even talking with Aidan seemed like a red flag. She started to say as much but thought better of it. She was the catalyst in this whole thing, not Mollie, and not Aidan or his in-laws. Their fear had only reared its ugly head when she and Aidan had gotten engaged, his late-wife's parents abruptly deciding that Aidan marrying Savanna meant they'd better scramble to secure their rights, as if she was some wicked stepmother. She was doing everything in her power not to take it personally, but it sure felt personal.

"Mediation is a good thing," he reiterated, propping elbows on knees now and peering at her. "I don't want you to worry."

"There must be some way for me to show them I have no intention of interfering with the relationship they have with Mollie. Did you ask Jillian about my idea to write them a letter?"

He nodded. "I did. She said no, in case this goes to trial. I know it doesn't really make sense," he added. "She feels anything in writing could be misconstrued or taken out of context to use against me. She wants it to remain between me and the Becketts."

She sighed. It didn't feel exactly right to her, with the three of them about to become family. But she'd decided two months ago when he'd told her about the grandparents' rights case that she'd do whatever it took to ensure nothing interfered with Aidan maintaining full custody of Mollie. "It does make sense," she said. "I get it."

Aidan waited until she met his eyes. "It doesn't mean you aren't important, or that our future family of three with Mollie isn't important. I have to trust that the attorney knows the best way to navigate this. We don't want to regret making a decision based on emotion."

She nodded. "Of course. You're right. Your attorney is right. I do trust her. I know from Skylar how good Jillian is."

"The mediation will probably be next week. Jillian hopes to have this all tied up before Christmas, well before the wedding. All good news. Tell me about your meeting with the famous ice sculptor."

"I'll have to fill you in later; I've got to run to Lansing. I, um. I got a call from Chicago. My former boss at Kenilworth was attacked during a break-in." She paused, uncertain how to explain.

"Your former boss…" Aidan frowned. "Your ex-fiancé's father?"

"No. His mother, Faye. Rob called a little while ago and said he's flying in to talk with the Lansing museum director or security, and he asked for my help with something related to the theft at Kenilworth. I'm not really sure yet what it's about."

"Wouldn't Chicago law enforcement already be dealing with that?" he asked.

She nodded. "I'm sure they are. I'll keep you updated. Faye is in the ICU right now so this will probably be a quick meeting. I know I haven't talked much about my time in Chicago, but Rob's mother was wonderful to me. I feel awful for her. If there's anything I can do that might help, I need to do it."

"I hope she'll be all right," he said. "I've got to get back to the clinic anyway." His complete lack of reaction to the fact she'd be seeing her former fiancé made her simultaneously relieved he was fine with it while knowing she'd have been less than thrilled about him seeing an old flame if the situation was reversed.

In the driveway, Aidan held her car door open for her, stopping with one hand on the doorframe before shutting it. "Do me a favor and get Britt to sit in on the meeting with you, will you? You know almost no details yet. With Britt in the room, if anything dangerous is asked of you, they can at least be the voice of reason."

"I'm totally capable of handling this on my own."

"I know you are. But humor me. Sometimes your curiosity gets the best of you." He bent, curling a hand around the side of her neck, his fingers sliding lightly into her hair. He kissed her, murmuring, "I've grown pretty attached to you, y'know. Come back safe."

"I will," she promised.

"And if he wants you back, tell him he missed his chance," Aidan said, lips curving into a smirk.

She laughed, warmed at his words. "Obviously."

SHE CALLED BRITT on the way and had to leave a voicemail. She bypassed visitor parking for the employee parking lot near the side entrance, a swipe of her museum name badge getting her through the yellow-and-white-striped parking arm at the guard station and then into the building. She'd done this dozens of times this summer without giving much thought to the substantial security measures in place. She'd passed at least two surveillance cameras in the parking lot walking in. As the heavy steel door closed behind her, she greeted the guard inside the door. There was one stationed at every access point into the museum. Better to be safe than sorry; her small museum's security seemed just as tight as Kenilworth's.

The stairwell just inside the door was much closer than the elevator at the end of the hall. She took the stairs to the third floor where the administrative offices and extensive lab were housed and slipped into conference room A3 per Rob's text. She was surprised to find several people seated around the long table, including the Lansing Museum of Fine Art's director Lawrence Flynn, the museum's assistant CEO Melissa Aguilar, and more security guards than she realized the museum staffed, some dressed in plainclothes.

At the far end of the table, Rob stood and moved toward her. His sandy-blond hair was cut shorter than she remembered it, the Italian silk suit and the gold Audemars Piguet wristwatch sending the message they were meant to, reminding the important people in this room that he was the son of Vincent Havemeyer, a constant presence on the Forbes Top 200 list. She was suddenly glad she hadn't changed out of the outfit she'd worn for her Frosty Fest meeting. Her red velvet wrap dress with an A-line, knee-length skirt trimmed with a thin, white fur hem, sleek black boots, and a delicate gold snowflake necklace was perfect for the holiday season and exactly the type of outfit deemed inappropriate for Kenilworth staff. Red—or any actual color, for that matter— was too bright and cheerful for her stuffy former employer. Britt had admired the look, saying it was *giving a hot young Mrs. Claus*. She only wished she hadn't ditched her jingle bell earrings.

She and Rob met in the middle, Savanna acutely aware of her colleagues and superiors watching. She extended her hand, knowing immediately it was a weird way to greet someone she'd dated for seven years, while Rob leaned in, clearly aiming for a hug. Recovering, he flushed red and quickly took her hand, shaking it too enthusiastically.

"It's good to see you," he said.

"You too." She broke contact and took her seat, nodding to Director Flynn. Where was Britt? She'd been certain they'd be here. Britt didn't live far from the museum and had just left her a couple hours ago in Carson. She sent a follow-up text to the one she'd sent in the stairwell on her way up:

"Where are you?"

It wasn't like them not to respond, but she hadn't thought to ask them anything about plans they might have had for today with Helene.

"I appreciate you all meeting with me on short notice." Rob spoke from the head of the table. "I'm sure you've received the cautionary statement this morning from our CFO. Kenilworth's head of security is working closely with authorities to determine how exactly our encrypted system was breached and who's behind this. We've taken a roughly twenty-eight-million-dollar loss from the theft, one guard is dead, and my mother is in surgery as we speak after being attacked during the break-in."

"How horrible," Director Flynn said. "Our condolences to your guard's family. I hope your mother will be all right."

"Thank you."

Flynn leaned forward on the table. "Kenilworth did contact us. It seems there's a concern that this may be a coordinated effort—the perpetrators may be plotting multiple thefts?"

Rob sat down—collapsed—into his chair. Dark under eye circles, Savanna hadn't noticed at first, hinted at what he'd dealt with the last two days. No amount of money or status mattered when a loved one was in the hospital. "We didn't just *lose* twenty-eight million dollars' worth of art. The pieces that were stolen make up a little over half that amount. The thieves also defaced and virtually destroyed millions of dollars' worth of displayed artwork with graffiti. Our most valuable Minkov was stolen, but the other one in the exhibit was slashed with some kind of blade and then spray-painted. It makes no sense. We've contracted additional art restorers to help our division work on the damaged pieces, if they're even salvageable." He pulled several enlarged photos from the briefcase he'd brought and slid them to the director on his left. Savanna's eyes widened. Even upside down, the crudely spray-painted red outline depicted in each photo was clearly an image of a devilish face: two curved horns and two x's for eyes.

"What in the world?" Savanna murmured.

"The thieves also posted this on an anonymous social media account." Rob nodded at Flynn. The director tapped a few keys on his laptop and the integrated LCD display on the wall behind him came on, the large screen filled with the same graffiti image sprayed onto a framed painting she recognized.

She gasped. "That's a Francois Laurant piece. Oh my— it's *Charmante Femme Agée*." She covered her mouth. Much of her junior and senior year of her fine arts degree was spent studying the impressionist era artists. She'd done her thesis on impressionist painter Sergei Minkov; she was afraid to ask which piece was destroyed. Destruction like this was a federal crime. Minkov was more widely known than Laurant, but both were excellent. The Laurent piece on the screen depicted a middle-aged woman, lovely face bare of makeup as she faced the morning sun, a darkened room behind her. The chiaroscuro technique typically used by Laurant for a dramatic contrast between light and dark layers of brush strokes wasn't apparent in the painting on the screen, but that was likely due to the graffiti taking up most of the image. "How could anyone ruin such an iconic classic? Wasn't this one originally displayed in the Louvre?"

Rob met her gaze. His singular, silent nod told her he was just as dumbfounded. "We acquired it from a private collector in Paris a couple years ago."

A security guard she recognized, Donald Tate, spoke. "What makes the police think this is a coordinated effort?" Tate served as museum security team lead. He'd been hired in this past summer shortly after she started working with Britt. He was older, around her parents' age, and reminded her of her mom's brother, Uncle Freddie—quiet but observant.

"Yes, I'm wondering too," the director said, "and why would we even be at risk here? Lansing Museum of Fine Art is smaller than, say, the Detroit Institute of Art and several others. We have far fewer valuable pieces. Maybe your theft was a one-off."

"We weren't the first museum hit," Rob said. "Three days before our break-in, the Morton Samuel Museum in

California was robbed. Only Impressionist pieces were taken, and they also left a few paintings severely vandalized. I'm told the FBI's Art Crime Team is now involved."

"We do have quite a large Impressionist-era exhibit," Savanna mused. Faint prickles climbed the back of her neck, the sensation that she was seeing an incomplete overview of these and possible future thefts. But what were they missing? And what about the remaining events of the season? "Tomorrow is the charity gala. Will that need to be canceled?"

Director Flynn pressed a thumb and forefinger into his closed eyes and groaned. "The gala. Tickets have been sold out for weeks. I'm not sure we could cancel it if we tried. Good Lord, I didn't even think of the gala." The conference room fell abruptly silent.

"Nothing said here is to leave this room." All eyes turned to the opposite end of the table. The museum's assistant CEO, Melissa Aguilar, stood. "We're not canceling the gala. The museum needs those funds. Mr. Havemeyer, I'm acquainted with your mother. I'll trust that her strength and your family's support will see her through this. Your family runs a tight ship at Kenilworth; the fact that you've suffered such losses is daunting for us and any other museum that might be in the sights of whomever is doing this. You were cleared to share all of this with us, I assume? By the Chicago PD or an FBI contact?"

Rob stood too, gathering the photos on the table. "Yes. An FBI field officer with the Art Crimes Team was in touch with my father. Most of what I've shared is already public knowledge. The graffiti tag or symbol was also left on the wall just inside the Impressionist wing. The thieves did the same thing at Morton Samuel Museum—tagged the wall of the exhibit in addition to a couple pieces. The images are gaining momentum online, but so far, no actual IP address or VPN has been isolated and there's been no luck in getting it taken down."

The CEO stared through him, obviously deep in thought. "That's good to know. If you don't mind, give us another few minutes of your time, Mr. Havemeyer. We'll want to swap out security so the rest of the team on site can be looped in. Officer Tate, go ahead and allocate guards to each station and have everyone else on duty come up here," Aguilar ordered. She turned back to Rob. "We can't thank you enough for this warning."

"No need for thanks," Rob said, his tone sincere. Perhaps the past two years had afforded him some humility; the Rob Savanna remembered was aloof and detached, unlike the man in this room. "We hope by enlightening you and the other museums at risk, you might not have to suffer the same losses. As my mother says, 'art is life and life is art.' She'll be devastated at the vandalism of some of our most prized pieces when she returns to Kenilworth. I wish she hadn't been working late that night; I wish we'd invested in newer software and more foolproof encryption codes. All of this might have been avoided with more strenuous security." His gaze came to rest on Savanna. "A mistake can be useful if we learn from it and adapt."

The group broke up. Security guard Tate waited in the conference room for the second round of guards to make their way upstairs once relieved. Director Flynn remained seated, leaning into a hushed conversation with CEO Aguilar.

At the head of the table, Rob took his seat. He adjusted his cuff links, raising his gaze to Savanna's where she stood in the doorway. "I'll be out shortly. Wait for me?"

She nodded. "Sure." She stepped out and was surprised to find Britt leaning on the wall by one of the floor-to-ceiling windows. "What happened to you?"

"It was a closed meeting," Britt said simply. "Except for ex-fiancés of Sir Havemeyer."

The snark wasn't lost on her. "I've been waiting for that to pay off. Hey, is everything okay? I was getting a little worried—you always text me back right away. Helene isn't with you?"

"She wasn't feeling great. She left for the day. So," Britt said, keeping their volume low. "Are you sworn to secrecy or can you share? Why is your ex here? I googled the Kenilworth robbery, seems like the FBI and local police are on top of it. What couldn't he tell you or Flynn over the phone?"

She frowned. "That's a good question. Nothing he said was actually shocking—Rob acknowledged that most of the story about Kenilworth's break-in is already on news outlets and social media. Including this." She turned her phone toward Britt, displaying the creepy, spray-painted red devil face over a different defaced painting. The Laurant had shaken her. "The criminals didn't just steal artwork; they vandalized some too. They ruined *Charmante Femme Agée*, the Francois Laurant piece. God. We handle these works with such extreme care; it's horrible that someone could destroy them in seconds. Why not just take it? What kind of art thievery ring throws away millions rather than adding it to their spoils?"

Britt made a face. "What kind of elite art thievery ring on a crime spree uses cartoonish graffiti like this?"

"I have no i—" Savanna cut herself off. Her friend Detective Nick Jordan and his partner were walking toward her from the stairwell, totally out of context, an hour outside their jurisdiction. She glanced at Britt. "What in the world are Carson Sheriff's detectives doing here?" Her heartbeat thrummed in her throat. Were they here for her? Had something awful happened in Carson? Since her father's near-death experience on Lake Michigan only a few months ago, she took nothing for granted.

Britt stood with her, watching the two men approach among a handful of uniformed guards summoned by Tate to conference room A3. Impatient, she hurried up the hallway toward them.

"Detective Jordan? What are you doing here? Is everything all right?"

Confusion crossed Nick Jordan's face. "Yes and no—you've heard about the thefts?"

"We moonlight here," Detective George Taylor said, picking up her meaning. "The director asked for all off-duty guards to come in for an emergency security meeting."

"Oh!" Relief rushed through her. That made much more sense than the wild fear her imagination had stirred up. "You guys work at the museum now? But—why? I mean—" She didn't mean to be insensitive. Jordan had just never struck her as hurting for additional income, though who couldn't use a little extra money these days?

Taylor tipped his head toward her and whispered, "They pay us." He cracked a grin.

Jordan side eyed his partner before addressing Savanna. "Taylor's been picking up a shift or two each week. June and I have some, uh, additional expenses lately. He got me in. The pay's not bad, especially midnight shift."

"Wow." She was tired just thinking about Jordan working his day job in Carson and then driving all the way here to work overnight. "That's great, I'm sure it helps you guys out." She scrutinized Jordan's expression. His explanation left a lot to be desired. She hoped his wife June wasn't sick, hoped the new expenses weren't due to something negative.

"Oh yeah," Taylor said. "It really does. He's almost saved enough to—"

Jordan spoke over him, interrupting. "To cover the trip we're taking next year. Europe. Pricey." His poker face was stony, unreadable, as always. Jordan was the king of giving nothing away. But she'd never seen him lie until now.

"Okay. That's awesome." Now wasn't the time, but she'd get the real story eventually. After so many cases solved together, Nick Jordan viewed her as a friend, even if he was too out of touch with his emotions to know it.

"You can't say anything," Taylor blurted. "In town. To anyone. Seriously, okay?"

"Moonlighting is frowned upon," Jordan explained. "Our sergeant wouldn't be happy knowing we're working here."

"I never saw you," Savanna said. "Don't worry."

"Nope," Britt added. "Didn't see either one of you."

ON HIS WAY out, Detective Jordan stopped and pulled Savanna aside. He waved Taylor ahead. "Hey." His expression was even more somber than usual. "I'm working the gala tomorrow. I was comped two tickets. June and her sister are coming. Will you be there?"

She raised her eyebrows. "Yes, Aidan and I have tickets."

"I just asked Tate to get June and my sister-in-law assigned to your table. Easier for me to keep an eye on all of you. Don't tell her I said anything about our finances, all right?"

"I wouldn't." Which part of what he'd just said should she dissect first? She'd met June once at Caroline Carson's birthday party. The detective's wife was a sweetheart. "Why do you need to keep an eye on us? And Nick, seriously, are you two okay? No one is sick, right?"

It was his turn to look surprised, and she knew why. So, it had taken her two and a half years to use his first name; so, what. His default setting was gruff with a dash of intimidating. Savanna had lived away during the time Nick Jordan dated her younger sister Sydney. With their history, older sister Skylar's working relationship with him, and the trauma they'd experienced this fall with Jordan guiding them through the fight to get Harlan home safely, formality had fallen by the wayside—for the most part. She was worried

29

about him. He was a friend.

"No one is sick. I didn't mean to alarm you," he said, his tone softening. "I'll explain another time. And I changed the seating because it's idiocy not to cancel the gala. Tomorrow night would be the perfect opportunity for this place to become third on the list of museums hit by the Impressionist thieves."

Chapter Three

ROB APPROACHED HER after Jordan left. She made introductions between him and Britt.

"We've met," Britt said, shaking Rob's hand. "Four years ago, at Kenilworth when I was consulting on a pair of Julian Rothman paintings."

"Right," Rob said, nodding. "I thought I recognized you."

Savanna held her tongue; Rob had no recollection of meeting her friend, she was certain, but Britt didn't need to know that.

"Well, back to work. I'll see you and Aidan tomorrow night," Britt said. They turned to Rob. "Will you be staying for the ball?" Savanna knew she wasn't imagining the little lilt of pleasure in Britt's voice at mentioning Aidan in front of her former fiancé.

"No. I've got to get back. Mother's out of surgery just now." When Britt had gone, Rob turned to her. "I'm glad you waited for me. Is there somewhere we can talk?"

Prickles of irritation crept up the back of her neck. Irrational irritation, to be sure. He'd flown in to share an update that could keep her museum safe from losing lives and millions and done so while his mother was in a hospital bed.

They'd broken up over two years ago. They were both adults. "Of course. How about the café?" They were both adults, but that didn't mean she wanted to go somewhere private with him while he rehashed what had happened between them.

"Sure. The café is fine."

They navigated through museum patrons and staff, the café inviting with skylights and lush, green plants. Rob had a momentary issue upon learning the museum's café didn't carry kombucha tea on tap. "I missed the gym today; I can't miss my kombucha too." He stared at her worriedly. "Do you have another restaurant or a beverage bar here?"

She bit her tongue and swallowed her first response; sarcasm was uncalled for. It wasn't entirely his fault he was so entitled. "Nope. This is it, sorry. The coffee is good, though, and there are a ton of different teas over here." She showed him the dozen or so choices of tea bags beside the hot water dispenser. The distaste in his expression told her how subpar this was.

"I'll get something on the way to the airport," he murmured. "This will do for now." He plucked a decaf green tea packet from the selection and filled his cup with hot water.

Rob took the lead, heading toward a table, while she got stuck in small talk with Joy, her favorite cashier. When she finally broke away, she located him at a fairly secluded table in one of the alcoves near the windows. He waited until she sat down to take his own seat.

"We really appreciate—" she began, at the same time he spoke.

"I've wanted to talk—you first," he said.

"You didn't have to help us out here. I know I speak for everyone in that room; thank you for the valuable information about what Kenilworth went through," she said.

He shrugged. "I hope it helps. It was really just a good excuse to see you."

She froze with her coffee cup halfway to her lips. "I don't—that seems like a bad idea," she said slowly, measuring her words.

"Nothing's been the same since you left. I miss you, Savanna."

As far as she was concerned, they'd had their closure. A month or two after she'd moved home to Michigan, he'd called, saying he'd made a mistake. He expected her to come back—as if she was just on vacation and he hadn't called off their engagement. There was no actual apology; the Havemeyers never apologized. But it didn't matter to her by then. "You didn't need to come all the way here to tell me that, Rob. That's crazy. Your family needs you in Chicago."

"I need you in Chicago," he said. "Will you at least think about it?"

Was he delusional? Or just arrogant enough to think she'd been living here, pining for him, waiting for him to beg her to move back? "No," she said, incredulous. "We're over—we've been over for a long time." She nearly added *and I'm engaged*, but it shouldn't matter, should it? She didn't need a new fiancé in order to know she didn't want the old one back, didn't want any part of her former life back. She'd known that since shortly after coming home almost two and a half years ago—when she'd realized how much she'd missed her family, how much she adored teaching, and how quickly and easily her heart had been stolen by cardiologist Dr. Aidan Gallager on Caroline Carson's porch in a tangle of poodles.

Rob shook his head. "I thought we could maybe—I'd hoped—"

She cut him off. That prickle of irritation had morphed into a searing urge to knock him off his pedestal of entitlement. "I'm leaving now. This conversation is over. Give my best to your mother." She pushed her chair back, began to stand.

"I got spooked," he blurted. "Right after we got engaged, I ran into my father at Mastro's. You remember, he and my mother ate there almost every Sunday. He was with his mistress and their daughter. Their *daughter*. I know because I wasn't going to leave without finding out what was going on; I asked them. The three of them were having a nice Saturday evening dinner. With the same wait staff, the same maître de and chef and sommelier who always catered to my mother on Sundays. It's all fake. All of it—them, him, marriage."

"Oh my God. Your poor mom." She didn't know what to say. Rob abruptly breaking up with her was beginning, finally, to make sense. "You never told me."

"How could I? I was a dolt. It doesn't justify me ending things the way I did. I never knew, not until that night. It completely threw me. I had to get away—but it didn't matter how far I traveled. You can't outrun family, even a messy, broken, dysfunctional family. The mess stays with you."

Savanna exhaled, stunned at his insights. "That's an awful, rude awakening. I'm sorry you were dealing with that."

"I'm sorry I hurt you." He reached for her hand.

She moved hers away, folding her hands on the table in front of her. "I'm getting married." She should have told him much earlier; she might have saved him from going through all of that with her.

Rob looked stunned. "You're getting married? When? To whom? To *Aidan*? Your date tomorrow night?" He spoke the man's name with such distaste it distorted his lips.

She ignored the childish reaction, forcing herself to allow him some grace. "Yes. On New Year's Eve. He's a wonderful man. He's a doctor in Carson." She found a recent photo in her phone, Aidan, Mollie, and herself on her Catalina, snapped by a nice older couple from their yacht a few slips over. She turned her phone to show Rob.

He stared at it wordlessly.

"That's his daughter, Mollie. Aidan is... he's everything I've dreamed of."

Rob nodded, still staring at the picture. "Okay. All right." He looked at her. "You're happy."

"Very."

"Okay. Well. You're sure you're happy, Savanna? You'll have an instant family to take care of." He pointed at Mollie. "This is what you want?"

"This is exactly what I want. I'm positive," she said.

He stood when she did. A heavy silence hung between them in the elevator car. "My driver is out front," he said in the lobby, turning to go.

"I'll walk you out." She couldn't put her finger on why she felt heavier, too, now; none of this was her fault. They were different people on different paths. She wouldn't rewind the clock for a million dollars.

Outside on the pavement, he turned, staring up at the Lansing museum. He dropped his gaze, meeting hers. "I will be happy for you, eventually. I'm working on being more honest now. So, I can't say I'm happy for you right this second—I'm sad. For me—for us. But you deserve good things. You deserve to have the life you want."

He surprised her. The old Rob had none of this self-awareness. "So do you. I hope you're happy, Rob. If you aren't, I hope you will be." The sudden relief in knowing this would be the last time she'd see him lifted her mood. Reminders of her time with him only made her wish she'd woken up sooner, taken the reins to her own life earlier. But then she might be a different person still than the one she'd now become. And she and Aidan might never have had the chance to fall in love.

"Would it be out of line if I hugged you goodbye?" Rob asked.

She hugged him. She sent silent little wishes for his mother's health and his happiness.

His driver waited inside the rented high-end white Lincoln until they'd separated before hurrying around to the passenger side, holding the sedan door for him. The Havemeyer family always hired the most tactful, discreet help.

It wasn't until she was nearly back home that she realized what had been needling her during the art theft meeting. She might be way off base, but what about lesser-known, high-value Impressionist exhibits? Did the FBI Art Crimes division believe only large facilities were being targeted? Was there no concern about smaller collections—and if not, why? Those would certainly be much easier to infiltrate. But there was no point in raising alarms based on a feeling.

SAVANNA'S PHONE WOKE her up Saturday morning. She snaked an arm out of the warm bedding and slapped her alarm clock's button, but the annoying ringing just continued. She fumbled for her phone, silencing it, but now she was up. Thanks to Skylar. "Ugh. I'm seeing you in like, an hour," she grumbled, glaring at the missed call notification. She blinked at Fonzie, who'd leapt onto the bed, wiggling with excitement that she was awake. Her dog had no sympathy; he was ready for breakfast. She rubbed her eyes and tried to focus on the new text just in from her sister. Since the call wasn't enough. It must be super important to warrant rudely waking her before seven a.m. on a weekend.

The message was long. Her older sister had a habit of sending either very long voice notes or text messages anytime something was going on within their family. Skylar was the fixer, the problem solver, among them, whether she realized it or not. But right now, Skylar herself *was* the problem.

Goodness. The message went on so long it was continued in a shorter, second message. Reaching the end, Savanna had to reread the last sentence (Skylar also only texted in full, complete sentences with accurate punctuation and no abbreviations). There was no way she was going to do what her sister asked: *"I think it's best if they all hear it from you that I'm moving. You left and the world didn't end. They'll be fine, they just won't think so at first. Make sure to do it before Sunday dinner."*

Her sister was loopy if she thought she could convince Savanna to break this kind of news to their parents. Savanna had been keeping Skylar's secret now for three months. Skylar's husband had an amazing promotion opportunity in Florida. After some turmoil, Travis and Skylar had agreed he'd accept it. To start, it was a two-year commitment in Venice, and the kind of salary increase that could dramatically change their future. She texted back just one word: *"Nope."* Skylar had to face this and do it herself.

She threw on her comfiest pair of old jeans and a Hamilton Musical tee, scooted Fonzie into her car, and headed for Main Street Sweets and then the coffee shop. She and her sisters had been working to carve out time for get-togethers; their Wednesday lunches at Fancy Tails and Treats had tapered down with busier schedules lately. Syd's holiday grooming appointments were booming, and Skylar's impending move required a lot of extra time in coordinating details. Between Savanna's approaching New Year's Eve wedding, Frosty Fest, the usual holiday rush, and now this art theft problem on her mind, she was also feeling time crunched.

She was mentally ticking off her to-do list for the day, carrying three coffees custom made by her friend Griffin at Holy Grounds Coffee, when Skylar pulled up in front of

Fancy Tails. By the time Savanna made it to her older sister, Skylar had unloaded six-year-old Nolan and a folded stroller onto the sidewalk, slung a diaper bag over one shoulder, balanced baby Hannah on her hip, and kicked the car door closed with a ballet flat clad foot. Savanna set the coffees on the brick ledge of Sydney's shop and stole Hannah from her sister. Seeing Skylar in action always made her realize she herself wasn't quite as busy as she thought! She bent down, eye to eye with her nephew who seemed to be an inch taller every single time she saw him. "Hi there, mister. Carry this please." She handed him a bakery box tied with string.

He grinned brightly, his fluffy white-blond hair sticking up in odd places from static and sleep. "Mine? Thank you, Auntie Vanna!" He peeked into the box and then ducked under Sydney's arm holding the salon door open, squealing as Fonzie took off after him. "Dogs can't have jelly donuts! These are all mine."

Once they were finally seated around the shop's mid-century modern red-and-chrome café table in the customer waiting area, Savanna distributed coffees and placed a jelly donut in front of Nolan. With two overstuffed aqua chairs flanking the big window that looked out over Main Street and a stocked beverage mini fridge, the area was inviting and comfy. A long, glass display case held dozens of cute, pet-themed organic treats that looked good enough to eat—but were not for humans. Sydney baked everything herself. The rotating display stand beside the goodies held colorful leashes, collars, and knitted dog sweaters for sale—one of her crafty patrons kept up a constant supply on consignment.

On the other side of the shop, divided with a painted daisy archway in the center, the reception desk for grooming appointment bookings faced the front door, large bathing and primping quarters housed through a set of double doors behind reception. Syd's employee Willow would be arriving in an hour or so to open shop.

Two years younger than Savanna, Sydney was a newly-wed, married three months ago to Aidan's med-flight paramedic brother Finn. With a boho-chic style and a talent for weaving feathers and ribbons into her long red braid, proprietor Syd looked more concert-ready than flea-bath ready. She loved her job and knew the name and treat preference of basically every dog in Carson.

"Are you still coming over this afternoon before the gala?" Sydney asked.

"If you don't mind. I need you to tell me which gown is better and help do something with my hair," Savanna said.

"Hmm. Maybe we'll put it up." She pushed the bakery box across the table to Skylar. "You're quiet today."

Skylar looked up from her phone. "What? Sorry." She dropped the phone into her purse and picked up her coffee. She was the picture of distraction.

Savanna seized the opportunity. If her sister was too worried about making a big announcement, why not practice first on Sydney? "Sky, you mentioned there was something you wanted to talk to us about, didn't you?"

Skylar flashed bug eyes at Savanna, then quickly recovered. She perused the baked goods. "No. I don't think so."

"I think you did," Savanna pressed.

"What. Come on," Sydney said. She rolled her eyes. "You guys always do this. Skylar, what?"

Skylar shook her head. "Nothing."

"Dude." Savanna leaned forward, staring at Skylar. "You're making it worse."

"Oh. My. Gawd. You're both making it worse!" Sydney's tone rose at the end; she looked genuinely worried.

Savanna felt bad now. "It's okay. I'm sorry. I thought she could do it. Syd... Skylar is going to be moving. Travis got an insane promotion and transfer offer, they've talked it through, it's near his mom, and they've decided to do it."

Sydney didn't move—none of them did. The salon was abruptly silent except for the sound of Fonzie snoring.

"I've been trying to work up the nerve to tell you, to tell the family," Skylar said softly. "It's only for two years. At least at first. And I'll come back, like, all the time. And you and Finn will visit. Lots. I just—I didn't know how to share this kind of news without it being upsetting."

"You told Savanna though."

"I uh... I kind of had to. She thought we were getting divorced or something. It was rough for a bit, between me and Travis. But this is my decision. I know it's the right one," Skylar said.

"Florida?" Sydney asked. "You said by Travis's mom, she's in Florida, right?"

"Yes. She's in Tampa. We'll be in Venice—I haven't even had time yet to check it out. It's supposed to be nice."

"How close to the beach are you?"

Skylar laughed. "Close. A short walk. Travis says we can

see the ocean and Venice Pier from our living room." She got up and wrapped her arms around Sydney, kissing her cheek. "I'm sorry to leave. It's not forever. I wanted to tell you. Oh—the house has five bedrooms. One for each of you when you visit. Does that help?"

"A little," Syd replied grudgingly.

"That didn't go so badly, did it?" Savanna asked. "How about we help you tell Mom and Dad and the uncles tomorrow at dinner?"

Skylar agreed.

THAT EVENING, AFTER an afternoon of Sydney acting as her own personal cosmetologist and bringing out a glamorized version of her that she could still recognize herself in, Savanna watched headlights sweep across the dunes beyond her house. She stood in the open doorway, breathing in the chilled air blowing in from the lake. Aidan appeared on her deck looking like he'd stepped off the cover of *GQ*. This was the second time she'd seen him in a tux, and she had no complaints.

He tipped his head to the side, one hand on his chest, lips curving up at one corner and spreading into a smile that sent zings swirling up her spine. "Good God, woman," he murmured, his low tone making her blush. He dipped his head and kissed her, trailing his thumb along her jawline to her neck and the long tendrils of hair her sister had left loose from the elegant, rhinestone-studded chignon. "Sometimes,

Savanna…" He held her gaze but didn't finish his thought.

She toyed with the button on his jacket and he captured her hand, bringing it briefly to his lips. "Sometimes?" she asked.

He shook his head, taking a deep breath. "Ready? We should go."

She frowned, curious. She was about to push but held back. Sometimes his lighthearted demeanor shifted, and the intensity was overwhelming. Even more so than herself, he'd lived an entire, fulfilling life—complete with wife and child—before ever meeting her. She wondered sometimes if he missed it, missed Olivia, and what they had; of course, he must. She hoped what they were building together could make him just as happy.

In his SUV on the way to Lansing, the charged space between them mellowed, the mood shifting again as she recounted that morning's coffee chat with her sisters and Sydney's reaction to Skylar's news. He laughed. "So, all your sister really needed to say was that she's moving to a beach house where your family can vacation for free anytime."

"That's actually a great way to spin it tomorrow when she breaks the news to everyone else," Savanna agreed. She made a snap decision. "I kind of need your objective opinion. Y'know the meeting yesterday at the museum?"

He raised an eyebrow at her. "The one with your ex that you've said nothing about so far?"

He surprised her. "I didn't—Aidan, I'm sorry. I wasn't purposely avoiding updating you. I told you the authorities think other museums will be robbed by the same people."

"You did, yes. I'm not mad, Savanna, you've nothing to apologize for. It's um. It's none of my business how it went seeing him yesterday. But… since you brought it up, how did it go?" He glanced at her again before returning his attention to the road.

"It was weird. It made me so glad he ended things two years ago. I think I was just in a routine and had no idea that wasn't what I wanted for my life."

"How did he handle seeing you?"

She stared out at the dark highway. "That was also weird. I guess it was probably good for both of us. He had the idea that maybe I missed Chicago—and him."

"I knew it. I knew that was going to happen." He kept his eyes on the road, saying nothing else.

"You did, huh? Were you worried?" she teased, aiming to keep things lighthearted.

He didn't answer her. The muscle in his jaw pulsed. Stunned, she scooted closer to him and circled her hand around his arm above his elbow, his bicep firm under her fingertips. She leaned as close as she could across the console and hugged his arm. How on earth could he have been afraid she'd have even the faintest inkling of getting back together with Rob?

"Aidan, there is nobody on this planet I'd rather spend my life with than you. I won the lottery running into you—literally—that day on Caroline's front porch. I still don't know why me, of all the options you had, but who am I to question your choices," she said, hoping for some sort of smile from him.

She was rewarded with half a smile. "So, I take it you told him you don't miss… Chicago?"

"Yes. And that I'm thankful to have left… Chicago. I never had any doubt. I thought you knew that, my love." She kept her voice soft.

"It's still good to hear." He cleared his throat. "What do you need my objective opinion on?"

"The thieves are targeting Impressionist paintings. Do you think it matters that Caroline Carson still owns a few valuable Impressionist paintings?"

"Hmm. Have there been private homes robbed in the same way lately?"

"No, not that I know of. It's only Kenilworth and the Morton Samuel in Los Angeles at this point."

He shrugged. "I don't know. It seems like even assuming your museum or DIA or any of the New York museums could be next is kind of a stretch… two similar thefts don't really mean it's going to turn into a whole *Ocean's 11* thing, right?"

She laughed. She hadn't even thought of those movies. "You're right. But if we spot Clooney tonight at the gala, we'll know something's up."

Thirty minutes later, she tipped her head back and stared up at the painted panels overhead in the auditorium. In one day, her museum had been transformed. White twinkle lights crisscrossed the vaulted ceiling. Neutral shades of organza and larger soft white light strands added ambience to white linen-covered tables and tasteful décor. They made their way to their designated table, Savanna stopping to chat here and there with colleagues. She delighted in the warmth of Aidan's hand on the small of her back through her thin silk gown as they drifted through. She introduced him to Director Flynn, the imposing Melissa Aguilar, and the few security guards she knew, including Donald Tate. It took her a bit to spot Detective Jordan. She thought at first that he must not be stationed inside the gala hall, until he came into view near one of the room's exits. Jordan raised a hand in greeting to her and then touched the earpiece he wore, speaking to another guard somewhere, maybe his partner. She wondered if George Taylor was working too. He probably was. Security was beefed up considerably tonight.

She was glad to be seated with June Jordan and her sister April; they were both lovely in tea-length gowns. Across the table were two empty place settings—Britt and Helene's. Savanna texted Britt, hoping they were simply running behind. She was dying to see the fancy attire they'd both mentioned choosing. When the first two courses had been served and cleared and Britt still hadn't texted back yet, she called them. The gala was well underway. Britt always loved a good party. She hung up on the outgoing voicemail message. Britt almost never walked away from their phone, and even when they did, their smartwatch was a good substitute. They were compulsively prompt in replying to her. Until yesterday.

"I'm going to step out into the hall and try Britt one more time," she told Aidan. "I'll be back before they serve the main course, don't worry."

He stood, pulling out her chair for her. "I'll come with

you."

"That's not—never mind. That sounds good." He was about to become her husband. She could ease up on constantly trying to prove she was independent, could handle anything on her own. She could—she knew that, and she was pretty sure Aidan did too. But it didn't mean she *had* to. "We'll be right back," she told June and April.

They were stopped by a security guard she didn't recognize at the first exit they chose. They were redirected to use the main entrance or the designated doorways that led to the restrooms. She and Aidan left the same way they'd come in. Savanna dialed Britt again, double-checking she'd chosen the correct contact. She had. When she was sent again to voicemail, she left a message this time.

"I don't get it," she told Aidan. "Britt and Helene were involved in planning the gala. Where are they?"

"Have you tried calling Helene? Maybe something's wrong with Britt's phone. Didn't you say you had trouble getting ahold of them yesterday too?"

"Yes, that's right. Let me try Helene." She hit the call button just as Detective Jordan burst through to the lobby from an adjacent doorway.

"What're you doing out here? Is June still inside?" Jordan's normally calm and cool attitude had evaporated.

"Yes, why? What's happened?"

"Power's out in the whole west wing. Lights, door locks, everything. The system isn't connected; that should be impossible. Locks override outages. Or they're supposed to. Something's happening. Get back inside," he ordered. Panic laced the edges of his words, amping up her own worry. "The auditorium's the safest place right now."

"Savanna!" Britt was strolling across the lobby toward her. "I can't find Helene. We were supposed to meet in my office upstairs. She asked me to bring her gown, she was running behind." A heavily sequined black hem spilled from the bottom of the garment bag draped over Britt's arm. Her friend was flawlessly elegant, their floral burgundy suit as striking as she'd expected. "Have you seen her in the auditorium? Maybe she's looking for me," Britt said.

"No. She's not in there. I've been trying to call both of you." She heard Helene's voicemail pick up and hit redial, showing Britt her phone. "I'm trying again."

Another guard showed up, coming in the same way Jordan had. "We've got a partial grid back up, but the video feed's gone." He frowned, halting. "Does anyone hear that?"

"Shhh." Jordan put a hand up.

The five of them froze, listening. In the distance, triggered alarms were blaring, whether from the outages or something worse, she didn't know. And then she heard it—they all did. A muffled ringing was coming from the bank of elevators behind them. Savanna stared at her phone screen. Feeling as if she was moving in slow motion, she moved toward the center door where the sound was coming from. The ringing stopped.

Chapter Four

BRITT STARED AT Savanna, then down at her phone bearing Helene's contact card on the screen. They pressed the elevator call button repeatedly. "Helene. Helene! Can you hear me?"

Savanna put a hand on Britt's arm. "I think the elevator power is down—look."

They followed her gaze upward. No lights were on above any of the elevators. They pushed the button again, but it didn't light up. "Helene. Say something if you can hear us—or make a sound! Knock or kick the wall!" Britt leaned on the metal doors with both hands, unable to budge them apart.

"Call her again," Aidan suggested.

She obliged.

"Maybe she can't hear us from in there," Britt said.

"But we can hear her phone," Savanna said. The phone inside the elevator was ringing again. Savanna joined Britt in pounding on the doors, trying to reach Helene—she was probably terrified, sitting in a dead elevator in the dark.

"Maintenance is on the way," the young guard informed them. "They might have tools to open the door."

Detective Jordan stepped between Britt and the metal

doors. "Careful. The techs are working on getting power back. We don't know if the elevator car is right here"—he gestured—"or halfway between floors. These are just the outer doors, even if we could get past them it doesn't get us into the elevator. When were you last with Helene? She's your date?"

"She's the curator. And my date, yes."

"Does she have any health conditions?"

"No, I don't think so. Why isn't she answering her phone?" Britt swayed on their feet, willowy frame sagging. "Where is maintenance?"

Detective Jordan's two-way radio crackled. He stepped away, crossing to the other guard, but not before Savanna caught three words that told her exactly how serious this was— *"they shot Collins."*

"Oh God," Savanna murmured, staring wide eyed at Aidan. This was exactly what authorities investigating the Kenilworth break in had feared. But worse. Instead of thieves choosing some quiet night to breach the system after closing, steal artwork, and leave, there were roughly 200 extra people on-site tonight—additional potential liabilities, witnesses, and shooting victims. And plenty of built-in chaos to shield the criminal activity.

Aidan put his lips close to her ear. "Let's go. We have to get out of here. Grab Britt." His gaze was fixed on something behind her; she turned to see Detective Jordan flip open the top of his gun holster, hand at the ready. Two more guards had joined him.

"What about June?" Savanna asked Aidan. "We can't just leave them."

He nodded. "I know. It's okay, we'll get them. I'll tell Jordan. Let me—"

The lobby and auditorium were plunged into darkness, or near darkness, the only source of remaining light emanating from recessed footlights Savanna had never noticed before. A dim glow was cast from the open doors of the auditorium. This must be the result of whatever that guard had said about a partial grid. Frightened, panicky voices floated to her from the gala—men arguing, a shout, a woman's high-pitched scream. A loud crash of glass and china shattering on marble, a dropped serving tray or overturned table, drowned out the voices for a moment, and then to their left, somewhere down the long hallway to the Impressionist exhibits, the unmistakable sound of a gunshot.

Aidan's arm shot out and forcibly swept her behind him. He turned, quickly whisking her with him to crouch down behind the half wall sectioning off the elevator bank from the wide-open lobby. His gaze was intensely focused on the front entrance, much too far away. Savanna's heart pounded so hard, she felt it beating in her throat, in her ears. They waited... and waited. The lobby had fallen completely silent. Time wasn't real; they crouched, frozen, for an hour or a few minutes, she had no idea. She'd lost sight of Jordan. Aidan was right, they had to get out of here, but how?

The decision to leave was taken out of their hands. Two couples rushed from the auditorium, barreling through the lobby to the wall of exit doors—and slamming into them. One woman shrieked, "We're trapped!" The trio with her raced frantically from one side to the other, more gala patrons joining, shoving against glass doors that were immovable.

Nick Jordan darted from the stairwell where the group of guards had gone. He ran into the auditorium, providing Savanna a shred of relief—at least June and her sister would be with the armed detective. The glorious sound of sirens approaching filled the air.

Around the edge of the barrier, she watched first responder vehicles arrive, one after another—police cars, an ambulance and then another, a firetruck, more police. The group trying to escape through the lobby doors abruptly fell forward as lights came back on and the locks disengaged. At the same time, the elevators now behind them dinged, doors sliding open.

Aidan looked first. He blocked her, shielding her view. "Savanna. You don't need to see. It'll be all right," he said, nodding to the officers rushing up the museum steps. As if straight out of a movie, uniformed SWAT team officers took over the lobby. One signaled to the waiting paramedics, waving them through toward the elevators that were now working. Two officers motioned to Aidan and Savanna, barking orders to put their hands in the air. They were obviously dressed as gala attendees, but it made perfect sense that the authorities could make no assumptions.

Detective Taylor appeared from the stairwell with Security Team Lead Tate. Taylor crossed to Savanna and Aidan, getting them permission to lower their hands, while Tate addressed the commander clearly in charge of the SWAT team. "We saw three of them leave out the south exit. Might have been four. An unmarked box van, no windows. No inventory yet."

Savanna drifted toward the elevators. She had to see Helene.

Aidan stopped her. "Hey. Don't, Savanna. Please." He tucked a finger lightly beneath her chin to make her look at him instead.

She gently pushed his hand away. "I have to."

The center elevator doors were stuck in a constant cycle, closing halfway and then halting and reopening, over and over. Helene lay sprawled in a wide pool of blood on the elevator floor, one arm extended over her head across the sliding door threshold. Wide open dark eyes stared, unseeing, at nothing.

Savanna clamped her hand over her mouth, eyes flooded with tears. Aidan's arms wrapped tightly around her, and she turned her face toward his chest—and then gasped. Britt. She whipped around, scanning the lobby.

"Britt's in the auditorium," Aidan said. "Come on. Police aren't letting anyone leave—Britt won't see her like this, don't worry. I'm sure she'll be... taken away... before they let guests out of there."

Evidence techs arrived, two of them moving carefully around Helene's body. One pressed two gloved fingers against Helene's neck, shaking his head. Filtered through tears and the handkerchief Aidan handed her, Savanna saw Helene's cell phone drop into a clear evidence bag from an officer's gloved hand. Into another bag went a smaller black device—another phone? Or maybe it was a battery pack like the one she kept in her purse.

She finally gave in, letting Aidan lead her away. "This is going to kill Britt."

THEY WERE BACK in Carson from the gala before ten. Aidan had hardly spoken on the drive home. Savanna tried at first to talk through some of what they'd just experienced, fretting about Britt, about poor Helene, finally falling silent as well; she could feel the stress emanating from him in the dark car.

He saw her to her door and kissed her good night, leaving to go pick up Mollie from his in-laws.

She grabbed his arm, pulling him back and hugging him tightly, fiercely. He hugged her back, burying his face in her neck. "We shouldn't have gone," she said. "I should have known it was a bad idea. I… I didn't think of it as risky. I'm sorry Aidan."

He let go. "It's not your fault. I've never…" He scowled, looking up at the sky. "There's never been a time when I thought I wouldn't see my daughter again. Until tonight."

Her eyes burned with a rush of tears. "I can't… I know I can't imagine how awful that felt. I wish I could undo it, the whole evening."

He didn't speak; he'd gone somewhere else, wherever he'd been on the drive home, somewhere she couldn't reach him.

"We're okay. We weren't hurt," she said softly. "You're

going right now to get Mollie. You're okay."

"But I might not have been. Then what?" He pressed a hand over his eyes.

What was the right response? In a couple weeks, if, God forbid, something happened to him, she would absolutely care for Mollie the same as if she was her own daughter. But it wasn't a couple weeks from now, was it? Would the in-laws end up raising her, if something happened to Aidan—now or even after they were married? What would be best for Mollie? What about Finn, would he step in? What about *Mollie*, who'd already suffered the loss of her mother? Savanna shuddered, her stomach flipping over queasily, likely a mere fraction of the dread he'd felt.

Everything in her ached to comfort Aidan. Everything about him told her to let him be. To give him time. He was so tightly, intensely wound right now, she feared anything she said could make this all worse.

He met her eyes. "I love you, Savanna. I've gotta go." He was off her deck and backing out of her driveway in seconds.

She hated that she'd put him in danger, given him this eye-opening moment. She went inside, a heavy, hollow coil of worry sitting on her chest. Until five minutes ago, she'd been feeling sorry for herself, sad that he couldn't stay—ever. At least not until they were married. In September, she'd hosted an impromptu sleepover after an exhaustingly fun day at the beach with Aidan, Mollie, and her niece and nephew who she was babysitting for Skylar. Mollie and Nolan fell asleep on the floor, each in their own sleeping bag, watching a Disney movie. Aidan took the couch, and Savanna claimed the love seat. The entire day and night were nothing if not G-rated.

Shortly after, Aidan was served with a subpoena for the in-laws grandparents' rights case. Mollie had mentioned something about a sleepover. The protective, accusatory stance his late wife's parents had adopted seemed out of left field. As Aidan pointed out, he'd never stopped Mollie's grandparents from seeing her; they were currently her only set, since his and Finn's parents were dead. He'd remained in Carson after Olivia passed away mainly so that his daughter would know her grandparents.

Aidan's attorney had advised vigilant caution until after the wedding, so as to avoid giving the Becketts anything else to twist around and use against them. It was sound advice. But after the gala trauma, she'd have given anything for Aidan to just stay.

Now she kicked herself for being so selfish. Aidan was a dad. He was a single dad with no parents and only one sibling. Mollie's world was very small.

She sat outside, staring out over the dunes and vast lake, light from the full moon bouncing off the choppy waves. She had to start thinking like a parent. Mollie had to come first, no matter what, if this new life with Aidan was going to work.

Savanna left her bedroom window cracked open the slightest bit that night. There was something in the lake air. She could feel it. She fell asleep dreaming of snow.

HER DAD TOOK her out for pancakes Sunday morning. The robbery story was in the Sunday newspaper with details that were still a little too fresh in her mind to read about—and scary enough that her daily newspaper reading father had to lay eyes on her to confirm she was fine.

Seated across the table from her at the Mitten Inn café, the only place in town for a decent breakfast, Harlan Shepherd folded up his newspaper the way it'd arrived on the newsstand and set it beside Savanna's purse in the booth. "That's your copy, in case you want it. You're mentioned in the article. So is Britt. And there's a quote from Nick Jordan—since when does he moonlight in security?"

She glanced around. "He told us not to say anything around town. The sheriff's department doesn't like their staff working second jobs or security or something. But I guess the cat's out of the bag now."

"Well, I'm glad they were there. You're sure you're okay?" He frowned, assessing her.

"I promise. I'm fine. It was mostly just really frightening. It's awful about Helene. She and Britt had just started dating a few months ago. She was such a sweet person."

"Pass our sympathy on to Britt, would you?" Harlan set his coffee cup on the edge of the table for the approaching server to refill it.

She nodded. "I will. Dad… I've been thinking about my house. I'm just wondering, with where it's situated and the electric and sewer and everything, would it be at all possible to add on? I'm just thinking."

"There's always a way. We'd figure something out. If you

wanted to extend the second floor the length of the house and over the garage, that could get pricey, but I've done it before. It'd turn out nice, I'm sure. But we could also knock out the back wall of the living room and use part of the side yard you've got there for a bigger kitchen and another couple bedrooms. That might be the easier way to go." He paused, considering. "You'd be looking at a few months, minimum. Either way, it'd be a big project."

She was so lucky her dad was a contractor and understood this stuff. She and Aidan would be talking through concrete plans for where they'd live soon. She'd mentioned the idea of expanding her lakefront home and he seemed receptive, but she wasn't sure how attached he and Mollie were to their current house. "That helps to know. I'll think things over. Thanks, Dad."

Had her mother or sisters been at breakfast with them, there'd be follow-up questions: when were Aidan and Mollie moving in? Were she and Aidan going to have more kids? How many extra bedrooms would she need?

Her dad had no questions for her. He was comfortable in the moment, content with silence. She wished she was. She tried to learn from him. She could hardly believe that three months ago, he'd been thought missing or dead, and then turned up injured, had recovered, and could hardly wait to get back out on the water next spring. In his mid-fifties, Harlan was tall and broad shouldered and just starting to show a little silver in his thick brown hair. His work as a contractor, managing multiple construction contracts at once, meant he spent a good deal of time outdoors, even in the winter, working alongside his subcontractors when needed.

He sat back, dropping his napkin on his cleaned plate. "Best biscuits and gravy around. Who's cooking tonight? I know it's not my turn yet." For as long as she could remember, her family had gathered every Sunday evening for dinner at her parents' house. The rule was they each had to take a turn preparing the meal. Charlotte kept track. Savanna's mother was the only one exempt from making Sunday dinner. It was an accepted truth in the family that she possessed the least talent or skill for cooking, and they were all better off giving her a pass. She acted as scheduler for their rotating meals and let everyone else wear the chef's hat. Charlotte's brother Freddie and his husband Max had moved to town last year, meaning less frequent turns at cooking for the family. Uncle Max and Freddie's daughter Ellie was a college student, but she pitched in to help her dads whenever she was able to come home for a Sunday Shepherd family dinner.

"Skylar's making dinner tonight," Savanna said, suddenly remembering Skylar had a daunting task to complete this evening. She'd better come clean and break her news to the family; she was running out of time before her move.

SAVANNA STOPPED ON her way around to the kitchen door at her parents' house, stooping down to baby-talk to Pumpkin, the large orange tabby cat who seemed to station himself on the walkway no matter the weather during family gatherings, ensuring ample attention. Fonzie had already taken off ahead of her, chasing Daisy, the abandoned golden retriever pup her parents had adopted last spring.

Savanna knew what they were having for dinner before she set foot in the kitchen. "Oh wow." She closed her eyes and breathed deep, the delectable aroma of Skylar's ham and split pea soup filling the warm kitchen. With the chill in the air, it was the perfect meal choice. She nudged her sister over so she could peek through the glass lid of the Crock-Pot. "You haven't made this in forever. I can't wait; I'm starving."

Skylar lifted the lid and stirred slowly, grabbing a smaller spoon and holding out a taste for Savanna. "It's been simmering for around nine hours. Tell me if it's done."

"Auntie Vanna!" Nolan burst through the door; Travis with Hannah close behind him. "Where's Mollie? Is she here yet?"

"Not yet. She'll be here soon. The soup is done," she informed Skylar.

"But when?" The little boy climbed onto the stool at the kitchen counter. "Now?"

Savanna laughed. "Not quite. Why? What's that?" She leaned on the counter, pointing at the gray fluff clutched in his hand.

"It's called a dolphin," he told her, pronouncing the word slowly and carefully. He held the stuffed animal up, wiggling it. "Mama says they live by our new house!"

Savanna stared at Skylar, who was shooting daggers with her scowl at Travis.

"What?" he asked innocently. "You said you told—"

"I lied," Skylar said through clenched teeth.

Nolan hugged his dolphin, staring wide eyed across the counter. "You're gonna be in trouble Mama."

"I mean, I didn't lie. I made a mistake. I've been trying to tell them. I was going to tell them before dinner today," she said to Travis.

"Tell who what?" Charlotte Shepherd appeared through the doorway from the living room. "Hi there, cutie!" Savanna's mother gave Nolan a quick hug and circled the kitchen island, taking the garlic bread from the oven.

"Mom—where's Dad? I need to tell you guys something; I wanted to wait for the uncles too. Let me just…" Skylar grabbed her phone and sent a quick text. "Nolan, would you run out to the barn and tell Grandpa we're eating now?"

"Yep!" He hopped off the stool and sprinted out the door toward the large pole barn their dad called a garage, his workshop for collecting and restoring old vintage motorcycles in his spare time.

"Uncle Max says they're just around the corner," Skylar said. "Let's set the table. I added a little more minced garlic this time and soaked the peas longer to boost the flavor. I hope it's good."

Savanna followed her sister, carrying dishes to the long dining room table without a word. Sydney and Finn arrived at the same time Freddie and Max did, Ellie carrying a platter of homemade cream puffs for dessert.

When they were all finally seated around the dining room table, Travis stood, glancing questioningly at Skylar.

She nodded to him. He cleared his throat and addressed the room, speaking primarily to Harlan and Charlotte. "Skylar and I have some news to share. I've been given a unique opportunity. Greenway Engineering is opening a new office in Florida as a result of an international merger. They've asked me to step in as senior environmental operations manager as we grow the new company and location. I turned it down at first. But after a lot of discussion, we've decided it's something I can't pass up."

"It's a two-year commitment," Skylar spoke. "The new branch is in Venice. The company understands the upheaval involved in asking Trav to do this. His salary will nearly double." She'd slipped into lawyer mode—Savanna heard it in her sister's confident, no-nonsense voice, saw it in the set of her jaw. She was prepared to argue their case.

Charlotte spoke first. "Travis, is your mother still in Tampa?"

He nodded. "Yes, she is. We'll be able to see her often, Tampa's not far from the new place."

Their mom smiled. "She must be so happy. She hasn't had the luxury of seeing her grandchildren grow, like we have."

"She cried when we told her," Travis said. "She's very happy. We meant to tell you sooner. We weren't sure exactly how."

Skylar shook her head. "I wasn't sure how to tell you. This is an amazing step up for Travis, for our family. It's a wonderful thing. But leaving you all is going to be the hardest thing I've ever done. You have to promise to visit,

I'm serious. We have a lot of space."

"I'm thrilled for you," Uncle Max said. "This sounds like a great adventure for the four of you."

Harlan finally spoke. "What I'm hearing is that we'll be racking up some frequent flyer miles on plenty of vacations in Venice. Congratulations, son. I'm proud of you." He got up and shook Travis's hand, giving him a brief, back-slapping hug. He stopped and kissed the top of Skylar's head. "All good. Stop worrying."

"There's nothing quite as exciting as forging a new path into new territory," Uncle Freddie said. "Max and Ellie have done it twice—from London to Manhattan when we became a family, and again last year for Ellie's move to university. To new adventures in Venice—you're going to love the Gulf Coast." He raised his glass in a toast.

The split pea and ham soup was devoured; nothing was left in the enormous Crock-Pot. Over cream puffs, Savanna provided a bare-bones sum-up of the robbery last night in context with the other two similar break-ins at Kenilworth and Morton Samuel, painfully aware of Mollie and Nolan at the table and not wanting to further upset Aidan.

Uncle Max picked up on some woo woo telepathy stress she must be emitting. He clapped his hands loudly as he stood. "I'm off to play with the pooches—they've been waiting long enough. Would anyone like to come? I might need some help. We all know Fonzie can be a bit cheeky."

Nolan giggled, repeating the funny word.

"Yes? You, young sir? And what about you, little miss?" Max asked, waiting while both children hurried to put their coats on and follow him and the dogs outside to the yard.

"How long has Jordan been working security at the museum?" Skylar asked. "I see him all the time through work and he never mentioned it."

"I don't know, a couple months, I think," Savanna said. "I was surprised too; it's hard to believe the pay is worth the long drive and the nights away. His partner Taylor does it as well, though. Maybe they carpool, who knows."

"Have you heard anything yet about what was stolen?" Sydney asked. "Or how they even got in?"

"I don't know anything yet about which pieces are missing. Britt isn't answering their phone, Helene is… gone… and those details aren't being published by media outlets so far. As to how they got in, something happened with the power. Jordan said something went wrong with the security system and how it's supposed to work."

"Huh," Finn said. "My paramedic buddy in Ingham County was one of the first responders. He said something like that too—there was some kind of delay in the police getting the alarm notification."

"What do you mean?"

"I don't really know. I'll ask him."

"Are the police even confirming yet that this is connected to the Kenilworth robbery?" Uncle Freddie asked.

Harlan spoke up. "No. Nothing in the article I read this morning mentions it."

Savanna retrieved her phone from her purse, tapping the screen and setting it on the table. "This was posted on social media three hours ago. If you look closely at the gilded frame's bottom edge, below the graffiti, you can see the Lansing museum's title placard. Swipe up, and you'll see the one before it with the same creepy, spray-painted face was posted Wednesday after the Kenilworth break-in."

Chapter Five

S NOW. THE SCENT of it was in the air, wafting through Savanna's bedroom. The slightest crack she'd left between the window and frame was enough to invite it in. Was it real? Or was it wishful dreaming? She rubbed her eyes, blinking in the dimly lit bedroom. She'd been dreaming of snow again.

Last night after they'd finished at her parents, she, Aidan, and Mollie had ended up on her deck, gathered 'round her warm firepit roasting marshmallows. Savanna'd rescued a box of graham crackers from the back of the pantry along with the last few chocolate bars her class had sold during the holiday fundraiser. She'd assembled s'mores using the marshmallows Mollie roasted in abundance. The little girl had been fascinated by the process, watching closely. Savanna walked her through creating her own, putting two graham cracker squares on a paper plate, a generous portion of chocolate bar on one, and then showed her how to sandwich the hot, gooey marshmallow from the roasting stick between the graham crackers. The look on Mollie's face was priceless as she proudly presented her first one to her dad, and then bit into her own.

She wished she and Aidan had had time to talk on their

own. Since the traumatic gala Saturday night, she'd only seen him last night for an hour or two with Mollie present. He texted her good night, as always. Things just felt strained between them now. They planned to attend the tree-lighting parade Wednesday evening. Maybe she'd be able to catch some one-on-one time with him before that.

Now, in her slightly chilly room that smelled like snow, she sat up, and Fonzie leapt onto the bed and burrowed in the comforter, rolling on his back with all four legs kicking in the air. She closed her eyes and breathed deeply. She wasn't imagining it. Pulling the curtains back at the window, she gasped, gratified and relieved. A blanket of white had fallen during the night, dressing up the tree limbs and covering everything in sight.

"Fonzie! Come on!" She padded in bare feet and pajamas downstairs and flung open the front door. Fonzie bounded onto the deck and sunk into at least four inches of snow. The rolling dunes were a soft, gleaming white instead of tan sand, the lake a salt-free ocean, endless white caps as far as she could see. The morning had barely gotten underway, most of the sky still black. A hint of golden sunlight filled the sky to the east behind her house. It was much earlier than she ever woke up, but she didn't mind at all.

Curling up with a blanket and steaming cup of coffee in the living room, she opened her weather app—she'd avoided looking at it since the meeting with Lars last Friday. It was now perfect ice-sculpting weather. She waited for the clock to change to eight a.m. and called Lars. He told her he was already on the road and would be at the park by noon, as soon as he and his crew stopped to check in at Mitten Inn.

She tried Britt again, unprepared when they picked up this time. "Hey Savanna. I meant to call you back yesterday."

"I'm so sorry, Britt. I still can't believe it." When she was met with silence, she continued. "I'm sure they'll catch whoever did it. Rob said the FBI got involved in Kenilworth's robbery; that'll probably happen with ours. Have you heard anything about inventory yet? About what was taken?" She couldn't think about what possible damage any of their Impressionist paintings had taken—that part of the Kenilworth theft made no sense.

"I have no idea what was taken. How would I know that if you don't?"

She pressed her lips together, cringing. Stolen paintings were probably far from Britt's biggest concern. "I—you wouldn't. I'm sorry."

A heavy sigh came through the phone speaker. "No, I'm sorry. I'm not myself right now. I'm going back to bed. I'll let you go," they said.

"Wait. Are you," she hesitated, about to ask if they were okay. Of course, Britt wasn't okay, "free today?" She held her breath, expecting them to snap at her again. There wasn't a thing she could do to make this easier. But nothing about her friend's voice sounded like her friend. Britt shouldn't be alone right now.

"I guess. The museum's still closed until tomorrow. Helene's family isn't holding her memorial until after Christmas. What do you need?"

"Nothing at all. Would you want to come hang out and

watch the ice sculptors get started, maybe? Or I could come to you if that's better."

"I don't know. I thought Helene said Lars canceled."

"What? No, I don't think so. He was already on his way when I talked to him a little while ago."

"I might head over to you later. I'll let you know."

Her poor friend. She should have just insisted on driving to Lansing to keep Britt company today. Maybe she still would, after she took care of some of her to-do list.

In town, Savanna stopped at Fancy Tails and Treats to drop off Fonzie. Finn greeted her from the reception desk. He was dressed in his navy-blue paramedic uniform and jacket, National Air Med Lifeteam patch on his sleeve.

"Hey there, sister from another mister." He propped his elbows on the desk, leaning over to greet the little Boston terrier. "He's reporting for work, I take it?"

Finn always had a way of cheering her up. "If you don't mind. Where's my sister from the same mister?"

"Coffee run. Willow's out sick today so it's just me and her, the way I like it." He must have either just finished a shift or would be going in to work later tonight. Finn hung out here often, obviously smitten with his new wife. Savanna loved that Syd had found her perfect match.

"The honeymoon isn't over, huh?" she joked.

"Never."

Across the street, Savanna smiled and waved to Uncle Max at In Bloom as she passed. He raised a hand in greeting before turning his attention back to the customer at the counter. Max was a trained botanist, and he'd fallen into his current flower shop gig shortly after moving to Carson. After Libby had been killed and the flower shop went up for sale, the uncles bought it and made a small change to the name.

Miss Priscilla's Dance School was dark inside, closed for the holiday break. A half block later, past the law office where Skylar worked, she turned right onto the sidewalk that led to the cluster of Carson Village offices and the sheriff's department.

Nick Jordan waved her into his office. "Shut the door."

She did as he said. "Are you okay? How are June and her sister?"

"We're fine. I was about to ask the same of you." His eyebrows were drawn together in concern. "One of the guards told me you saw Helene when the power came back on. That was brutal."

"I don't know what happened, why she was in the elevator, who would ever target such a sweet person. How did she die? There was a lot of blood."

"I can't disclose that."

"The evidence people took her phone and then something else in the elevator with her—it looked like a flip phone, but I'm not sure."

He maintained his poker face. "That's odd. Ingham County is running the investigation, not us. The FBI was on scene Saturday night, too, before I left. Did you ask your friend Britt about Helene having a second phone?"

"Britt's not really talking much right now. They'd only been dating four or five months, but they were so happy. Britt sounded very down this morning, understandably," she said. "You don't happen to know which pieces were stolen, do you? That info seems hard to find."

"Nope. They haven't released it yet, to my knowledge."

She nodded. "I kind of thought so." It wasn't public information yet, but she'd be willing to bet Rob knew something. With his family's prestige, Rob seemed to be privy to far more details about Kenilworth's robbery. "Hey, are you in trouble now with your sergeant for moonlighting?"

"Nah. Well. Maybe a little. He'll get over it. He can't fire both me and Taylor."

She wanted to ask if he planned to continue at the museum but couldn't summon the nerve. It was none of her business. The best she could do was—"I was so glad you were there Saturday. Aidan and I both. We appreciate you watching out for us. I should go." She stood. "I just had to make sure you and June got out of there all right. It was really nice spending a little time with her Saturday until all heck broke loose. She's so funny—you never mentioned her great sense of humor." She was accustomed now to Jordan's serious, no funny business demeanor, but she hadn't expected his wife to be the complete opposite. She was delightful.

"She said the same exact thing. She really enjoyed talking with you." He was quiet until Savanna reached the door. "Maybe you and Aidan would come for dinner sometime? In the new year, when things settle down a little."

She looked back at him. "I'd love that! I'll take you up on it."

Savanna popped into the building next door to the police department, which housed Carson's parks and rec department and the new mayor's office. She'd had an idea brewing the last couple days. Her friend Yvonne looked up from her desk.

"Hey girl! Oh, my goodness, I'm so glad you're okay!" She rushed over and hugged Savanna. "I saw the news this morning. Holy cow, what an awful tragedy. Two guards dead plus the curator. How is Britt? Did either of you know the people who were killed?"

"I—it was on the news?" She shook her head. "I didn't see it. We knew the curator. She was Britt's girlfriend. We talked a little this morning, Britt is taking it really hard. I didn't know two guards died." She opened the internet browser on her phone and searched the museum. Sure enough, a couple news clips came up. She bookmarked them to watch later.

"Oh dear. I'm sorry. Yes, I can't remember names though. I'm so glad you're all right. They showed a clip of the gala during cocktail hour. I caught the two seconds of you and Aidan walking in. That *gown*. You were totally channeling Audrey Hepburn. Or maybe Jessica Rabbit."

She laughed. "Oh wow. That paints a picture! I feel so gorgeous now. You're so sweet." Yvonne was almost always a ray of sunshine no matter what the situation. "Well, I know I'm a movie star and everything, but I'm still running Frosty Fest until Hollywood calls. It's actually back on! We've already got like five or six inches on the ground and it's still coming down."

"When was it not on? I know the weather wasn't cooperating but come on, we're lakefront. The cold snap was bound to hit before Christmas."

"Good point. We do always have snow by Christmas, don't we? Britt practically guaranteed it too."

"The festival kind of revolves around the ice sculpture show, and I was so excited when we were able to get enough funding," Yvonne said. "When is the ice sculptor coming back? You sent him home after Friday's meeting, right?"

"Not exactly, but he didn't want to hang around town with no sign of a freeze. I get it. He was already on his way down from the U.P. this morning when I called him." She peered through the doors to the Parks and Recreation department; it looked deserted. Even the mayor's assistant across the lobby wasn't at his desk. "It's kind of slow right now. Would you want to come with me to check him out? To check out the ice-sculpting process, I mean," she corrected. She pulled at a loose thread on her sleeve, hoping Yvonne wouldn't see through her. She'd never been good at subterfuge.

"Sure! I'm curious how it's done. They use chainsaws or something, don't they?"

"I think so. The artist seemed really nice, I'm sure he'll give us a demonstration."

"Awesome! Let me grab my coat." Yvonne hurried through the door behind her desk, disappearing down the hall. She returned, handing Savanna a gift-wrapped box with a sparkly green and red bow. "In case I don't see you again before Christmas."

"Yvonne! You really shouldn't have. I've got something for you at home, but I haven't even started wrapping presents yet. I'm cramming everything into this week now that school's out." She turned the box in her hands. "Should I open it? Or wait?"

"Open it now!" Yvonne donned the cute jean jacket that was much more suited for spring than winter. She caught Savanna staring at her. "Don't yell at me. I should have been ready, but I wasn't; I couldn't find the storage bin my winter stuff is in."

"I won't yell at you. Sheesh, you're gonna freeze though. Here." She handed Yvonne her hat to wear. Discarding the paper and sticking the pretty bow on the lapel of her warm pink wool peacoat, Savanna gasped as she carefully extracted a beautiful snow globe from its foam nest. "Oh, my goodness! I love this!" She gave it a gentle shake, her heart swelling as she took in the scene within the glass globe. Snow floated down over a snow-covered park complete with an ice-skating rink, big decorated Christmas tree, and figures walking and sitting on park benches. Upon the ice rink, turning slowly in a circle, were two women skating, one blonde, the other brunette. The word BESTIES was painted in cursive on the glass globe. She grabbed Yvonne and hugged her tightly.

Her friend laughed. "I'm glad you like it!"

She was shocked by the tears that rushed to her eyes. Blinking rapidly, Savanna laughed, too. "I really love it. You're amazing. Thank you."

Yvonne patted her arm. "Aw, I didn't mean to make you

cry."

"You didn't—I'm not," she protested. "It's just… I love my sisters like crazy, but you're the first real best friend I've had since, like… I don't know. Since college probably. Thank you, Yvonne."

They hopped in Savanna's car in front of Fancy Tails and drove the rest of the way to the park; the temperature, a perfect thirty degrees this morning, had dropped into the teens. Lars Anders and his two assistants were already in the process of setting up. His ancient camper van was parked next to a large freezer truck.

Lars spotted them approaching and set down the large plastic bin he was carrying, coming over to them.

"You made great time," Savanna told him. "Thank you so much for doing this. I wanted to introduce you to my friend from the parks and rec office, Yvonne. She's the reason we were able to get enough sponsors for the event—she got nearly all the Carson businesses on board. Oh, and she also made the map I gave you! Yvonne, this is Lars Anders."

The big man towered over her petite friend. He removed his black knit cap. He shook Yvonne's hand, hers disappearing in his. "Hello Yvonne. It's nice to meet you. I like the map." He pulled the folded Frosty Fest map from a pocket. His eyes crinkled; he must be smiling, but it was difficult to tell with his ample red beard.

Yvonne stared up at him. "Hi Lars. Yes. It's nice to meet me. *You.* It's nice to meet you, too." She laughed at herself, a little too loud, and then stopped abruptly, her cheeks a brighter red than they'd been a moment ago from the cold. "So how did you get that ice all the way over there? It must be heavy. I never even thought about where the ice comes from. What if you run out or make a mistake? What do you carve the ice with? I wonder—" She'd started out so awkwardly and now she seemed to be trying to cover it with a machine gun barrage of questions.

Savanna rescued her. She linked an arm through Yvonne's, snapping her out of it. "We're fascinated by this process. I don't think I've ever seen it done in person. Do you have time to walk us through how it all works?"

Lars nodded. "Yes." He gave Yvonne an appraising look. "Are you cold? Here, take this." He shrugged out of the lined red and black flannel, leaving himself in coveralls and a black T-shirt.

"Oh no, I couldn't! You'll freeze." Yvonne pushed it back toward him, but he shook his head, holding it out.

"I don't get cold. You're shivering." When she didn't take it, Lars wrapped it around her shoulders and stepped back. "We have a hydraulic system in the ceiling of the freezer truck, let me show you how it works."

They followed him to the freezer truck, Yvonne shrugging into the thick flannel and buttoning it up. It went down to her knees. "It's so warm," Yvonne whispered, giving Savanna a wide-eyed glance.

Savanna smiled at her. "He seems super nice, right?"

Yvonne stopped walking and frowned at her. "Uh huh. What're you doing?"

"I don't know what you mean."

"Pfft. Ulterior motive much?" Yvonne said. She resumed her pace, dipping her head and sniffing the collar of the shirt. "Super nice."

Savanna burst out laughing. Lars turned, waiting for them by the truck. "Like you mind," Savanna whispered back, rolling her eyes.

"I don't mind at all." Yvonne jogged the last stretch over to Lars and stared into the open back of the truck. "Holy cow. Look at all the ice! Does that metal arm thingie pick up these big blocks? But then how did you get them all the way over there?" She sounded genuinely curious now, awkwardness gone.

"Like this. The hoist is used to move the ice from the truck onto that tilt cart, which allows us to load and unload vertically or horizontally." The sculptor showed them how the hooks went into the sides of the block of ice that must weigh two or three hundred pounds, attached to a Y connector chain which was lifted by the hydraulic arm built into a reinforced steel track in the ceiling. Lars maneuvered the ice block onto a sturdy-looking metal cart parked on the pavement. It had padded rails on the top and curved supports on the bottom. He steered the whole thing from the parking lot to the walkway that circled through Carson Park. He explained that he used something called crystal ice, ice prepared in a special manner in a Clinebell machine to remove trapped air for the clearest quality ice.

Savanna lost track of time as they got a private front-row demonstration of how ice sculptures were made. Lars began on the untouched ice block, firing up his chainsaw and carving out the crude shape. He paused and had his assistant step in to take over, and he crossed to a large, asymmetrical piece of ice that had already been pared down. Savanna couldn't guess what the end result would be. She and Yvonne stood, mesmerized, as the sculptor used a variety of chisels, circling the ice, until the head of a reindeer began to emerge, antlers and all.

"Would you look at that!" Yvonne marveled. "Oh, he's lovely. You're very talented, Lars."

Savanna excused herself, saying she needed to check in with the skating rink attendant on something. She actually did—during Frosty Fest, patrons had the option to "pay" for their rink time and skate rental with the festival tickets that could be purchased online or upon entry. She and Yvonne had arranged the payment system with sponsors. Confirming details with the rink manager took around two minutes; easy peasy. But she'd left her friend with Lars on purpose. Yvonne hardly dated, but she'd confided to Savanna this fall how discouraged she was with the occasional dates she did go on. She'd always been painfully shy and had trouble meeting men her age. The ones she did attract often turned out to be jerks. Lars Anders seemed very different than anyone Savanna had seen Yvonne date. His artist bio said he lived alone with his two cats, so he wasn't married. If he didn't have a girlfriend, maybe Yvonne would catch his interest. Judging by her friend's reaction, Lars had already succeeded in catching hers.

She bought a cup of hot chocolate from the rink concessions worker and found a bench in a sunny spot near the small evergreen tree. The hand-painted red and white sign read THE GIFTING TREE. She leaned forward, peering at the hangtags she could read as they turned in the breeze. Some were simple and sweet: *I wish for a kitten.* Others were practical: *I wish for grocery money* and *I wish my car had heat.*

Yvonne joined her. "I can't believe you did that. You're so sneaky."

"Yep." She smiled. "If I had said hey, come with me so I can introduce you to this really sweet, interesting, lumber-jack-looking artist dude, would you have come willingly?"

She giggled. "Probably not."

"It's not my fault—I had to be sneaky. It was just an idea. He does seem very nice, though, doesn't he?"

"Very nice and very... rugged. And did you notice his eyes when he smiled? He asked if I'm free for dinner."

Savanna squealed. "I love it! You're welcome."

"I'll let you know how it goes. Are you adding your wish to the tree?"

"No... not yet. I don't know what to wish for. I don't need anything," Savanna said. "So, do you set this up each year through the parks' department? It's such a great idea."

"Oh no," Yvonne said, shaking her head. "Not us. No-body knows who started it."

Lars was unloading another huge block of ice from the freezer truck as she and Yvonne were leaving. With a pang, she realized she hadn't said a word to the man about Helene. They were acquaintances, at least; maybe they'd been friends. Did he know?

Savanna put the car in park, telling Yvonne she'd forgotten about something and would be right back.

"Lars, do you have a minute?"

He stared at her, both gloved hands steadying the ice block suspended mid-air by large metal hooks.

"Sorry! Finish that first." She watched, wide-eyed. Some facets of the ice-sculpting process were more dangerous than most people realized. She hadn't meant to distract him while he was maneuvering a 300-pound weight down the skinny metal ceiling track. The last thing she needed on her conscience was the crushed foot of the artist she'd hired for Frosty Fest.

He lowered the ice onto the trolley in the parking lot and removed his gloves, slapping them on his thigh. A replacement flannel shirt had appeared from somewhere, this one thinner, not thickly lined like the one he'd given Yvonne. "Everything all right?"

"Yes. I mean, yes but no. It's about Helene Devereaux, the curator who put us in touch with you. I'm not sure if she's just a professional acquaintance or maybe a friend, but—"

"She's not a friend," he said firmly.

"Okay then." She tamped down her surprise at his response. "Well, there was a robbery at our museum. You haven't heard what happened?" She hated to be the bearer of bad news, though it didn't sound as if Helene's death would devastate him.

He shook his head. "I don't watch the news. Or read it. What happened?"

"There was a robbery Saturday at our museum. Helene

was killed." She scrutinized his reaction, but nothing at all changed in his expression. "I guess I just felt like I should have thought to mention it earlier, in case you knew her well. Two guards were also killed. Anyway. So, now you know," she finished awkwardly. She wasn't sure what she'd expected, but a complete lack of response to learning people had been killed, even for someone who had not been a friend, wasn't it.

"Okay," he said. "Thanks for telling me." He turned his attention to the tilt cart and went back to work.

On the short drive back to the village offices, Yvonne ran through the possible outfits she might wear, clearly excited for her dinner date tonight with Lars. "My sister says I look best in pink, but I just bought this pretty royal-blue blouse. I could wear that with my…"

Savanna was having trouble concentrating on their chat, an uneasy feeling creeping around her shoulders. She'd researched Lars Anders thoroughly for Frosty Fest, read articles on his sculpting talent, how he'd gotten started, his move from Norway to Quebec before coming to the States, his parents and siblings he'd left behind. Helene had known Lars a long time—at least since the museum had acquired two of his sculptures years ago. She'd vouched for him and connected them. There probably nothing to worry about.

"… the brown boots or black ones?" Yvonne asked.

She'd missed the whole question. "Hmm. Maybe go with whichever you're most comfortable in? They'd both look great." She parked in front of Yvonne's office.

"You're right. Nothing's worth getting sore feet—I should throw the black ones away. Thank you for my long lunch break, Savanna." Yvonne gave her a quick hug. "And thanks for the setup!"

"Anytime," Savanna said, smiling. She hoped she hadn't made a mistake. Now that she was thinking about it, she didn't really know Lars Anders at all. "Hey, call me when you get home and tell me everything! And if he turns out to be a bad date, text me and I'll make up an excuse and come rescue you." Her laugh sounded as forced as it felt. She was probably just being paranoid.

"Don't worry, I have a feeling he's a complete gentleman. I'll call you later!"

Chapter Six

TUESDAY MORNING, SAVANNA waited on her usual stool at the long, stainless steel lab countertop in the laboratory at Lansing Museum of Fine Art. Director Flynn had called her in, saying he needed *all hands on deck*. She knew nothing else yet, and she was the first one here. It was oddly quiet, being here on a weekday morning. Her usual hours as a consultant were evenings and weekends for the most part. Turning in slow circles on the stool, she texted Britt, but she didn't want to call and bother them; they'd been terrible lately at answering or returning calls. She'd wait for Britt to arrive and then they could both seek out the director together and hopefully be enlightened.

She called Rob while she was waiting. She'd been meaning to check on how Faye Havemeyer was recovering. True to his word, Rob hadn't called her again since last week; not even with the robbery Saturday night. She was certain he had plenty of thoughts on that. But he was maintaining healthy boundaries.

He answered on the second ring. "Hi Savanna." His subdued, quiet tone put her instantly on edge. Something had happened.

"I'm calling to check on how your mother's doing," she

said. "I know her situation was a little precarious last Friday."

"Hold on. Let me step into the hallway." After a minute of shuffling sounds, Rob said, "She's not doing well. They think she might have some kind of post-op infection. She's not progressing the way we expected. She's still in the ICU."

"Oh no. I'm so sorry." What to say? She couldn't help at all with this. "How's your sister taking things? And your father?" She crinkled her nose, glad he couldn't see. Even before Rob had confessed what made him break off their engagement, she'd never been a fan of his father.

"I don't know. Tiff and I trade off sitting with Mother. My father has been working even longer hours since it happened. He pretty much lives at Kenilworth," he said, his words laced with disappointment. "I saw that your museum was hit. It's a shame the FBI turned out to be correct. Detroit or New York will be next, if they're right. Was the robbery at yours targeted only at the Impressionists as well?"

"I haven't seen anything yet about what was taken. It's super frustrating. I can't even get into our west wing where the Impressionist works are. It's still cordoned off with police tape." She'd been checking online for updates since Saturday.

"I was just curious. My father says the FBI is watching for anything leaving the country. They've got feelers out through Interpol. The whole thing seems crazy to me. I doubt it'll be easy for the thieves to liquidate what they took, unless there are already buyers lined up."

"There are always buyers," Savanna said, more to herself than to Rob. Art dealers or gallerists would snap up a great deal on a prized piece of art, sometimes turning a blind eye if a piece was lacking adequate provenance, to then sell to private buyers or at auction for a great profit. A reputable collector would never accept a piece without provenance. That was precisely her area of expertise, or at least it used to be in Chicago, and as an independent contractor for the Lansing museum. Detective Jordan had once compared provenance to chain of custody, but for art: documented, certified proof of every location and owner a piece had, every change of hands and every expert who'd ever certified it as genuine. If a piece of artwork was authentic, she'd be able to prove it with provenance, except in cases where the historical record hadn't been maintained or records were lost. Even in those cases, there were other ways of authenticating a piece in terms of making sure it wasn't a forgery—artist's individual techniques, brushstroke methods, paints and pigments used and more. "A thief can always find a buyer," she reiterated.

"True. Good point. Remember that 'famous forgeries' course we had together junior year? The percentage of high-profile paintings that are fakes is so much higher than most people think."

"Yes, I remember being continually shocked in that class. I'm sure I'll find out soon enough which pieces of ours were affected—stolen or otherwise. Our director called me and the rest of the lab staff in this morning."

"Well, I hope it's not too bad." Voices in the background and a series of beeps filtered through, reminding her he was at the hospital.

"Listen," she said, "I hope your mom's recovery makes a turnaround soon. Let her know I'm thinking of her and sending prayers."

"I will," he said. "Should I… do you want me to update you if… if it doesn't?"

What was he asking? She was grateful for the boundaries he'd maintained with her, but now he was almost playing the martyr. "Of course, I'd want to know. But she's going to get better, Rob. I believe that."

As she dropped her phone into her purse, the art restoration expert Paisley Leonard came through the doors. "Hey Savanna. This should be interesting, huh?"

"Definitely," she agreed. How many pieces had been defaced? Was Director Flynn going to have to contract out for more restoration specialists, like Kenilworth had?

Britt came in next. Savanna grabbed Britt and hugged them the moment they arrived. She didn't let go until Britt did. She searched their face. "I've been worried about you."

Britt gave her a one-shoulder shrug. "I'm fine."

"Are you? Because I don't think I would be. What can I do to help, Britt? Is her family taking care of arrangements on their own? Did you have to call any of her friends?"

"There's really nothing you can do. I love you for asking, truly. Her friends all know now; her parents and brother gave me a few to call and they handled the rest, plus her ex-husband." That piqued Savanna's interest—she hadn't realized Helene had been married before. Britt continued, "Let me know if you want the details for the memorial next week."

"Of course, I'd like details, I'll be there. We can go together if you want," she told them. What wasn't Britt saying? Her normally chatty friend was obviously hurting and trying to keep it all bottled up. She started to say as much; ignoring grief never made it go away. If anything, it only made things worse in the long run. "Britt—"

Two of the restoration techs entered, both young men in their twenties, their conversation dying down upon seeing somber Savanna and Britt. Director Flynn pushed through the lab doors a moment later, accompanied by security guard Donald Tate. Tate hit the automatic open button, ushering in a handler pushing a long-padded table resembling a hospital gurney with a wrapped piece of art atop it.

"Good morning, all," Director Flynn said. "We've got some work ahead of us. I appreciate you being here, especially in light of the upsetting experience on Saturday."

She raised an eyebrow at Britt, who rolled their eyes and mouthed the word upsetting. As if the gala had run short of prime rib or the band hadn't shown up.

Flynn donned purple nitrile gloves, matching the handler, and they carefully moved the wrapped mystery piece onto the lab counter. He nodded and the young man took off wheeling the table, accompanied by the guard. "We have two more coming." He shook his head. "This is a travesty. I cannot fathom who would do such a thing." He opened one of the several laptops on the lab counter and navigated through a few screens. The large LED screen over the counter lit up.

Sergei Minkov's famous *Taiga Desolation* filled the screen, the landscape scene grotesque now with the bloodred spray-painted devil's face, too familiar after seeing it on social media.

"Why?" Paisley asked, her tone horrified. "This is going to be painstaking to fix, if it's even repairable. Why would anyone do this?"

"They had access. Why not just take it?" Britt asked.

"It feels like an insult," Savanna said. "Not just the vandalism, but the graffiti, this graffiti. It feels elementary. Like a sick joke."

"Yes," Director Flynn said. "I agree with that. We're being mocked. My only hope is that the FBI's Art Crime Team will get to the bottom of this, who's involved, and what's behind the aggressive destruction aimed at such a specific type of art. These are the others." He clicked through the other two: a Julian Rothman painting of a similar theme Savanna recalled writing a paper on as a college freshman, and a Francois Laurant valued at 6.2 million.

Director Flynn helped the returning guard and handler with the remaining paintings until all three were laid out on the laboratory workstation countertop like some ugly parody of a fine art display. He gave them their assignment. "With the holiday nearly upon us and patronage temporarily down, the museum's board of directors appreciates any headway we're able to make. Since the thieves had access, each piece will need a new certification, including validation and update of existing provenance, before restoration can begin."

Savanna followed Flynn into the hallway, noticing he'd stationed Donald Tate at the door. She nodded at the guard, glad for the added security. "Director Flynn, I have a question."

"Yes? Oh. Ms. Shepherd, I know you're here on a consulting basis. I should have clarified—any amount of time you're able to spend on this is great. I believe you work full time somewhere, if memory serves?"

"Yes—"

"No problem. I'm glad you're here now. Whatever you can do is fine. Be sure to invoice payroll."

She nodded, grateful (and not for the first time) for this side gig Britt had pulled her into. It allowed her to keep her authenticating skills sharp and put some extra money in her bank account. "Thank you. But that wasn't my question; can we get a list of the other museum's defaced and stolen pieces please?"

"What for?"

"I think it'll help as we move forward with certification and restoration," she said, off the cuff. "It's a unique situation. Having the ability to coordinate with other specialists if needed would be helpful." That part was true. But she had an ulterior motive for wanting the lists.

Flynn raised his eyebrows. "I see. I hadn't thought of that. Let me find out what I can do."

She pressed her luck. "And our loss? Do you know where I might get an itemization of what was taken Saturday?"

"Of course," he said. "I'll forward that to you when I get back to my office."

All she had to do was ask. She spun around to head back inside, self-satisfied smile on her lips, and found Britt waiting by the guard outside the lab. She tipped her head curiously. "Hey there. Were you looking for me?"

"I was. I called dibs on the Laurant for us to get into,"

Britt said. "If that's okay with you?" Despite their current work in marketing and acquisitions for the museum, Britt's career had begun in authentication and they were excellent.

"You just had to take the most valuable piece, didn't you? But no pressure," she said, elbowing them.

Back in the lab, the first thing Savanna did was to put in a requisition for the Lansing Museum of Fine Art's own provenance records on file for the painting. It was the quickest, easiest way to begin Francois Laurant's *Notre Dame de Paris*.

She spotted the email from Director Flynn with the full list of missing and defaced works from all three museums. This was a much more comprehensive view of the thefts. She sorted through them mentally and decided she needed to see it on paper. She hit print, and then as an afterthought, clicked back to the images Flynn had shown them of the vandalized works and printed those too.

"I think we can get a chip of the spray paint from this thicker area here, without going all the way down to the original surface," Britt said, pointing with a thin scalpel.

She nodded, glancing around. The other staff in the lab were involved in various stages of the same tasks, but no one had yet decided to dive into analyzing the type of paint used for the graffiti. She issued a heads-up, letting Paisley and the others know they'd update the room with any results found.

Ever so carefully, nitrile gloved hand holding the large painting in place, Britt used the pointed blade to extract a speck, a scrap of dried red paint about the size of a sesame seed. Tiny flecks of red dust floated into the air along with it, eventually settling back onto the canvas. Savanna caught that—she hadn't seen that happen before. But she'd also never seen a thick spray-painted graffiti image on a museum piece before. They were into new territory.

They placed it on the glass slide she offered. Savanna secured it with a smaller, sterile glass square and placed it on the waiting pedestal of the laboratory's polarization microscope. This common authentication tool enabled a detailed analysis of paint layers and pigments, which would help target the right technique for removing the graffiti without rendering the valuable, irreplaceable work of art worthless.

She brought up the slide onscreen so they could both see. Individual paint layers came into focus from bottom upward, a variety of shades now visible. She saved the data supplied and removed the slide, carrying it around to the opposite side of the counter.

"The transmission electron microscope will give us a better idea of what we're dealing with," she said. "Okay, check this out."

Britt joined her, taking a turn to peer through the lens. "So, we have an oil-based spray paint with a petroleum distillate binder or carrier but an unknown type of solvent. But knowing it's an oil-based paint should let us get started removing it from the piece, right?"

Savanna took another look. "No. Removal shouldn't begin until we know for sure what VOC we'll have exposure to. I'd normally assume it's just a common, run-of-the-mill brand oil-based spray paint, which wouldn't have any restricted compounds like toluene or benzene, but nothing about this theft and vandalism crime has been common or run-of-the-mill."

"Can you even get spray paint with benzene in it anymore?" Britt asked. "I thought they stopped using it, it's too dangerous as a solvent. As far as volatile organic chemicals go, I'd rather be exposed to lead or pretty much anything else rather than benzene, even if we're just cleaning it away."

"Totally agree. I don't know how much off-gassing would occur during removal for a project like this." Savanna frowned, thinking. Chemistry and hazmat classes had been part of her training in authentication, but she'd rarely had to consider exposure to dangerous compounds in her work—at least until now.

"Wait—" Paisley looked up from the Minkov she was examining. "I'm not risking my health for any job. How can we make 100 percent sure there's nothing in this spray paint like benzene or otherwise? If it's on our Safety Data Sheet, we shouldn't be messing with it and breaking it down. Oh my God. Should you have had a respirator on before cutting that spray paint sample out?" She pointed at Britt.

Savanna spoke up. "I'll call Director Flynn."

Paisley pushed her stool back and stood, crossing to the door and grabbing her coat. "I'm out. I want to see confirmation that these pieces have been cleared for us to safely work with them." She disappeared through the lab doors.

"Let's all step out while we get ahold of Flynn. I'm hoping the FBI would have already been on top of it if there was any issue with the graffiti's chemical composition. But we can't assume that; we need to make sure."

THE TWO RESTORATION techs carefully removed and discarded their gloves, Savanna and Britt doing the same. The image of that red dust drifting into the air with the paint chip removal stayed with her. What, if anything, had they already been exposed to?

The four of them filed out into the hallway where Donald Tate was still stationed. "All finished for the day? That was quick."

"We're not done. We've barely started," Savanna said. "But there's a potentially hazardous issue with the graffiti and restoration process. We need to talk with Director Flynn before continuing." She pulled out her phone and called the director's office number on speaker, hoping Flynn could put their minds at ease so they could get back to work. When it eventually went to voicemail after several rings, she groaned, frowning at Britt.

"Try again," Britt said.

While she did, Tate tapped the screen on his phone, motioning to her to hang up. "His schedule shows him off-site until tomorrow. Security has access to the director's schedule in case of any issues," he explained. "Looks like he's back in the morning but is reachable by cell. You said something about a potentially hazardous concern?"

She nodded. "We need some clarification from him before we can continue working today."

Tate turned his museum issued phone toward her, showing her the director's personal cell phone number. "Go ahead and call him, I'm sure he'd want to know."

"Thank you!" But when the additional attempt also proved fruitless, Savanna gave up and left Director Flynn a voicemail, asking him to get back to her as soon as possible and letting him know they'd had to pause working.

The younger of the two assistants shifted his weight from one foot to the other, watching Savanna's phone still in her hand. "Does he usually call back pretty quickly? I've got Christmas shopping to do if we really can't get back into the lab today."

"Yes, usually," Donald Tate said.

After another several minutes of their little group hanging out around the closed laboratory doors, Britt finally called it. "Even with the HEPA filters in there, we're going to have to wait for information from Flynn before we can do anything else today. I'll let him know I made the decision for our team to head out for now. I'll get ahold of you guys as soon as we hear from him."

"I GUESS I'LL lock up then. Everyone have what you need from the lab?" Tate stood in front of the security keypad, his back to them blocking the device from view. Savanna had noticed all of the guards used the same close proximity stance at entrances and exits, obviously for good reason. The guard swiped his badge and punched in some numbers and the audible sound of the locks engaging on the laboratory doors told her the room was now secure, but she'd seen nothing—

as it should be. There were multiple levels of clearance for the various roles within the museum.

"So," Britt said as they took the stairwell down, "lunch? Anywhere but here?"

Oof. How had she not even considered how painful it must be for them to be here? Now it made sense that Britt had chosen stairs over elevator. They exited at ground floor, right by the door to employee parking. She linked an arm through their elbow. "Yes please. I'm starving." She held up the sheaf of papers she'd grabbed off the laboratory printer as they were rushing out—the list of vandalized and stolen items from each of the three museums, and the printed images of the three vandalized pieces at Lansing. She'd find time later on to take a closer look at them.

Chapter Seven

WEDNESDAY MORNING BEGAN in the best way possible—with Aidan and Mollie in Savanna's kitchen, having coffee and hot cocoa, respectively, and fresh from the oven cinnamon rolls. Aidan's call had woken her this morning at six, well before her usual Christmas break wake-up time, and she didn't even mind. They'd barely had a chance to talk since Sunday dinner.

He'd felt terrible waking her, but Mollie's babysitter had come down with the flu. Savanna immediately told him she'd love to watch Mollie for the day. She'd offered to pick her up so he wouldn't be late for rounds at the hospital, but he'd already shuffled around his schedule for a later start.

He poured himself more coffee and topped off Savanna's cup. "I'm so glad you don't mind doing this today. You're sure it won't interfere with anything you've got planned?"

Director Flynn had never returned her calls yesterday. Now she was glad to have the unexpected free day. "The only thing on my schedule today is lunch at Caroline's. My work today fell through," she told Aidan. "Is it wrong that I'm happy about it?"

"Nope. Mollie and I are happy about it too." He drained his coffee, rinsed it and put it in the dishwasher, and crouched down in front of his daughter, who was dressed in a red, velvety dress with a green sequined Christmas tree on the front and matching green tights. "I'm a little jealous. You two are going to have so much fun. Be kind, and take care of your things, okay?"

She nodded, her pale blond hair pulled up in two pigtails moving with her. Savanna spied a small Santa Claus barrette near each pigtail, holding the loose wisps in place. "Daddy, you be kind and take care of your things too. Ms. Shep—I mean Ms. Sav…." She frowned, biting her lip. "I m-m-mean, Savanna and I are gonna take Fonzie to get some treats."

Savanna's throat felt thick with tears. Mollie's stuttering problem had nearly evaporated around her, even at school, as she'd grown more and more comfortable with her the past two years. This bit of confusion over what exactly she should be called, and the accompanying stuttering, was new. She had an inkling of why.

She left the little girl at the kitchen table with Fonzie at her feet and walked Aidan out. After he'd kissed her goodbye and gotten behind the wheel, she motioned for him to roll down the window. "Hey. Try not to worry, okay? I'll make sure she has a good day and forgets all about that," she said, inclining her head toward the house.

"I'm not worried. She loves you, and she always loves seeing Caroline and the poodles. Can we talk more later?"

"Absolutely." Her gaze caught a small Santa Claus pin attached to his tie. They'd been together long enough now that her mind automatically searched for whatever matching item he and Mollie had chosen that day, a custom that had begun after her mother died when she was three.

"Thank you again, Savanna. I appreciate you taking care of her."

She leaned in and planted another kiss on him. "Please stop thanking me for taking care of Mollie. She means the world to me." As she watched him pull away, she wondered whether he'd tried the in-laws before calling her. She chose to believe he hadn't.

Director Flynn called as Aidan was pulling out of the driveway. Flynn was about two hours too late—she was booked for the day. He apologized, saying of course the FBI Art Crimes division had already run toxicity tests on the graffiti and confirmed they were safe for restoration work to begin. "I should have made that clear yesterday morning. I'm emailing you and the team the analysis reports from the vandalized pieces at Kenilworth and Samuel Morton museums as we speak," he said. "No worries about today. I appreciate whatever availability you have."

As irritated as she'd been yesterday to have to leave the lab without any answers, Savanna was grateful for the flexibility of her side job. She headed back inside to collect Mollie and Fonzie and get the day started.

At the baked goods counter inside Fancy Tails and Treats, Sydney handed Savanna a white box tied with string, the box printed with tiny Scottie dogs dressed in red plaid. "Princess and Duke love these, I promise. The chicken churro treats are their favorite," Syd told her. "I threw in a few holiday ornament cookies, too, just for fun. If Caroline asks, they're made from peanut butter, unbleached flour, honey, and egg. The color in the icing is from chicken broth."

"You're amazing." Savanna peeked under the lid. The golden ornament cookies looked good enough to be people food—except for the thought of chicken flavored cookie frosting. "Are you going to the tree lighting tonight?"

She nodded. "Finn's working, but I'll be there with Kate. I'll look for you!" Sydney was friends with most of the small business owners up and down Main Street. Kate of Kate's Yoga held class in the building across the street, next door to Uncle Max's flower shop.

"Syd, why is the smaller tree not included in the tree-lighting parade? The procession goes straight past the ice rink and that tree to get to the big evergreen."

"You mean The Gifting Tree?"

"Yes, that one. And who on earth is behind that? It's been going on for the last few years, but no one knows. How can that be?"

Syd shrugged. "I don't know. I've never seen anyone setting it up or maintaining it or anything. But I did go put a bow on one of the hangtags. It was for someone who needs a winter coat for their kid. The weather's only going to get colder; I hate thinking that people right in our town don't have the means to keep warm, or give their children nice presents, or even afford enough food."

She nodded. "I know. So, that's really how it works? All I have to do is pick a tag with a wish I can fulfill, and attach a bow? That's so it's clear which ones are already spoken for?"

"Yep," Syd said. "That's the idea. I always do a couple on behalf of Fancy Tails. Didn't you chip in on the gifts Mom and Dad bought last year for the tags they chose?"

"I did, yeah, but I didn't really understand. It's such a nice idea, I love that someone just sets it all up each year. After I put a bow on one of the tags, how do I know where to take the gift? I didn't see an address on the couple I looked at."

Over in the grooming side of the salon, Mrs. Sims spoke up. "Folks can choose to be anonymous or not. Some have names and addresses, but some don't."

"You didn't read the instructions at all, did you?" Sydney teased.

"It's all right, hon," Mrs. Sims told Savanna, coming over to the treat counter. "Good for you for asking. All the tags are numbered. For the ones without an address, you just label your gift with whatever number is on the tag and drop it off in the ice-skating rink across from the tree. December 24th is pick up day. Whoever made a wish at the tree goes to the ice rink lobby and finds their numbered gift."

Her sister chimed in. "So, if you're thinking of contributing, you only have until this Friday to do it. Saturday's Christmas Eve."

"Okay, I'm definitely doing it. I'll pick a good one tonight, or maybe after Mollie and I go see Caroline."

Mollie perked up at her name, hopping out of the overstuffed aqua chair by the window. She packed her coloring book and crayons into her little backpack. "Where are we going?"

"We're going to see my friend, Mrs. Carson," Savanna said.

"I know Mrs. Carson! Daddy takes me there sometimes. Is that for Princess and Duke?" She pointed at the box.

"It is. But we need some treats, too, don't we? Do you think the sweets shop has anything we'd like?"

Savanna let Mollie and Fonzie lead the way to Main Street Sweets. After a stop at the deli to pick up soup and sandwiches, they drove the short distance to the Carson Mansion.

Jack Carson, Caroline's son, opened the front door of the Carson Mansion, smiling widely. "Hello there! Miss Mollie and Ms. Shepherd, it's great to see you." He ushered them in. With Caroline now a sprightly ninety-two, her family visited often in case she needed help—but she usually didn't.

The *Ms. Shepherd* caught Savanna's attention as he said it. It made sense, Jack calling her that in front of Mollie. Jack was the elementary school librarian and computer teacher right across the hallway from Savanna's art classroom. She'd grown oblivious to hearing *Ms. Shepherd*, she heard it so many times on any given day. But the fact that Mollie heard her called Ms. Shepherd and sometimes Savanna and sometimes Auntie Vanna or Savvy must be a lot for an eight-year-old to keep track of and wonder about her own place in Savanna's life. She and Aidan had encouraged Mollie to call her Savanna last year when they'd begun dating seriously, but even that was tricky during school hours, as she'd seen Mollie work to switch gears and revert to Ms. Shepherd.

They followed Jack through the gorgeous historic home

of the town matriarch, the poodles meeting them halfway down the hallway, prancing and dancing around Fonzie, who Caroline had said was welcome anytime. Savanna had grown up believing, at least until she was eight or nine, that Caroline Carson was her grandmother. Even after she and her sisters were old enough to understand that their families were just close friends, lazy Sunday afternoons and long summer days had been spent on Caroline's wraparound porch and the beach beyond.

In the parlor, Caroline greeted them from her wingback chair, enormous windows behind her looking out over Lake Michigan. The adjacent wall held the picturesque mural Savanna had painted for her of her late-husband Everett's sailboat depicted on the waves of blue water.

"Whatever did I do to deserve a visit from two of my favorite people," she exclaimed, inviting them in. Her coiffed silver hair and fashionable floral scarf complemented her beige linen pantsuit paired with bejeweled sneakers. Princess hopped up on the chair, settling in beside Caroline, and Duke curled up in his little dog bed by the cozy fireplace.

Mollie pointed at the older woman's feet. "I like your fancy shoes."

Caroline laughed. "They're pretty, aren't they? My granddaughter insists I wear only sneakers these days. No more mules or slides since my recent near-miss fall. But if I have to wear sneakers, I require them to be fancy. Lauren decorated these for me."

"Fancy is always better," the little girl said.

"You're very wise to already know that," Caroline said. "I

A STROKE OF MURDER

like your fancy Christmas tree dress."

Savanna gave the woman a brief hug and excused herself to help Jack set up lunch in the kitchen. As she left the room, she heard the exchange continue.

"Daddy let me wear it even though it's a dressy dress. And then we picked our matchy Santas, see? I have the Santa barrettes and Daddy has the Santa pin for..."

In the kitchen, Jack handed her soup bowls and plates. They worked together setting the table. Savanna arranged an assortment of sandwich portions on a big platter in the middle of the table and filled the soup tureen with the deli's to die for hearty chicken noodle soup, perfect for the chilly weather outside.

"I keep meaning to call your coordinator at Carson Ballroom," Savanna said. Last year, Jack and a silent partner had purchased the long-standing ballroom and adjacent theater and launched a large-scale, much-needed renovation. Since it'd finished, both spaces were now in constant use. She was lucky the ballroom happened to be available on New Year's Eve for her wedding, thanks mostly to Snow Fest being the main event most folks would be attending that night.

"Did you need to make some changes to the setup?" Jack asked. "I can have her call you if you'd like."

"No, nothing like that, just to confirm we're all set with details. Thank you again... you should really raise the rental fee. I think you're undercharging."

He shrugged. "We're a new enterprise. Maybe next year we'll bump up the fees." He put a kettle on the stove. "Tea with lunch? Grandmother was so happy you called last night.

You're sure you wouldn't rather use the dining room?"

She laughed. "For a weekday lunch of soup and sand-wiches and tea? I mean, I know we love fancy but that seems excessive. Right here is just fine." The Carson Mansion dining room was like something out of a princess movie. Jack was one of the most down-to-earth people she knew, especially at work, but sometimes he accidentally reminded her that he was indeed a Carson through and through.

"I get it," Jack said, smiling. "We always eat right here in the kitchen anyway. She prefers it. How are you and Aidan since the scary experience in Lansing Saturday? Are you both okay?"

"We are now. I am, at least. I think he's still rattled. It was an awful night." She didn't elaborate. Awful didn't seem a strong enough word, especially given the fear he'd voiced to her. "That's part of the reason I called though. I can ask her this, but you might know the answer. Your grandmother's finished liquidating pretty much all of her fine art collection, hasn't she? After the whole ordeal with the forgeries we found in her collection, I remember she'd only kept a few select pieces, right?"

"You remember correctly. I know the large one in the library is her most prized possession, but I don't know artists very well. There are a couple others still here. My grandfa-ther was the avid collector, more so than Grandmother. I don't think she's acquired any new pieces. She'd be able to list the ones she kept. Why do you ask?"

"The one in the library is a genuine Sergei Minkov. I don't even know the value of it anymore. A couple years ago we estimated its worth at around 2.5 million, but since then, many of the paintings thought to be Minkovs have been exposed as forgeries. Some were tied to the forgery ring involved in your grandmother's pieces but others with private collectors mainly in Europe were also discovered to be fakes. With there being fewer genuine Minkov works in circulation, the value of that substantial painting in her library will have gone up considerably."

Jack raised an eyebrow. "Are you suggesting she sell? You have a buyer?"

"What? No. I'm concerned that painting may be at risk. Jack, for some reason, the thieves who robbed my museum also robbed Kenilworth a few days prior. They started in California at the Morton Samuel Museum. The FBI thinks it's the same person or persons each time. They're only taking Impressionist paintings." She waited for his reaction, but it was slow in coming.

"So... Grandmother's painting in the library is... by an Impressionist artist?"

"Yes. Minkov pieces have been taken from each museum."

"But only museums are being robbed. Surely there's no interest in breaking into a private home just to steal one painting?"

"I think you're underestimating the value of that one painting. Listen," she said, "I'm actually glad I could run this by you before talking with Caroline about it. I don't want to upset her. I haven't even had a moment to ask Detective Jordan if he thinks it's a legit concern or if I'm being overly cautious. Maybe I should do that, before causing any anxiety or worry for your grandmother?"

High pitched giggles and a few barks came from the parlor, accompanied by Caroline's singing. Mollie was in heaven hanging out with the pups and delightful Caroline. Jack sat down at the table and poured himself a cup of steaming hot tea. He didn't answer Savanna right away.

She mirrored him; tea was always better here for some reason. She propped elbows on the table and leaned in, risking having poor manners to make her point. "Jack. I don't want to put you in an odd position, asking you to decide. I can talk with Caroline about all of this if you think that's best. Or I can wait. Either way, I'll be running this by Jordan later today. If he has any concerns, I'm sure he'll assign someone to keep watch for a while."

"How would these elite art thieves even be able to find out Grandmother has that painting?" he asked. "I think it's a little far-fetched. It'd be like a needle in a haystack, wouldn't it? The thieves searching for private collectors' pieces that fit what they want, when they could just as easily keep targeting big museums."

"That's a good question. I've thought about it too. Breaking into a private home brings infinitely less risk than breaching a high-tech security system. As for how anyone would know she has that Minkov, all it would take is an online search. Each authentic work of art has its own unique historical footprint of sorts detailing past and present owners from creation onward."

Jack's eyes widened. "All right. That's good to know. I

had no idea. I don't think you're crazy."

She smiled. "Excuse me? I don't recall anyone saying I might be crazy."

He laughed. "Overly cautious then. I'm glad you told me about your concern. But..." Now he leaned in as well. "You know she's under Dr. Gallager's care. She has a heart condition that she's on two medications for. What if I just stayed over the next few nights, until you and the detectives figure out if we should take measures to protect her better or move the painting out of the house. I'd rather not worry her yet."

"I agree with that. I'll keep you updated. In the meantime, I think I remember her door and window locks being beefed up two years ago after the whole forgery debacle thing, right?"

"Yep. Dead bolts at most of the doors and keypad entry, and the window screens are all hardwired into her home security alarm system. We'd know immediately if anyone tried to get in. I don't think Grandmother will know anything's amiss if I just tell her my power got knocked out due to weather and I need to stay here for a bit."

"Perfect. I hope I'm wrong—but I appreciate you taking it seriously."

"Of course! I—"

Mollie appeared in the doorway, Caroline close behind, a little slower with her cane.

"What are we taking seriously, kids?" Caroline asked.

Jack pulled out her chair for her. "Um—"

"Training for the new lesson plan software," Savanna said. "The school district overhauled the way we lesson plan each week and the training sessions were intense last week before break."

Jack picked up where she left off. "I wasn't a fan of the new software. But Savanna's right; I've gotta get with the program. We start using the new system as soon as school starts up in January."

Everything they'd said was true, so fudging on giving Caroline the answer she'd asked for didn't feel too much like a lie. Savanna ladled soup into each of their bowls. "Oh!" She'd suddenly come up with a much safer topic. "Caroline, you have to tell me: What's up with The Gifting Tree in the park? Whose project is that; who sets it up each year?"

Caroline shrugged. "I haven't the slightest notion, dear. Why do you ask?"

"I don't know. Just curious, I guess. It's a sweet idea. It just seems wild that nobody knows who does it."

"Not everything is a mystery needing to be solved," Jack said pointedly. "Maybe whoever does it doesn't want the recognition."

"Hmm." She made a face at him for the mystery comment. She wasn't trying to be nosy. The unexplained, in general, tended to nag at her, making her pick at it like a loose string until it loosened and eventually it all unraveled. That tendency was the reason Detective Jordan now entertained her theories and listened to her questions that admittedly were sometimes far-fetched.

AFTER LUNCH, SAVANNA had a surprise for Mollie. She'd reserved two spots for them at The Crafty Kiln. The new shop opened last month in the vacant storefront next door to Sydney's place and was the first of its kind in Carson. Savanna had already stopped by and scouted it as a possible field trip location for her art classes. She got to choose one destination each year for two of her classes. The Crafty Kiln was a pottery painting and glass fusing DIY experience she knew Mollie was going to love. Several long tables occupied the center of the space, the walls lined with racks and display shelves full of bare ceramic pieces in every shape and interest category one could imagine, from animals to musical instruments to fashion, flat ornaments and mugs and bowls and piggy banks, plus a tall case of drawers that held bits and pieces and chunks of glass in a rainbow of colors. The glass fusing craft was more advanced, maybe something she and her sisters would try sometime.

But today at two o'clock, she and Mollie would each get to choose and paint whatever pottery piece they'd like, for as long as they'd like, with the hundreds of paints and brushes available. In three days, their pieces would be ready for pickup, vividly glossy and lovely after being fired in the kiln. She'd only hinted to Mollie what their afternoon project would be. She wasn't sure who was more excited, her or her soon-to-be stepdaughter.

First, though, she and Mollie stared up at the modestly sized evergreen near the ice-skating rink at Carson Park. There must be fifty or sixty tags on ribbons hung on branches. Many of them had been claimed and bore a bow as indication that someone would fulfill that wish. Each intact hangtag was large, the size of an index card, but in the style of an old-fashioned raffle ticket, with a perforation halfway down and duplicate info on top and bottom—one to be left on the tree from the person filling out the tag with their wish and the other to be torn off and taken by the person agreeing to fulfill the wish.

She saw now that if she'd taken the time to read, the wooden Gifting Tree sign bore simple instructions:

TO MAKE A WISH:
- WRITE YOUR WISH ON A TAG, ONCE ABOVE THE PERFORATION AND AGAIN BELOW
- INCLUDE YOUR ADDRESS OR PHONE NUMBER, OR MAKE A NOTE OF YOUR TAG NUMBER
- WISH FULFILLMENT OCCURS BETWEEN DECEMBER 1st – 23rd
- WATCH FOR DELIVERY TO YOUR HOME OR TO THE ICE RINK LOBBY

TO GRANT A WISH:
- CHOOSE A WISH FROM THE TREE AND TEAR OFF THE BOTTOM PORTION
- STICK A BOW ON THE TOP HALF
- GRANT THE WISH—DELIVER TO THE WISHER'S HOME OR THE ICE RINK LOBBY BY DECEMBER 23rd

"What do you think?"
Mollie looked up at her. "This is hard. I can't decide."

Savanna nodded. "You said it, girl. This is really hard. I want to grant all these wishes."

"What's that one up there, with purple writing?"

"Let's see. Want me to pick you up?" Mollie nodded so she did, letting her reach for the still intact tag filled out in purple pen. "What does it say?"

"I wish I could af-af-ford the Barbie Dreamhouse my d-dog-dau-daughter wants for Christmas," she read, sounding out the tricky words but not stuttering. Mollie looked sad. Savanna set her down. "That mama or daddy can't get the Barbie house for her? Do you think Santa will bring it?"

"I don't know. Santa does a lot, but he can't think of everything. Maybe I should grant this wish, so the little girl will get the Dreamhouse?"

She nodded. "Yes. Grandma Jean got me that last Christmas. That little girl should get one too. Her dolls need a house."

Savanna tore off the bottom half, noting an address, thankfully. That seemed easiest, but she understood why some folks might not want their address on the tag. "Pick a bow," she told Mollie. When she'd stuck a silver bow on the back of the still hanging top half, she bent and flipped over another one on a low branch that she'd seen earlier. She loved the thought of gifting a toy, but Mollie should know that some people also were hoping for more basic necessities.

"Hey, did you see this one?" she asked, holding it out for her to read.

Mollie read, "My dad's boots have holes and his socks get wet at work. I wish he had new boots size ten," she read smoothly without pause. "Me and Daddy could do this one! Daddy just bought new boots, I bet he knows the good kind to get for that daddy."

Savanna nodded. "That's a great idea. Tear off the bottom and I'll put it in my purse for you to give your dad. Don't forget to put a bow on the part that's left," she added. The more she was around Mollie, the more she loved her.

Mollie slipped her hand into Savanna's as they turned to go. The girl had grown quiet, her pace slow as a snail. Savanna stopped. "Hey Moll, everything okay?"

"I never made a wish."

Savanna felt like a heel. "I totally forgot! Here you go." She grabbed a tag and the purple pen from the plastic bin.

Mollie hunched over the tag, taking several minutes to write her wish—twice. The clock at the entrance of the park read 1:58 p.m. They were going to be late for The Crafty Kiln appointment. Mollie was still writing. Savanna tilted her head, trying to discreetly get a peek at her progress. She must be almost done by now. She had no luck seeing any part of the tag—the little girl kept one mittened hand atop the paper as she wrote, shielding it from view. Her wish was top secret, apparently. Savanna pressed her lips together, ignoring the clock. She refused to rush the girl.

She finished and found an empty branch, hanging the purple ribboned, purple inked tag on it. "No looking," she said, staring up at Savanna.

"Of course not. Don't worry." Now she was truly curious.

Mollie slipped her hand into hers again and this time

went willingly. Savanna glanced back at the purple-themed wishing tag, trying to memorize exactly which branch it was on.

Chapter Eight

CARSON'S ANNUAL TREE lighting always took place on December 21st, celebrated with a parade down Main Street leading to the mammoth evergreen. The Shepherd family watched from the sidelines as holiday-themed floats rolled by, most created by participating high school groups and businesses. A big yellow school bus covered in red and green flashing light strands passed, followed by two Clydesdale horses drawing the Christmas sleigh carriage that would be used during Frosty Fest. Carson residents up and down Main Street whistled and cheered for Santa and Mrs. Claus in full, fancy red and white velvet Christmas regalia. The couple grinned from ear to ear, waving and tossing candies into the crowd. Savanna wasn't certain, but Santa's beard closely resembled Joe Fratelli's, the talented and kind chef at Guiseppe's restaurant up the street. Mrs. Claus looked a lot like Mia, the proprietor of Mitten Inn. Savanna made a mental note to ask her mother whether Mia and Joe had gotten back together. They made a cute couple, especially as Mr. and Mrs. Claus. Jack Carson would be playing Santa for the few appearances made by the beloved character during Frosty Fest, but he was currently across the street with his girlfriend Elaina and his grandmother, seated and bundled up comfortably.

Santa's sleigh signaled the end of the parade, which meant it was time to light up the two-story high Christmas tree at the entrance to Carson Park. The townsfolk slowly made their way to the tree, where Mayor Lopez and City Councilwoman Linda Rae waited to flip the switch. Savanna had coordinated with Lars to simultaneously illuminate the ice sculpture show with the LED lights and spotlights in various colors that he'd integrated into the displays. She'd meant to text a reminder to him but had forgotten.

With Main Street's Christmas music playing in the background, Mayor Lopez led the town in counting down from ten. They reached *one* and the huge tree lit up with dozens and dozens of multi-colored light strands, the crowd cheering and clapping. Beyond the tree into the park, the lights came up for the ice sculptures, eliciting a collective gasp and more applause.

Aidan tightened his arm around Savanna's waist. "You did great. Look at our little park—wow. Walk me through the ice sculptures?"

With Mollie between them, they began at the gazebo and followed the path of the beautiful art Lars had created. The trio of reindeer she and Yvonne had watched emerge from the ice a couple days ago were embedded with tiny white lights. North Pole-themed sculptures were interspersed with smaller pieces, like the ice-skating snowman as they approached The Gifting Tree and skating rink. In the time crunch caused by the weather, there were two large blocks of ice still in progress. Lars and an assistant actively chiseled and cut away at the ice, entrancing the folks gathered round watching. She guessed it might be a larger-than-life Santa Claus, based on the hat. It was his idea to leave a couple pieces incomplete to gradually work on in the next few days, piquing interest and bringing patrons back to see the progress.

Yvonne had texted after her date with Lars, saying he seemed nice but was very quiet. They'd chatted over text, deciding he must simply be an introverted, loner artist, especially living way up at the top of the U.P. Savanna kept an eye out for her friend—she'd have been lost without her help with the festival. She figured she'd spot her near Lars but perhaps she wasn't here yet.

"Swing me!" Mollie pulled on both their hands, noodling her legs and taking Savanna by surprise.

"Whoa!" She steadied herself with help from Aidan, and then got a better grip on the little girl. Mollie swung between them a few inches off the ground, whooping with laughter. Savanna's mind flashed an image of both her parents smiling down at her, swinging her between them when she was very small.

"Again," Mollie begged.

"Let's give Savanna a minute," Aidan said, lifting his eyebrows at her. "We have to power back up first."

"I'm ready," Savanna confirmed, smiling down at Mollie. "Ready? One, two, three!"

The little girl had time to push off the ground, gaining more airtime. She giggled wildly as they ended the ride and set her feet on firm ground again. "Hey! There's Makaela!"

Aidan nodded, letting her sprint through the light snow to a cluster of girls building a snowman near the swing set. Savanna glanced at The Gifting Tree they had almost reached. She hoped to get a peek at Mollie's wish. There was no way she was letting it go unfulfilled. The crowd around the tree, waiting for admission to the ice-skating rink, put her off; she'd have to try another time.

"Sorry about that," Aidan said. "It's good you've got great reflexes, or she'd have pulled you down. She hasn't done the swing thing in years."

"Really?" That surprised her. "I remember my parents doing that with me."

"Finn and I used to swing her after Olivia died. But I know it wasn't the same for her."

"Aidan, I'm not sure how to help her through the struggle with what to call me. That was frustrating for her this morning. Do you think it'd help if we talked with her about it?"

Across the way, Mollie was engrossed in getting stick arms to stay in the snowman while a friend helped. "I think she's okay," he said. "I made an appointment for us with the child psychologist she used to see, so we can work through some of the adjustments and changes coming."

"That's a great idea. When is the appointment?"

He looked at her, caught off guard. "Oh. I—"

"Us, meaning you and Mollie. I'm sorry. I shouldn't have assumed," she said, not feeling the words coming out of her mouth. Why wouldn't she assume the appointment included her? She was the reason the adjustments and changes were about to happen.

"Hey." Aidan took her hand, gently turning her toward him. "It makes sense that the three of us should go. I should have considered that. Let me get through this one with Mollie, and then I'll schedule one for next week with all of us. I want her to have the space to feel whatever she needs to without the pressure of worrying about what we might think or do. I'd only planned to be in the room for part of this session tomorrow."

"I know you're right. I don't want to interfere with her reactions. And she—and you—should be allowed to still miss her mom. I understand that." There was so much more she wanted to say. They had to start communicating better or this would only get more difficult.

"That's not really it—" He stopped as her phone rang.

Savanna pulled it from her coat pocket to silence it. *Rob Havemeyer* was displayed across the call screen. She turned the ringer off, catching Aidan's expression.

"What does he want? Do you need to answer?"

"No. He'll text if it's something important." It was the wrong thing to say.

Aidan turned back to watch Mollie. "Perfect."

"About Faye, I mean. Or the thefts. That's all."

He nodded. That little muscle in his jaw pulsed, but he said nothing.

"She's doing worse," Savanna said. "She's still in the ICU and not recovering the way they'd hoped." She glanced at her phone. "He didn't leave a voicemail or text. It's probably nothing—but I asked him to keep me updated if… if she doesn't pull through."

"Call him back." His tone held compassion. "I get that you were close to his mother."

"It's really okay." Rob called again, stirring dread in her gut. She held up the phone. "I have to answer." She purposely stayed where she was, resisting the urge to politely walk away and take the call. She'd never observed any sort of jealousy from Aidan, but this might be a smidge. She didn't want to feed into it. "Hi, Rob."

The line was quiet at first, and then she heard sniffling. Her stomach dropped. Faye was dead. She should have gone. Should have taken the opportunity to see her one last time. No broken engagement or the mistakes of an ex-fiancé should have allowed her to ignore what she knew she should have done.

"Rob? What's happened? Is she…" She kept her tone quiet, but background noise in the park was substantial. She covered her other ear with a hand, straining to hear him.

"They had us call her priest. Her breathing is worse; she wouldn't want to be put back on the ventilator, but they say if we don't, she might not survive." He drew in a hitching breath just barely covering a sob.

"Is your sister with you? What does she think should be done?"

"Yeah, she's here. We don't know. But—" He sniffled again, and her heart hurt for him. She wouldn't wish this experience on anyone, not even Rob. He continued. "But that's not why I called. They said we should tell my aunts and anyone else important to her what's happening, in case they want to see her or say something to her. Soon. Because…"

"Yes," she said quickly, cutting him off so he wouldn't have to finish that sentence. "Thank you. I, uh." She took a deep breath, fighting for the right decision. She turned to find Aidan had moved away from her, giving her privacy. He was sitting alone on a bench near where Mollie and her friends were playing.

Rob cleared his throat, his voice a little stronger now. "I promised to let you know. So… that's why I called. She knew how much you loved her, Savanna. After we broke up. She was mad at me for months." He tried for a laugh but failed. "Anyway. In case it helps, she did know you loved and appreciated her. I'll let you go."

"I'd like to come. If it's okay with you. I'd like to see her one last time. I'll get a flight."

"Okay. She'll like that. Thank you."

She was about to hang up when he stopped her with, "Savanna wait—there's something else." She held her breath. In spite of whatever ping of jealousy the call had sparked in Aidan, Savanna had truly felt right up to this moment that she and Rob were on good terms. Ex terms. She hoped he wasn't about to ruin it.

"I've done nothing but sit here in the hospital room for days, so I don't know what's happening with the theft investigation, but I think I might have found something. Last year someone keyed my BMW in Kenilworth's parking lot. They scratched up the whole driver's side."

Savanna rolled her eyes silently. It was time to hang up.

She didn't care about Rob's car obsession, why was he telling her this?

"It pissed me off, so I added a 360 Dash Cam. If I'd had it before, I could have caught whoever keyed my car." He must have sensed her impatience; he hurried ahead. "The dashcam app on my phone records anything the software deems suspicious, like someone circling the car but not getting in or whatever, and it just sent me my weekly wrap-up like it always does, which I usually don't bother to go through, but it captured something in the background at Kenilworth the night of the robbery. At least, it looks like something that could be important."

Now he had her attention. "But you said you weren't working during the break-in. Your car was in the parking lot? Why?"

"Oh." He sounded nonplussed. "Er. My girlfriend drives it sometimes. She works front of house at Kenilworth; her shifts go late sometimes. I took her car to the gym since my stuff is in it, so she took—it doesn't matter. What matters is, the dashcam caught movement near the employee entrance a little while before the robbery. Security uses their own entrance in the back, so I know it wasn't a guard."

"You just said your girlfriend was there. Are you sure it wasn't her?" *And why were you pleading for me to come back when you have a girlfriend??* Now she was mad on the girlfriend's behalf.

"I'm sure. The person on camera is a man. I screenshotted him and can almost make out his face but it's too pixelated. But I figure it'll be a great lead for the FBI, they probably have equipment that can clean it up and zoom in close."

"You have to tell them. You could give them access to your app so they could see whatever else might have been captured. This could help with our Lansing robbery, too. This is great, Rob."

"Right? I'm gonna call the field agent first thing in the morning. I can send you the log in, so you can take a look, if you want."

"Yes, for sure. Send it. All right, I'll text you when I know my flight time."

"I'll send my driver for you. His name is Alec Green. He'll find you."

As she hung up, she saw that a couple was talking to Aidan. She began to head over and stopped cold—it was Tom and Jean Beckett, Olivia's parents. Aidan's in-laws did not look happy. They left as quickly as they'd shown up.

She joined him on the bench, sliding close and wrapping her arm around his.

"Hey there." He kissed her temple. "Is it what you thought? His mother, is she gone?"

"No. But they're preparing for it. They've called in her priest. He said they've been told to let Faye's sisters and anyone else know that they should say their goodbyes soon if they want to."

"Oh no. I'm so sorry, Savanna." He was quiet for a beat. She didn't know if it was simply the way he was wired, or part of his intuition as a doctor, a healer, but she wasn't surprised when he said, "You're going to say goodbye."

She nodded. "I would like to. I feel like I should. Faye's a big part of why I found my niche in art authentication. She started out as an authenticator. She hired me when there were better qualified candidates, spent time she didn't have to giving me pointers; she always had my back."

"You should go. I'd never want to be the reason you didn't get a final goodbye with someone you cared about."

She turned on the bench, facing him, making him look at her. "You do know we're talking about Faye Havemeyer right now, right? Not her idiot son." She held his gaze, making sure he got it.

His lips curved up on one side. "Yes. I believe that." He cupped her cheek, fingertips sliding into her hair. "I'm not wasting any energy on anyone's idiot son, don't worry."

The best kisses were sometimes the ones that fell apart because of laughter. She couldn't help it. The way he'd phrased it made it sound even more ridiculous than it already was. It applied to both of them.

She wanted to ask if everything was all right with the Becketts—no, she wanted to ask what in the world they wanted, why they'd stop and talk with him when they were already making his life harder with their unnecessary lawsuit.

Instead, she kissed him again, and this one didn't fall apart.

Chapter Nine

MOLLIE FELL ASLEEP on the way back to the car, cheek smushed against Aidan's shoulder, after declaring her tired legs wouldn't carry her another step. She'd had a very full day. Savanna drove them home. She remembered to give Aidan the bottom half of the hangtag Mollie had chosen from The Gifting Tree and let him know the little girl had decided to leave a wish on the tree too. Aidan carefully extracted the sleeping girl from her booster seat in the back. He handed her his keys to unlock the front door and she held it open for him. Their fluffy mutt Jersey greeted them, nuzzling Savanna's hand for ear scratches and pets.

"I'll be right back," he whispered.

She sent a quick text message to Nick Jordan while she waited. She'd planned to go in the morning to discuss her question about Caroline's Sergei Minkov, but there was a cheap flight to Chicago at six a.m. out of Lansing. The sounds of Aidan settling Mollie in bed drifted to her from the hallway. She'd never dated a doctor before, but early on, she'd imagined Aidan's home to be big and fancy with expensive furniture that was pretty but uncomfortable. She couldn't have been more wrong.

Aidan's living room was furnished with soft, comfy

couches and oversized armchairs, throw pillows and blankets here and there in earth tones, and a convertible coffee table that held Mollie's arts and crafts. Jersey's big poofy dog bed sat in front of the hearth. The inviting space was neat and tidy thanks to a weekly housekeeping service. He'd knocked down the dividing wall between kitchen and dining room at some point in the past in favor of a big, bright kitchen at the back of the house with swivel stools lined up at the kitchen island countertop and an oval dining table under two gold and white sunburst chandeliers.

The house was lovely. She could move in and not change a thing, if that was best for Mollie. She shuddered involuntarily—she wasn't sure if this could ever be their house, hers and Aidan's and Mollie's. There were still traces of Olivia everywhere, little things she knew Aidan wouldn't have chosen or designed. The home felt comfortable because it had housed a happy family—it still did. But it wasn't her family, not yet. Not until ten days from now, and then what? She sighed heavily, forcing her worries into their assigned corner of her mind that seemed to be steadily growing lately.

They'd figure it out. Once the holiday this weekend had come and gone, there'd be so much more time to focus on what really mattered—the new life they were starting together in ten days.

Aidan returned empty-handed just as her phone dinged. He cocked an eyebrow at her. He said nothing but she read his mind. "It's just Jordan. I asked if he had a few minutes for me to fill him in on Caroline's Minkov, just to make sure he thinks she's safe."

"Good plan. Can I do anything? Do you need a ride to the airport?"

"You're so sweet to ask. No way, that'd be awful to wake Mollie so you could take me that early. I'm just going to drive and pay for parking. It's a short flight, I'll be back tomorrow afternoon."

He walked her out, Jersey leaping into her car and then out again, probably looking for Fonzie. He leaned down, a hand overhead on the roof of her car. "Text me when you land. And when you're heading back. And if anything changes… or if you need me."

"I always need you. I will text you constantly, my love," she said, batting her eyelashes at him and making him smile.

She read Detective Jordan's response before pulling out:
"Stop by the station if you want. I'll be here a while yet."

Nick Jordan waved her into his office, telling her to shut the door. He and George Taylor were staring at a wall covered in photos and notes and string and thumbtacks, exactly like she'd seen on *Law and Order.* "Holy cats. So, you guys really do this stuff, huh? Is this for something in Carson?"

Jordan pulled a projector screen down in front of the crime board. "Can't say."

She addressed George. "It's not related to the museum thefts, is it?"

"No," he said, at the same time Jordan repeated, "Can't say."

"You two are funny together."

Jordan gave her a look, his signature Detective Nick Jordan look, mostly disinterested, impossible to rattle, and completely out of patience. Not even out of patience, because she'd never known him to actually have any in the first place. Just devoid of patience.

She smiled in return. She knew that behind the look was a kindhearted law enforcement officer who cared deeply about his community.

"Sit. You said something about Caroline Carson's artwork?"

"Yes. I don't know if you remember, but after everything she went through a couple years ago with that art forgery ring, she mainly just has the large Sergei Minkov left in the library. It's a high value Impressionist painting," she clarified.

"I remember."

Detective Taylor interrupted. "I'm gonna go bug tech to hurry up on that report. I'll be back."

Jordan nodded and turned his attention back to Savanna.

She thought out loud. "With the FBI Art Crimes Team confirming the museum thieves are only targeting Impressionist-era work, and Caroline's painting being worth millions, do you think there's any possibility she's at risk? Maybe it sounds crazy. But I checked and the current market value of her Minkov is estimated at 9.2 million."

The detective had the good grace to lift his eyebrows slightly in surprise. "That's an expensive piece to keep around the house."

"I know. I just don't want anything to happen to her. It's not just the fact that she has a high-end Impressionist painting. The Lansing museum's Minkov, *Taiga Desolation*, was part of the same limited collection as Caroline's Minkov, painted during the artist's green period. That may make hers even more likely to be targeted."

"That's concerning," Jordan said. "And an art thief would view her as an easy mark." He rubbed at his mouth thinking. "No security to stop them, no sophisticated anti-theft cases or displays."

She nodded. "Exactly. That's why I wanted you to be aware."

"What if we have her move the piece? To a bank vault or send it on loan to Lansing or something."

"Unfortunately, I don't think that will keep her safe. She's the registered owner. Even if she moves it—even if she were to sell it tomorrow—an art thief will go by the most recent information."

Jordan leaned forward and tapped a few computer keys. "We'll put a couple officers on it, at least until there's a break in the case. I'll station Morris there tonight in a patrol car and then Taylor or I will go talk to Mrs. Carson in the morning about why there'll be a police presence at her place for a while."

Savanna stood. "You're the best. Thank you. That'll give me a lot of peace of mind while I'm gone; I appreciate it."

He held the door open for her. "Where are you going? You need a pre-wedding vacation or something?"

"That'd be nice, but no. I'll just be in Chicago for the day tomorrow. My ex's mother hasn't recovered from the attack on Kenilworth. They think she only has a short time left. I'm going to say goodbye." The next twenty-four hours were going to be tough; losing Faye made her so sad.

"I'm sorry, Savanna."

"Thanks. Oh—but," she lowered her voice as they were now standing in the open doorway, "Rob thinks he caught something on his 360 Dash Cam the night Kenilworth was robbed. The app sends a weekly summary and the camera caught a man going through the employee entrance after hours."

Jordan frowned. "Who? Security?"

"No. He says security has their own entrance at Kenilworth. He's telling their FBI field agent there, don't worry. Rob can't see much detail when he zooms in, but maybe the FBI can."

"That's great to hear—it's a good development."

That was about as excited as Nick Jordan got. She'd take it. "I thought so too. Okay, early flight tomorrow, gotta get to bed. Thank you for taking care of Caroline."

SHE TEXTED ROB that she'd landed and was on her way to the hospital. He'd scheduled his driver, the same somber-faced, middle-aged man who'd flown into Lansing with Rob, to fetch her from O'Hare. Alec Green waited at the exit for her holding a large sign with her name. He led her to a pearl-white luxury sedan, this time from the family's fleet of Bentleys and BMWs. What particular model this one was, she had no idea. It was one of a long list of items that hadn't mattered to her but was important to Rob and his family: how they represented themselves, the way they'd be perceived upon arrival and departure wherever they went. Right now, she was regretting her decision to snag the six a.m. flight. It was the only one that fit her budget, but it was now seven forty-five a.m. and she felt as if she'd been awake an entire day instead of since four in the morning. With morning traffic, she should be at Chicago's Northwestern Memorial Hospital by around nine a.m.

Half hour into the trip, when he hadn't texted back, she tried calling instead. What if Faye had passed during the night? The last thing she wanted was to intrude on a mournful family gathering at the hospital. Her call went straight to voicemail, ramping up her worry. She tried sending another tactful text message, but with no response.

Savanna groaned and did the only thing left she could think of besides just showing up without knowing whether Faye Havemeyer had made it through the night. She searched her contact list, unsure if she'd deleted the number or not. But she still had Rob's number, so she'd probably still have his older sister's.

Tiffany Havemeyer answered on the first ring. "Oh my God, Savanna how are you? I miss you!"

Savanna smiled. "I've missed you too. I should have called."

"I should have too. It's not your fault," Tiff said. "We can blame my brother."

Savanna left that alone. As warm as Tiff sounded, she was Rob's family. She wasn't about to trash him to his sister.

"I hope… I hope your mom is… Tiff, I'm so sorry to hear about Faye. I'm sure this has been horrific for your family."

"Thank you. Mom is tougher than they think. She's still with us, still fighting," she said, answering Savanna's question. "Hold on, let me step into the hallway." When she spoke again, her voice was quieter. "The doctors said she wouldn't last the night, but she's proving them wrong. All we can do is be with her and pray."

"I've been praying," she said. "I'm about twenty minutes away. Rob said she might like to see me… I hope it's okay?"

"He's glad you're coming. He knew what time you'd be here?"

"Yes, I texted him the info."

"Typical. He's probably still asleep. He went home last night to shower but he said he'd be back. I thought he was coming back last night… he's not answering his phone," Tiff said. "It's kind of weird. I even called Effie in case he was with her, but she's at work."

"Effie's his girlfriend who works front of house?"

"Oh good, I'm glad he told you about her. I never know with him," Tiff said. "Hey, where exactly are you, Savanna?"

She leaned over, looking out at the city through congested morning rush hour traffic. "We're on I-90 just past Division."

"I don't want to leave Mother. Our dad hasn't been here since last week, I can't get him to come. I can't leave her alone to go drag my brother back up here. We're both exhausted, I'm sure he just crashed last night, but I need him here. Would you mind stopping at his place?"

"I can do that. Is he still at The Sinclair?"

"Yes, same as me. Just tell Alec, he'll take you and wait while you grab my brother."

When they'd hung up, Savanna pressed the intercom button. "Hello, Alec?"

The driver lowered the smart glass partition between front and back seats. "Yes, ma'am?"

"Would you take a detour please? Tiffany wants us to stop by and pick up Rob."

"Of course." He nodded once, frowning. The man's brows were as bushy as his sideburns. He changed lanes and the partition slid closed.

She glanced down at her outfit, checking for crumbs from the croissant she'd had on the plane. She'd dressed in all black today and pulled her hair into a smooth chignon, small gold earrings her only jewelry. Her usual colorful A-line dresses seemed completely inappropriate for today, or for the Havemeyer family in general, no matter how this all turned out.

At the curb in front of The Sinclair apartment complex, Alec Green was around the car opening her door before she could do it herself. "Ma'am." He held out a hand and she crossed the sidewalk to the doorman. The driver accompanied her, stating her name to the uniformed young man. "Savanna Shepherd is here for Robert Havemeyer, sent by Ms. Tiffany Havemeyer."

Alec retreated to the car while the doorman ushered her through into the lobby of The Sinclair, handing her off to the reception desk with, "Savanna Shepherd for Mr. Havemeyer—she's expected."

The lobby security guard consulted the screen in front of him. "I see that. Ms. Havemeyer notified us. Good morning, Ms. Shepherd." She followed him to the elevators where he swiped a fob over the elevator keypad and entered the car with her, typing a code on the number pad next to the floor listing and accompanying her up to the thirty-fifth floor. The Havemeyer name opened doors—literally.

She exited at Rob's penthouse apartment, nodding in thanks to the guard still in the elevator. "Thank you. I'm okay from here," she said, though she was uncertain whether Rob had changed his key code.

"I'm required to wait, in case Mr. Havemeyer isn't home." The guard folded his hands in front of him, the elevator door locked open.

"Of course," she murmured. She entered the six-digit code at Rob's apartment door and was met with a flashing red LED light above the keypad. She tried again, more carefully this time, gratified by the green light and simultaneous click under her fingers on the door handle. The elevator doors slid closed behind her; the guard satisfied she wasn't some grifter.

"Rob?" She poked her head in. Not much had changed in his décor since she was here last. She committed and stepped inside, closing the door behind her. "Rob, hello? It's Savanna." She slowly moved through the spacious apartment, not wanting to startle him or find him in a compromising position. There was no way to know if the girlfriend was here. "Hello, Tiffany asked me to come by.

Are you here? Rob?"

She came around the corner into the bedroom, a hand shielding her eyes in case she walked into something she shouldn't see. "Rob?"

Nothing. His bed was neatly made. Clothing was strewn across the floor leading into the bathroom. The light and fan were on under the door. She heard water running. Great. This was way more than she'd bargained for. She could easily leave and tell Tiff he'd likely be heading to the hospital soon. She'd more than completed the favor asked of her. Instead, she knocked loudly on the bathroom door. Three quick raps. "Rob! It's Savanna. Tiff sent me. She needs you at the hospital."

Nothing came from the other side of the door. "Rob!" she called again. This was crazy. She pounded on the bathroom door. Nothing. No sound at all other than the running water and bathroom fan.

Savanna's mouth went dry. She took a deep breath, then another. She was here. She'd flown all the way here to be supportive of Faye; how the heck had she wound up in Rob's apartment, afraid of what she'd find on the other side of this door? Okay. She might as well see it through. She tried the door handle and it turned. She nudged the door open an inch, two inches. "Rob?" Reflected in the mirror was a small smattering of blood on the glass shower door. She forced herself to look down, pushing the door open all the way with one foot. Savanna shrieked and clamped a hand over her mouth.

Rob lay face down on the bathroom tile, black bath towel wrapped around his waist. There were flecks of blood on his neck and shoulder, a small puddle of blood beneath his head. A can of shaving cream, razor, comb, nail file, various other toiletries were scattered around him. The towel rack near the sink had been wrenched away from the metal mounting brackets and was clenched in Rob's hand on the floor. She moved carefully along the bathroom wall, craning her neck to see his face. It was half covered with dried, crusty shaving cream, but it was him. His eyes were closed. The blood... there was only a little. Maybe he'd fallen and hit his head?

She crouched down and carefully, gingerly put her fingertips at the side of his neck, searching for a pulse. His skin was freezing. She shot back, hitting the wall and backing out of the room, head spinning, and dialed 911. She told them what she knew, her voice sounding tinny and distant to her own ears.

She waited. She found herself perched on the edge of the couch but didn't remember getting there. Her phone buzzed in her hand—Tiff was calling. Oh God. She leaned forward, holding her head in her hands. First Faye, now Rob. She couldn't tell his sister. She couldn't be the one to tell her. A text came through from Tiffany and Savanna squeezed her eyes shut. How long did it take for the police to get here? She didn't hear sirens. With a shaking hand, she set her phone on the glass coffee table and pushed it away. She should tell his sister, she shouldn't make her wonder and worry, but she couldn't do it.

With no clue how much time passed, ten minutes or forty, her head snapped up at the sound of the door opening. Police and paramedics filed in, issuing orders at her, at each other, shouting clear from each room. Clear, as if they were checking the whole penthouse for someone—for whoever did this to Rob. Had anyone done this to him, or did he just fall? There'd been no one in the apartment when she arrived—had there? The thought never crossed her mind until right now.

Someone wrapped a blanket around her. More Chicago PD officers arrived, each crossing to the master bedroom and en suite bathroom. Her phone buzzed again, loud on the glass table. A uniformed officer stood in front of her, speaking to the paramedic sitting with her. "Body temperature and lividity indicate time of death last night between eleven and midnight."

"Ms. Shepherd. I'm Detective Amberly. Can you recall where you were last night between eleven and midnight?"

"I was at home. I went to bed around ten thirty."

"In Michigan," Tiffany Havemeyer said from the foyer. She rushed to Savanna and hugged her, disregarding the officers and detective. She straightened up. "She flew in this morning. I got a call telling me to come. Please say he's okay? Is he hurt, but okay? Please?" Her tears overflowed as the detective took her aside to break the news to her.

Seeing Rob's sister was the jolt Savanna needed. Tall, strikingly beautiful in a somewhat severe way, Tiffany was a commanding presence even clad in the maroon track suit she wore presumably for Faye's bedside vigil.

Savanna shook her head, trying to shake the wooziness.

She downed the water bottle someone had put in her hand. "I shouldn't be here," she told the paramedic still sitting with her.

"It's all right. You're okay here. No one's going to make you leave."

"I don't want to stay here. I shouldn't even be here," she repeated. She stood up, bracing herself, but her head was less spinny. "Can I?" She pointed to Tiff sobbing across the room from her.

"Of course." The paramedic steadied her and then let her go.

Savanna joined Tiff. She transferred her blanket to Rob's sister, wrapping it around her shoulders, and then took her cold hand between her two, squeezing. The detective explained that it looked like an accident, but they wouldn't know for sure until the medical examiner was able to evaluate.

"It wasn't an accident," Tiffany said. "He had no health conditions, wasn't on any medications. He didn't just fall or pass out."

"What about substance use? Drugs? Alcohol?"

Tiff scowled at the detective. "No drugs. My brother quit all that after college. And he just recently stopped drinking. Someone did this. Someone did something to him to cause this."

Detective Amberly didn't comment but made a few notes in a small book similar to Jordan's. When he left them for a moment, Tiff turned to Savanna, eyes puffy and red rimmed. "I can't believe this is happening. And I left Mother all alone at the hospital." She covered her eyes. "I can't do this alone."

"Where is your father?" Savanna asked. "Is he at Kenilworth?"

Tiff nodded. Savanna started to speak but Tiffany cut her off. "Don't bother. He doesn't care. Don't even try, Savanna, I mean it." She drew in a shaky breath. "It's awful that you had to find him like this. I hate to ask, but…"

When she didn't finish, Savanna nudged her. "Ask. I'm here. I want to help."

"Would you go sit with Mother? I can't stand the thought of her alone, especially if she—when she—gets worse. If that happens call me right away. Oh, and you'll have to say you're her niece or something. It's immediate family only."

Savanna dismissed the fact that Tiff could still make a request sound like an order. All of this was incredibly heavy for anyone to carry. Tiff pushed through the door to the master bedroom and demanded to see her brother's body, despite advice from the officer at the door not to do so. Detective Amberly took Savanna's official statement and had her sign something saying he was allowing her to leave the state despite being the person to discover Rob's body, with her agreement to come back should there be further need or questions.

The immediate relief she felt as soon as the cold winter air hit her face outside of Rob's building was followed quickly by sadness, the emptiness embedded within loss, even loss of someone she didn't love anymore. He wasn't a bad person. He'd still had a lot of living left to do. On the short ride to the hospital, her mind spun faster than she could process. Alec Green looked at her oddly as she climbed into the back seat. Her shell-shocked red face was probably telegraphing the distress of discovering the dead body of someone she cared about. Should she say something to the driver? Or not? Maybe not? In the end, as the car arrived at the hospital, she left it to the authorities. Maybe it made her selfish, but she assumed that Alec had been close to Rob, at least as an employee, and she couldn't deal with sharing this news and managing his reaction on top of her own.

She walked through the hospital hallway, echoes of her conversation last night with Rob playing in her mind, his discovery on the dashcam app, his intention to tell the FBI. Who else had he told besides her? She'd told only Jordan.

Chapter Ten

IN A CHAIR pulled up to Faye Havemeyer's bedside, Savanna held the older woman's hand and told her everything she'd want to know. She covered moving back to Carson, living with her younger sister for a year while she found her footing, discovering she loved teaching elementary art and she'd missed her own painting so much. She described her adorable lakefront home and Fonzie's love of the sand dunes. She described her nephew and niece and rehashed a little of the ordeal her father had been through this fall during the sailing regatta. She worked her way around to the topic of Aidan, how they'd met, his sweet little daughter who she hoped to call her own, and their upcoming wedding. She sat for a long time in silence, Faye's even breathing and the rhythmic beeping of the machines oddly soothing.

She hadn't changed at all besides a few new lines around her eyes. She'd bestowed her beauty on Tiff and still wore hers well at sixty-eight. Rob and Tiffany's mother looked as if she was asleep, not in a medically induced coma meant to allow her to fight and heal, if she could.

Savanna could not imagine the heartache of Faye recovering only to learn her son was dead. She couldn't imagine the devastation of Tiff losing her mother and brother at once. She didn't know what to hope for in all of this, so she simply hoped for peace—eventual peace for each of them, even Rob's absent father.

Tiffany returned at four, a half hour before Savanna's flight home would leave without her—at the airport an hour away. Savanna sat for a while with mother and daughter in silence. She went online on her phone and found the next flight home, checked her bank account balance, and cringed as she paid the ticket change fee and additional cost for the last-minute, prime-time flight.

"Is there anything I can do? Seriously, anything at all." She searched Tiff's face, meaning it. "I feel awful for what you're going through. I'm so sorry—none of this is fair."

"None of it seems real yet. My aunt and uncle are on their way here, that will help a little. I don't know how I'm supposed to navigate this alone. I'm so angry. I know the grief is coming..." Her gaze rested on her mother in the hospital bed. "But right now, I'm furious. I want them caught. Whoever did this to my family—I want them to know the same pain they've caused us."

"I understand," she said. She had no idea anymore who to trust, but there wasn't a chance Tiff could've brought this destruction upon her own family. "Your brother shared some information with me last night that may shed some light on the case. I'll make sure the right people are told about it. I gave your mom my life story since I left Chicago, I figure maybe she'd want to know. One of the doctors who came through said she's doing better than twenty-four hours ago. When she wakes up, when she's doing much better, will you give her my love?"

"I will. I promise."

SAVANNA CLIMBED THE steps to her deck feeling like she'd been gone a week rather than sixteen hours. She could already imagine her head hitting the pillow. Kicking up a new dusting of snow, Fonzie sprinted ahead of her and triggered the motion sensor light. Savanna let out a shriek seeing the figure sitting in silence on the bench until she registered it was Aidan.

"Oh, my goodness." She pressed her hand to her chest. "If you knew the day I've had, you wouldn't be risking giving me a heart attack. It'd be the second near miss in one day. I—" His expression stopped her from finishing.

He looked defeated. He stayed seated where he was and she realized for the first time that he always stood and greeted her when they met like this, anytime she encountered him waiting for her anywhere. But he didn't move.

"You're scaring me, Aidan, what happened?" And suddenly she remembered. The mediation with his in-laws had been today. She mentally kicked herself. How could she have forgotten? She hadn't texted more than a word or two to him all day, with the chaos in Chicago. "The mediation today. It went badly? Come inside. It's freezing out here." She held out her hand and he took it. Once inside and warm and settled on the couch, she gently asked again, "What happened?"

"Nothing happened. The Becketts filed for a delay. They postponed the mediation. They're making an issue of the fact that I asked you to watch Mollie when the babysitter was out sick, instead of asking them first."

"What? That sounds insane. She's your child. How can they—"

"Because they can. Because while their case against me is pending, they're granted specific grandparents rights and their attorney is saying they get right of first refusal when Mollie's pre-scheduled childcare falls through. My attorney's saying they're stretching and misinterpreting the wording in Michigan's grandparents' rights legislation."

"I'm so sorry. If I'd known, I would've told you to call them yesterday. I was just so thrilled to spend the day with her. I feel like... Aidan, I feel like we're both trying so hard to keep things amicable with them and follow the rules and avoid causing problems and none of what we do matters. None of the effort you're making is enough for them. When did they begin to hate me so much?" Her eyes burned but she refused to cry. She refused to make it about her.

"They don't hate you."

"Yeah. They do. Think about it. Every complaint they've had so far involves my existence in Mollie's life. They had no issue with you until you decided to marry me."

"Savanna, how could anyone hate you? They hate that their daughter's gone."

Her eyes widened. "But I'm not trying to take Olivia's place in Mollie's life."

"It's not a rational thing. If it was, I wouldn't be looking at a two month delay in the mediation."

"So, nothing will be decided until when, February?"

"Right."

"But we'll be married two months by then. Are they going to also stop me from adopting her? Do they know that we talked about that?"

"They know more than I wish they did. I don't see how they could interfere with that... but I didn't see any of this coming in the first place. I have to stop underestimating them; who knows what they'll use to twist around next."

Her heart sank. Not being Mollie's legal parent obviously wouldn't change how much she loved her, but it would mean that, at least on paper, Mollie still had only one parent. Savanna would have no rights when it came to helping Mollie with her health and medical care, finances, insurance, or being allowed in spaces where only a parent could be. If anything ever happened to Aidan, it would be as if Mollie was orphaned. She'd be placed into foster care while the courts decided whether Savanna was fit to raise her rather than her grandparents. Mollie might be too young to understand now, but as she grew, how would Savanna explain to her why she'd never taken the extra steps to adopt her?

"I'm a little lost," Aidan admitted. "I don't know the right way to handle this. I'm meeting with Jillian right after Christmas, next Monday, to discuss how to move forward without risking losing more time with Mollie."

Savanna closed her eyes and took some deep breaths. She tried to force the thought from her mind, the one that'd occurred to her the other day and kept drifting back against her will. Without her in the picture, the Becketts wouldn't have a reason to contest Aidan's fitness as a father or their grandparents' rights. It would all go back to the way it was before. She could suggest postponing the wedding. Maybe, with more time, things would mellow, and they'd begin to see that her presence in Mollie's life would never diminish their daughter's.

She bit her lip, trying to summon the resolve to do it.

"There's nothing else I can do until then," Aidan said. "Jillian will have a plan. I'll let you know Monday how it goes. Now, tell me how Faye is. You must've gotten to spend a fair amount of time with her—was she conscious or did they have her sedated?"

He knew nothing. She'd avoided trying to text it all or squeeze in a conversation from the back of an Uber, planning to just tell him in person about Rob. She started at the end, saying Faye was hanging in there and possibly starting to do better.

"Rob is dead. It seems that he fell and hit his head or had some kind of, I don't know, medical event. I found him dead in his apartment bathroom." She registered Aidan's stunned expression. "I was almost to the hospital when his sister asked me to stop by his place and try to get him to come relieve her—he hadn't answered his phone since the night before. She got the staff of The Sinclair where he lives to let me in. The police came and estimated that he died last night, but it's not clear how."

"I—I don't even know what to say." Aidan's brows drew

together, his jaw set. "Are you okay, Savanna? It sounds awful."

"I'm fine," she said. "I feel terrible for his sister. And sad for him. I can't help wondering…"

Aidan's frown deepened, worry coloring his features.

"He told me just last night that he'd found footage on his dashcam of someone entering Kenilworth through the employee entrance around the time of their break-in. He was going to call the FBI field agent this morning and share what he had, in hopes they could clean up the images enough to see who it was. I can't help wondering if someone knew and stopped him before he could do that."

Aidan exhaled forcefully and sat back. He smacked a hand over his eyes, leaving it there for a second and then scrubbing it back through his wavy black hair. "Good grief. I thought you were going in a whole different direction with that."

"What?" She was confused. She replayed what she'd said, distracted by his muscled bicep on the arm he'd left in the hair, hand cupped at the back of his neck. The only times she'd ever seen him do that was under extreme stress. Her mind flashed back to Aidan at Caroline's house in this same pose after he'd tried and failed to resuscitate poor Eleanor. She was somehow the cause of his stress at the moment and she hated knowing that. She touched his arm, bringing it down and taking his hand. "Aidan?"

He brought her hand to his lips. "Never mind. It does sound like you're onto something though. Have you told anyone about the dashcam footage?"

"I told Detective Jordan last night."

"Well, besides him. Anyone at the museum? What about Britt? Who in Rob's family or friend circle might he have told, besides you?"

Her eyebrows rose. "Why Britt? And I'm not sure if Rob would've mentioned to anyone what he found. But... he was pretty excited to tell me about it. Maybe he told Tiff or his girlfriend."

A hint of a smile crossed his features. "He had a girlfriend?"

She nodded. "You surprise me, Aidan. Girlfriend or no girlfriend, I keep telling you I'm so happy to be exactly where I am. Why would you doubt that for a second?"

"Stupidity." He shrugged. "Your ex is on the hundred most eligible millionaire bachelor list, has a penthouse apartment at The Sinclair, and is heir to the Havemeyer fortunes. He's a catch."

"Was," she corrected.

"So, you agree?"

"I do not. He was not a catch. I should have tossed him back when I caught him. Can we stop arguing about a dead man please?" Aidan truly did surprise her. She'd never noticed anything unattractive about him before this moment. Rob was dead, and even when he was alive, he was a blip on the map of her past, where she wished he'd stayed. "Besides, can we maybe feel a little sad that Rob lost his life? I'm sure his girlfriend and family are in rough shape right now."

"I'm sorry," he said, his tone sincere. "I'm sorry for what

happened to him and for letting my insecurities get the best of me. Can we rewind about a half hour? Or maybe an entire day?"

She hugged him, snuggling as close to him as she could. "I'm sorry too. It's been a bad day all around. Maybe instead of rewinding, we could skip ahead and forget this whole conversation."

"Skip ahead to where?" He planted a light kiss on her neck.

"I have some ideas."

FRIDAY MORNING, SAVANNA combed through her work emails until she found the one from Kenilworth's CFO cautioning the Lansing museum among others about the potential for theft. Buried toward the bottom of the email was a general phone number for the FBI Art Crimes Team. She called and had to leave a vague message asking for whichever agent was assigned to the Kenilworth robbery case to please call her. She could probably track down that agent's name and number through Tiff or by calling Kenilworth, but she was feeling uncomfortably paranoid about who she could trust. If she called Kenilworth, they'd want to know who she was and why she needed the information. Even worse, what if she got Rob's girlfriend when she phoned?

She dropped off Fonzie at Fancy Tails and made one more stop before heading to Lansing. Heading north along the lake for about a mile, she turned into the parking lot for

Mitten Inn. Carson proper only had two tourist accommodations: Mitten Inn, owned by Charlotte Shepherd's friend Mia, and Rose's B&B, a smaller establishment south of town. Mitten Inn was comprised of several connected two-story buildings in varying colors, arranged in a horseshoe around a large recreation area in the center. Snow covered everything now, but in the summer, the inground pool, firepits, lush gardens with oversized pink and purple hydrangeas and other flowers, and a picnic area with umbrellas over café-style metal tables occupied the space. At one end near the trail to the beach and bike trail was a tall multicolored sign with directional arrows that read:

PARADISE BEACH AND DUNES

MADE IN THE MITTEN ICE CREAM SHOPPE

CARSON HORSE STABLES

CANOE, KAYAK, AND BICYCLE RENTAL

Mitten Inn's tourism dropped in the winter, but the parking lot was still about half full. Savanna got out of her car and realized she'd never asked for room numbers when she had Mia set aside rooms for Lars and his assistants. At the reception desk, she was surprised to be greeted by Remy James, the sous chef who worked for Joe Fratelli at Guiseppe's, and Mia's son. Remy had left Carson for a while but ended up back here after going to culinary school abroad.

"Hi there, Remy, how are you?" He was close to her age, taller than Aidan but very thin, and covered in tattoos over his arms, hands, and the side of his neck.

"Doing well, Savanna. How've you been?" Remy was one of the nicest guys she knew. He'd been a lifesaver last year with the Art in the Park catering, making everything run smoothly even though he'd had to step into his boss's shoes for a time.

"Really good. Busy, but aren't we all?" She smiled at him. "I need to drop these off to Lars Anders, from my mom. She can't stand the idea of anyone having nowhere to go for Christmas. With this weather picking up, she's worried he might not end up heading back home yet. Is he around? I don't know the room number."

"That's nice. Your mom and mine are a lot alike." Remy typed for a moment on the keyboard, clicking through screens. "He's here now, or at least his car is. We have secure parking; guests just swipe their room key to operate the barrier arm gate. He got back yesterday morning. I can deliver those"—Remy pointed to the envelopes in her hand—"unless you want the room number."

"Oh, you can please, if you don't mind," she said, handing the three-holly leaf patterned envelopes across the counter. "You mentioned he got back; he was gone?"

Remy consulted the screen and then raised his gaze to hers. "He's the ice sculptor the town hired for Frosty Fest, right?"

"Yes, that's right."

He shrugged. "Just asking. So, he's like, under contract currently for the festival you're managing?"

"Yes... why?"

"Just asking," he repeated. "We can't share private guest info but he's your employee, sort of. He's a cool guy. But a couple guests complained about his loud van waking them up when he got back early Thursday morning." He lowered his voice. "Ma wanted me to address it with him, but it was like five a.m., not crazy early for a weekday. Seems kind of dumb to complain about something like that. His old hippie van is sweet, it's just loud."

"I've seen the van, it's pretty neat. Very vintage. No complaints besides the early morning noise issue? Since he is my employee," she added.

"Nope. Nothing. He and his two workers like the fire-pits, they sit outside almost every night while he plays guitar. No wild parties." He laughed. "The ice sculptures they've made are crazy good."

"When did he leave on Wednesday?"

"Um." He checked the screen. "Looks like he swiped out twice—once in the morning, then came back at 8:02 p.m. and left again at 8:14 p.m."

She thanked Remy and wished him and Mia a merry Christmas. Savanna's mind spun during the drive to Lansing. Director Flynn's voicemail early this morning basically begged her to come in. With the day they'd lost, the lab team was now scrambling to catch up. Flynn hoped for some progress from anyone who didn't mind working the day before Christmas Eve.

She felt slightly icky from the exchange with Remy. Why had she felt the need to snoop on Lars? He was free to come and go as he pleased. He wasn't contracted to stay in Carson for the entire festival; she'd actually assumed he'd go back home up north for a few days and come back to do maintenance on the sculptures once or twice. But his reaction to Helene's death was like an annoying little bee, buzzing through her mind at random times. She'd assumed they were friends. But even if they'd just been acquaintances, artist and curator, what kind of person didn't even blink when they'd just been told someone they knew was killed? Lars hadn't even reacted when she'd added the news of the two guards dying.

It was the mention of an inn guest complaining about Lars's early morning return that brought the bee buzzing back. Where had he been that he was coming back to Mitten Inn at five in the morning? Two and a half hours. Chicago was a mere two-and-a-half-hour drive away. Five hours round trip. She'd only chosen to fly because it made for a quicker trip. With Rob's death placed between eleven and midnight, it'd be fairly easy for someone from this side of the lake to drive there, silence him before he could inform the FBI about his dashcam footage, and make it back to Michigan before anyone knew they were gone.

She wanted to see Anders's sculptures. She'd seen them online, the pieces on exhibit at the Detroit Institute of Art and New York's Museum of Modern Art. But she'd never bothered to go seek out the two sculptures at Lansing Museum of Fine Art. She'd have to do that, today or after Christmas.

There wasn't much to do now except hope the FBI field agent would call her. If she heard nothing by the end of the day today, she'd call the detective she'd given her statement to yesterday at Rob's apartment and maybe he could help. The authorities would have taken Rob's phone with 360 Dash Cam app installed. She just needed to point them in the right direction; they were the FBI, they'd be able to get into his phone and apps. But she'd never seen his phone yesterday. She thought hard, searching through the images in her mind like snapshots of the minutes she'd spent in Rob's bathroom, master bedroom, apartment in general. The shaving cream and other items on the floor hadn't included his phone. It wasn't on the credenza where he typically charged it—she'd have seen it. But it had to be there, and the police would've located and taken it with them.

George Taylor was stationed today outside the lab. "Good morning! Your colleague is already inside," he said, turning to swipe his badge to let her in.

"Great! Here," she said, giving up one of the two coffees she'd just bought at the café for herself and Britt. "Do you like French vanilla?"

Detective Taylor's eyes lit up. "Love it. You're the best; I didn't get my coffee yet today. Thank you! I hope you and your family have a nice holiday."

"I'm sure we will. What about you and Rosa? Doesn't she usually make a bunch of seafood dishes for Christmas?"

He nodded. "The feast of the seven fishes. She and her mother always go overboard with the food for Christmas Eve. The shrimp and stuffed lobster tail are always my favorite."

"That sounds amazing! Give her my best—I know neither of us is in a rush for winter break to end. Enjoy your feast of fishes," she said as he held the door open for her.

She must really love Britt. She handed over the remaining coffee to her friend. "Drink it quick before Flynn catches you," she warned. "How are you doing?"

Britt hugged her. "The bigger question is, how are *you* doing after yesterday? Are you all right? I'm sorry about your ex."

"Thank you. I'm—jeez. I'm so sorry about Helene, too, Britt."

"I appreciate that." Britt tipped the cup up, taking her advice. "Hot. Good though. Do you have any thoughts on who killed Rob? I can't believe you had to find him like that."

She'd texted Britt this morning to let them know Rob passed away yesterday, but figured she'd fill them in more in person. "They don't know yet how he died—if it was a fall or something like a heart attack or if someone caused it. How did you—it's in the news then? They mentioned me by name? Can they do that?"

"Not exactly by name. The reel I saw on social media said his former fiancée discovered his nude body on the bathroom floor."

"What?!" Her shout echoed in the nearly empty lab. "Britt. Come on."

"Sorry. I threw in the word nude. I just assumed. Seriously though, you're fine? It must have been traumatic. It's just us today, by the way. Yay," Britt said, smiling.

"Oh good! I miss you," she said. "I keep thinking about

you and… losing Helene. I hope you know I'm here for you, for whatever. If you're sad and want to talk or need a friend to share a bottle of wine with or maybe have some retail therapy."

"I know that. Thank you."

"Has anyone been in touch with you about that night? Like, have they figured out how she ended up like that in the elevator? It just seems so unfair. She wouldn't have been in the way of the thieves, and she didn't have the security clearance that the guards have. Why would they do that to her?"

"Why are you asking me?" Britt rose and went around to the opposite side of the long stainless steel counter, powering on the workstation computer. "I have no idea, Savanna. I know nothing. I didn't even get to see her that night before she died. She told me to bring her dress for the gala; she was stuck working later than she'd planned."

"So, you stopped at her place and got it," Savanna said. "She was going to meet you in your office upstairs, right? But she never made it."

Britt scrunched up their face in a scowl. "I've been through this with the police. And the FBI. And Director Flynn. I know as much as you all do."

She came around to their side, giving her friend a quick hug. "I know. I don't mean to make you relive it. I'm just asking these questions that have been bouncing around in my head, hoping something will lead to something else, y'know?"

"I guess. Look, the provenances are in for all three pieces.

Check your email."

She nodded, heading back around to her workstation computer. "Hey, did you end up getting a new phone?"

"No, why?"

"Remember? I couldn't get ahold of you at all last weekend. Your phone was being glitchy. The night of the gala, too, I tried a few times but maybe nothing came through to you?"

Britt looked up from donning gloves to begin working with the vandalized Francois Laurant's *Notre Dame de Paris.* "My phone is fine now."

She had to stop. All she was succeeding at was alienating her friend, and for what? She knew Britt too well to think they'd had anything to do with Helene's death. There was just… one last question. "I wish she'd been able to answer one of her phones. You were probably trying both phone numbers for her that night, right?"

"What do you mean, one of her phones?"

"The flip phone she had with her. In the elevator. She probably had that to avoid having her personal cell be bombarded with work calls all the time, is that why? I've thought about doing the same thing because of all the texts and calls from students' parents."

"I didn't know she had two phones," Britt said. "You're sure you saw a flip phone?"

Her question was answered. Britt didn't try to hedge. They were as surprised as she was to learn Helene had an extra phone. A pang of regret pinched at her for questioning her friend. Why had Aidan lumped Britt into the same category as potentially untrustworthy people who might've done something unsavory upon learning camera footage existed? Britt would never harm a soul. She shuddered. Too many people associated with the museum thefts had been hurt or killed. Too many that she knew directly—Faye, then Helene, the two guards at her museum who she hadn't known but was sure she'd crossed paths with, and now Rob.

Director Flynn came through the doors. "Hi there team. Half-team," he corrected. "The museum is grateful for your dedication; I appreciate you working today. Right about now, I'm really wishing we had funding for full time rather than contract. I know it makes it tricky at times, the odd schedule."

"We don't mind," Savanna spoke for herself and Britt.

"Now that we've been able to dig into restoration, I got some additional information from Melissa Aguilar on the FBI's findings. They identified the graffiti paint as a BBG brand shade called Violent Red. The thieves used the same at Kenilworth and the L.A. museum. The dark shade's going to make it difficult to remove, I'm sure."

"We'll do our best," Savanna assured him.

Flynn nodded. "Of course. Listen, don't share the brand or anything else outside this room; it might be important later."

As soon as Flynn left them, Britt got back to work with the graffiti while Savanna did what she did best—dove into the provenance details for the Francois Laurant, a bit challenging due to the travels this painting had in the last 150 years. Less than an hour later, she leapt off her stool, unable to believe what she'd just read. She leaned in, peering at the screen, and read it carefully again.

"Britt! Come here, come here right now!" She bounced on her feet, motioning them around to her screen. "Look! Read that."

"Read what? The location, St. Armands, Florida?"

"No, no, no. Right here. I want to make sure I'm seeing what I think I'm seeing. Read the authenticator's name who certified this piece."

"Ivan Kiernanski."

"Do you remember?" she asked, waiting. She'd called in a favor from Britt two years ago when she needed use of the Lansing Museum of Fine Art's sophisticated lab authenticating equipment. She'd been trying to prove there were forgeries within Caroline Carson's substantial art collection. She was confident Britt would remember the outcome.

Britt gasped, eyes wide. "No! Really?" They pointed at the computer screen, the painting, Savanna. "Oh. My. God. For real? But—Kiernanski was in on the forgeries you discovered at the Carson Mansion. So, this is a fake."

"Looks like it," she said.

Britt turned in a slow circle taking in all three defaced. "My word. Goodness, are they all?"

Chapter Eleven

IN SHORT TIME, Savanna had done her due diligence with the provenances for the other two vandalized paintings. Only the Laurant was authenticated by the infamous Ivan Kiernanski, if that was even his real name. The other two paintings' provenances appeared to be legit on first look, until her gaze caught on the name of the art dealer who sold the vandalized Sergei Minkov to the Lansing museum last year. "Look." She pointed out to Britt. "What are the odds it's just a coincidence and the guy also dealt in legit paintings?"

"Slim to none, I'd say. What the heck is going on? Are the other museums seeing similar connections to that case at Caroline Carson's?"

She shrugged. "It'd sure be interesting to find out." Savanna opened a new browser tab and searched online for the story from a little over two years ago, when several pieces in the Carson Mansion were found to be forgeries, unbeknownst to the Carsons.

"This is the article published two years ago by the Association for Research into Crimes against Art in the *Journal of Art Crimes*." She turned the screen more toward Britt. "It happened after Caroline's husband Everett passed away and she began downsizing and liquidating some of his substantial collection. Everett was an avid fine art enthusiast with several connections to gallerists and art dealers, but all it takes is one shady dealer to pass off a forgery as genuine. You remember some of what happened; I was painting a mural on commission for Caroline's parlor when I noticed an anomaly with a small Minkov she had. Even with a great art forger, there's always a giveaway—the one upside of that whole experience was getting to see you more in our lovely home away from home." She gestured at the lab as a whole.

"I'm confused, though," Britt said. "How did it work? Did Detective Jordan ever tell you the rest of the story, after the arrests were made?"

"No, not really. He did say a while later that what we discovered was having far reaching implications. Forgeries from that St. Armands art gallery they traced the Carson piece to were found in other countries, sold by more dealers than just the one who duped the Carsons. That dealer was given a prison sentence; I think he'd still be in but who knows. To my knowledge, the authenticator was never caught. Or so-called authenticator; Kiernanski was just a name to plug into the fabricated provenance. No one by any name like that with those credentials was located."

"Let's get Director Flynn up here. Someone's going to need to update the FBI Art Crimes Team."

"Good idea. Do you want to call him?" Savanna checked her phone, but there was no call back yet from the Chicago field agent. Maybe Flynn could put her in touch with whichever FBI agent was assigned to their museum's case.

Why hadn't she asked Rob to send her a screenshot of the person he'd caught on the dashcam? He'd said he would text her his log in and password, so she could take a look, but he never had. She tapped her phone again, scrolling through the texts from the last time she'd spoken to Rob. There was nothing. Unless—he was so careless with the ways he communicated. Sometimes he'd say he texted her, but he'd actually emailed instead and vice versa. She opened her personal email—and there it was.

The subject line read *my log in and password.* Sheesh. Good thing nobody was looking at her email besides her! She glanced over what he'd sent her, tapped through her phone to download the 360 Dash Cam app, and logged in as Rob. There were a ton of short clips stored in the app.

"Earth to Savanna," Britt said, peering over her shoulder. "Flynn's on his way up."

"What? Sorry." She shut her screen off.

"What's that?"

"What?"

"On your phone. Did you add a security camera to your car?"

"You know about those?" She bit her lip, staring at them. There just was no way Britt could be involved in any of this. They wouldn't have known about Rob's app footage, wouldn't have ever hurt Helene, and certainly wouldn't be involved in art forgery and theft. Britt was being less than honest with her about *something* that happened the night Helene died... maybe even the day before. She could feel it. But her friend wasn't a killer.

She reopened the app and album of clips and tapped the ones from the day of the Kenilworth robbery and the day before, choosing the bulk download icon. "Here," she said, and pushed her phone across the counter to Britt. "This is Rob's 360 Dash Cam app footage from the night Kenilworth was robbed. He said he accidentally caught someone sneaking into the building through an employee entrance. Some man. I haven't seen it yet, it's probably this one." They leaned over her phone, watching as a large figure entered the area captured in front of Rob's car in the employee parking area. The man stood near the employee entrance for five seconds, turning once to look over his shoulder. Then he slipped into the building. The footage ended.

"Go back," Britt said. "How did he get in? I didn't see him swipe a badge."

"Me neither." Savanna slid her finger along the screen, backing up the video and letting it play. She paused it. "Look. Right there. Do you see that? I think that's a hand pushing the door open just enough to disengage the latch." She played it again.

"Yes! You're right. Someone lets him in. It's time stamped, too, that's helpful. You've got to get this to the FBI. Sooner than later."

Outside the door, Flynn and Tate were chatting. Tones from the keypad sounded as the guard let the director in.

"Don't tell Flynn," Savanna quickly whispered to Britt. "We don't know who's in on it."

Britt's mouth dropped open. They recovered, closing it. "You're right, good thought," they whispered back as Flynn stepped into the lab.

"We have a breakthrough already?" he asked. "Remind me to give you two a raise."

"Oh, we will," Britt snarked.

"Director," Savanna began, "why don't you sit down, and we'll show you what we found."

She had to go through it twice. Flynn remembered the incident connected to the Carson Mansion artwork but knew few details. She could see the light dawning on him as she explained again about Ivan Kiernanski as the documented authenticator of Caroline's forged pieces and his name appearing on provenance for their museum's vandalized Laurant. Add to that the Carson case's crooked dealer being listed as the man who'd brokered the sale to Lansing museum's acquisitions team for their now vandalized Minkov.

Flynn didn't move at first, his gaze fixed to the provenance onscreen. "But why destroy forgeries? If we assume these are forgeries based on what you've just told me—"

"We don't know for sure yet," Savanna said, "but we've only just started the process of investigating each painting's qualities, brushstrokes, pigments; you know the drill. We will do that, obviously, which will likely support the fact that these are fakes. But we wanted to get you in the loop now."

He nodded. "Thank you for that. I understand. Still, though, I can't come up with a reason the thieves would go to all the trouble of breaching our multiple security safeguards for forged works. And not to steal the forged paintings, to vandalize them like this instead."

Savanna sat across from him. "Well, they went to the

trouble of getting through all the security roadblocks in order to steal authentic works, right? And then destroy the fakes once they had access."

Britt spoke. "Are we certain the paintings they stole are authentic?"

"Oh snap."

"Two of the vandalized pieces were in their own dedicated infrared secure display," Flynn said. "It still took effort to get to them. This was a very deliberate act."

"Most but not all of our Impressionist collection predates my work here," Britt said. "The incoming pieces we've acquired in the last handful of years have been mainly Postimpressionist works, though this Minkov looks like it was acquired last year here. I hope I wasn't the authenticator for any of the stolen or defaced Impressionists."

Director Flynn shook his head. "You would've caught a forgery. Besides, you know if a piece comes to us with a perfectly intact provenance, we don't typically conduct a full exam of the canvas."

"Don't worry," Savanna told her friend. She directed her question at Flynn. "Could you get us access to the provenance records for the stolen pieces?"

"Of course. The FBI was reviewing the hard copies, but I'll send you both the electronic records in just a bit. This Kiernanski discovery is extremely helpful. If I can get our assigned FBI agent here quick enough, will you run through this once more for her? I understand if you've got to leave before then, though. I'll be here late; I can also detail your findings for her. I hate to keep you both too late right before the holiday."

"I can stay," Savanna said. "Thank you for the flexibility though. I hope you can get out of here and enjoy your holiday, too, Director."

Her running mental to-do list was topped with gift wrapping the Barbie Dreamhouse she'd purchased for The Gifting Tree and dropping it off at the designated address by tonight. She wasn't sure if she was supposed to put it on the porch and run away or hand deliver it. She was leaning toward dropping and running. There was also a pile of gifts waiting at home for her to wrap tonight, the breakfast casserole she wanted to make for Christmas morning, two pies to bake for Christmas Day... but right now, she wanted nothing more than to unravel what was happening with these forgeries.

She and Britt dove into the meat and potatoes part of art authenticating—assessing and evaluating the actual piece of art with all the tools at their disposal. Instead of focusing on trying to remove the thick red graffiti paint, Savanna began with her go-to tool, the wireless Firefly, a powerful high magnification video camera microscope that she could sync with her laptop. Britt worked opposite her on the Sergei Minkov they now suspected was a forgery based on the art dealer's name on the provenance.

Moving slowly, Firefly held a few inches away from the canvas, she began at the top left corner and scanned the varying shades, the texture of the paints, the brushstrokes depth and patterns. Artists developed their own habits and techniques, making it easier to recognize their work or spot a poor copy. In Francois Laurant's *Notre Dame de Paris*, she should see marked contrast between light and shadow in at least some of the depicted scene. The artist was known for infusing his work with depth through this contrast, known as chiaroscuro technique. *Notre Dame de Paris* lacked the hallmark sign of a true Francois Laurant. The Laurant they'd viewed on screen during the meeting with Rob here last Friday likely also lacked it. At the time, Savanna had noticed the distinct lack of chiaroscuro method within the artist's *Charmante Femme Agée* but chalked it up to looking at the painting on a screen versus in person. Now she was almost certain Kenilworth's vandalized Laurant was also a forgery.

In case this finding alone wasn't enough to declare the painting in front of her a fake, there was another test she could run. Even with provenance, there had to be more— paint from different time periods, a clear lack of the typical brushstroke type, even when all else matched. Vincent Van Gogh was a good example of an artist with a signature style. A favorite professor had asked the class to imagine Van Gogh's *Starry Night* as painted by Pablo Picasso, which conjured quite a discordant image. One artist could imitate another artist's style, but the finer details were often the giveaway.

She fetched her large tote bag she called her brains and pulled from it the printout she'd gotten from Director Flynn detailing every stolen and vandalized item from all three targeted museums thus far. She made a few notes next to those two Laurants, both vandalized rather than stolen.

She wheeled the almost certainly forged Laurent on the lab's cart to the far end of the lab where the bulky X-ray equipment was located, behind an L-shaped barrier. She handled the imaging of the painting, which sent high energy protons through proton-induced X-ray emission, or PIXE, to be used in analyzing the chemical elements in the painting. This was another valid, noninvasive method used to determine the makeup of the paints used; often, forgeries were discovered when PIXE revealed chemical compounds not in existence during the time the artist was alive.

She was marginally aware of Britt moving about the lab using the diagnostic equipment, too, but with her laser focus on analyzing the chemistry, when she lifted her gaze from the computer screen she was shocked to see two hours had passed. "This one's a confirmed forgery," she told Britt. "No doubt about it. How's yours?"

"Definitely forged. The signature is the giveaway. It checks out fine at first, but under UVA the luminescence is all off. Two down, one to go."

While Britt finished with the other painting, Savanna studied the pages laid out in front of her, comparing two separate categories: stolen versus vandalized. Morton Samuel in California had three stolen Impressionist paintings and five vandalized Impressionist paintings listed. Kenilworth had five stolen Impressionist paintings and six vandalized Impressionist paintings. Lansing had lost three Impressionists to theft and three others were defaced.

She got a fresh piece of paper, wrote *Artists* at the top, and drew three columns, one for each museum that had just been robbed. She drew a horizontal line through them across the middle. Beginning with Lansing, jotting only the supposed artists of the vandalized pieces. Below that, she wrote the artists of the stolen pieces. She got the columns filled in quickly for her museum, Kenilworth, and Morton Samuel. Kicking off and sliding her stool down the counter back to the monitor that still displayed the *Journal of Art Crimes*, she scrolled through it, looking for artist names. Minkov, Laurant, and Rothman leapt out at her, probably because they were the ones she'd spent the most time evaluating.

But of all the pieces stolen, there were only a handful of artists listed. The three she'd already flagged, the late Impressionist era artist Josephine Claire, and lesser-known painter and sculptor Camille Winthrop. She tapped the keyboard, navigating to one of the vetted websites the museum used to research provenance for potential acquisitions, and began the arduous process of tracking the known histories of Winthrop, Claire, Minkov, Laurant, and Rothman.

She and Britt ended their day having made enormous leaps forward in deciphering what on earth was happening with the stolen and vandalized Impressionist pieces, but no appearance by the FBI field agent. She was almost back home when Director Flynn called. He'd finally heard from the FBI Art Crimes Team Lead.

"I know tomorrow is Christmas Eve," Flynn said. "I hate to ask, Savanna, but the agents are out on assignment until tomorrow. They'd like to go over all of this in person tomorrow morning. I can ask if right after Christmas would work instead… it's up to you."

As much as she wanted to wait, the video footage from Rob's 360 Dash Cam app felt like a ticking timebomb in her phone, as yet unseen by anyone of importance. Sitting down with the FBI to share that information and also delve into what she knew so far about the break-ins would allow her to redirect her focus and enjoy the holiday. "Tomorrow morning is fine."

Chapter Twelve

S AVANNA WAS JUST finishing wrapping the Dreamhouse Friday evening when her phone rang with a call from Anderson Memorial. Her heart beating a little faster as her mind sorted through the scary possibilities of who in her small circle of friends and family was in the hospital, she grabbed it. The girl on the other end of the line identified herself as a cardiothoracic surgical tech.

"Dr. Gallager asked me to call, is this Savanna Shepherd?"

"Yes, it is."

"He's sorry for the short notice. The heart surgery he's in is running long. He can't estimate when he might get out, and his sitter needs to leave on time today. He asked if you'd be able to relieve the babysitter and stay with his daughter until he's home?"

Savanna hesitated. Of course, she could—but what about his in-laws? He wouldn't leave it up to her to call them and make sure they didn't want to do it, but had the tech already asked them? The last thing she wanted was to give the Becketts more to be mad about.

In the brief silence as she wavered, the tech added, "He said to tell you that his in-laws are out of town. And if you're busy, I'm to call someone named Elaina Jenson."

"I can be there in ten minutes," she'd replied, relieved. She liked that his backup was Elaina too; Elaina's son Carter was good friends with Mollie.

She hung up, for the first time wondering if he and his late wife had had some kind of protocol or phone call tree for when he got stuck in a surgery and Mollie needed a caretaker. Mollie was only three when her mother died, but had Olivia been a stay-at-home mom or worked outside the home? Were her parents as involved then as they seemed now? Why had it not occurred to her sooner that the Becketts were probably always on call when Olivia was alive? It wasn't like Aidan had a job that he could just walk off of or clock out when his time was up. This type of thing must've happened on a semi-regular basis, judging by how often it'd happened since she was in the picture. Aidan's in-laws probably never had to deal with anyone else being called to care for their granddaughter until recently.

She still wished she could communicate with them. Write them a letter or sit down for coffee in public somewhere, where the conversation would have to be kept civil. She didn't have anything complex or shocking to say to them. She wished they knew she'd never try to take Olivia's place, never infringe on their time or keep them from seeing their granddaughter. All she wanted was to have a place in Mollie's life too. She hoped Aidan's next meeting with Jillian Black would yield some solutions… something better than what was currently happening. Because the whole situation seemed to be getting worse.

She slapped a big red bow on the wrapped Barbie Dreamhouse gift and made it over to Aidan's house in closer to five minutes to relieve the sitter. Savanna informed Mollie that they had a mission to fulfill, reminding her of their Gifting Tree commitment.

"Wait!" The little girl took her by the hand to the spare bedroom her dad had turned into a playroom. Spacious and bright, the room was less pink princess and more neutral earth tones than she'd at first expected. A hanging green pothos plant in the corner had grown and flourished so well, its long leafy branches were suspended with tiny clear adhesive hooks along the ceiling and around two window frames. A round, child-sized table and four chairs sat in the center of a large, fluffy rug, toy chests and shelves with games and Lego sets and crafts along the walls. Mollie's own Dreamhouse was set up on a low table against one wall with a second dollhouse beside it that Aidan had built, adding living space for her dolls. The hand-crafted house was three stories with cheerful wallpaper, swatches of carpet, and electric lights throughout. It reminded her of the dollhouse her father had made for her and her sisters as children, so cozy and pretty that Savanna would have moved in if it was life-sized.

Mollie fetched a cute purple and pink plastic camping RV, pushing it across the carpet to her. It opened on a hinge, revealing a tiny kitchen, living area, and beds. Cloth sleeping bags were unrolled on the beds, a miniature golden retriever in a dog bed below.

She bent down to peer inside. "This is adorable! I love

it."

"Me too," Mollie said. "Ms.—Savanna, I mean—can w-w-e give this to the girl too? Maybe she doesn't have one yet, and what if her dolls want to go camping?"

Savanna felt Mollie's difficulty with sorting her name out right along with her, hating that the stress briefly triggered her stutter. "I think that's a really sweet idea… but I'm not sure about what your dad would say. He probably got the camper for you so your dolls could go camping, right?"

Mollie hopped up and opened the closet, pointing to a second doll-sized RV just like the one on the rug. "I have two. Grandma Jean gave me this one, but it matches the one I already had from Daddy."

Knowing she couldn't contact Aidan, Savanna went with it. Aidan wouldn't be upset, she was certain, and it seemed like a great way to put the camper from Grandma Jean into play, make a little girl who didn't have much very happy, and maybe best of all, allow Mollie to learn the joy of selflessness all on her own. "This is really generous, Moll. You won't miss having two? I'm sure the girl is going to be so surprised just with the Dreamhouse."

"I won't miss it. But can I keep my dog?"

Savanna placed the tiny pup and dog bed in her outstretched palm. "Of course! Should we wrap it, so it's a Christmas gift too?"

Savanna parked in front of the house on Pinecone Avenue, double-checking the address on her half of the hangtag from The Gifting Tree. She met Mollie's eyes in the rearview mirror. The little girl was practically vibrating with excitement. Beside her on the back seat were two presents wrapped in Christmas paper, one decorated with sledding penguins in Santa hats, the smaller package in sparkly red and green polka-dotted paper Mollie had helped her locate in the house. It felt wrong snooping through the cupboards and closets in Aidan's house searching for gift wrap. She was glad when Mollie discovered it.

At six o'clock in December, it was already full dark as Savanna and Mollie quietly set the Christmas gifts on the porch of the house on Pinecone Ave. She pulled the half hangtag from her pocket and texted the number on it; she loved the Secret Santa premise of The Gifting Tree, but she didn't want to stand here with Mollie and make this family feel embarrassed or like they had to be profusely thankful. The simple text she sent read:

"Good evening! Your Gifting Tree wish has been fulfilled—check your porch. Best wishes for a happy holiday!"

She held out her hand and Mollie took it. "Run!"

They dove into the car at the end of the driveway, both giggling. Mollie sank down in the back seat, peeking over the edge of the car window. Savanna took her cue and waited, watching. They were rewarded a moment later.

A woman opened the door and clapped her hand over her mouth. She turned and ran away. A minute later she reappeared with two little girls. One looked a little older than Mollie and the other was younger. The girls ran out onto the porch, their whoops of joy loud enough to hear inside the car.

"Oh my gosh, they're so happy! Okay, now go!" Mollie ordered from the back seat.

Savanna complied, catching the girls jumping up and down and waving as she drove away. She glanced at Mollie. "That was so much fun. You made their Christmas extra special, Moll. I'm so glad you thought to be generous and give them your camper."

"I'm so glad too, their dolls are gonna love playing in the camper and Dreamhouse," Mollie said.

"We can set up the other camper from your grandma Jean when we get home," she suggested. "But first, we might have to make a quick stop at Lickety Split. I think we need some ice cream."

Two hours later while building a Lego city in the living room, empty ice cream bowls in the sink and Jersey and Fonzie asleep in front of the fireplace, Mollie interrupted her own chatter about which color Lego to use for the car she was building. "But," she said, as if they'd already been talking about it, "my wish at The Gifting Tree isn't something that someone can leave on the porch for me. So, does that mean I can't have it?"

Savanna tipped her head, studying the girl. She really needed to find out what Mollie's wish was—she hoped Aidan had found time to go look. "No, it doesn't mean you can't have it. I think," she said, "if it's not something that can be left on your porch, someone will find a different way for you to get it. Can you tell me what you wished for?"

"No way." She thought about Savanna's answer. "Like, if someone wished for a pony, then instead of a pony being on their porch, maybe the person will find a pony later on somewhere and get to keep it?"

She nodded. "Probably. Something like that."

"Okay, good." She resumed her work on the Lego car.

A few minutes before nine, Aidan called from the hospital. Exhaustion was embedded in his normally handsome face, giving him an almost haggard appearance on screen. He still wore the blue scrub cap, his eyes bluer than usual, and she saw stainless steel sinks in the background. He must've just gotten out of surgery. "Hey there. Long day. Have I told you lately how amazing you are?"

She smiled. "Nope. You'd better tell me."

"The scrub nurse got a text from a friend whose neighbor said someone just dropped off a big dollhouse and doll camper on her porch for her girls. The neighbor's daughter swears she saw her art teacher from school and Dr. Gallager's daughter in the getaway car." His tired smile sent a little zing straight to her heart. "So yeah. You're amazing, stepping in with no warning to watch Mollie and then sneaking around dropping off gifts like a couple of wish-granting bandits."

Sometimes she forgot what a small town Carson truly was; she should've known they'd be recognized by someone. "It was my pleasure hanging out with her," she said. "I'm glad you tagged me in. Are you all right? I'm sorry you've had such a rough day." She'd learned not to ask about the outcome of his surgeries on days like this. If the patient had pulled through after whatever complications occurred, he'd tell her. And if the outcome wasn't good or was precarious, he'd eventually tell her that, too, but in a few hours or days, when he was ready to talk about it.

He nodded. "I'm okay. The patient's okay. I just want to

come home. I've gotta change and I'll be on my way. Thank you, Savanna. I'll see you both soon."

SAVANNA STAYED IN the living room while Aidan carried his drowsy daughter upstairs to tuck her in. She added one last log to the fire, stirring the embers around and getting it going again; the radiant heat in the living room had very nearly knocked them out during the little girl's favorite movie, *The Princess Bride*.

"Savanna?" Aidan called from the top of the stairs. "Mollie wants to know if you'll come tuck her in with me?"

"Absolutely!" She jumped up, sprinting up the steps. "She asked?"

He nodded. "She mentioned how fun it was giving those two little girls her Barbie camper today to go with the Dreamhouse you got them."

She walked with him down the hallway to Mollie's room. "She convinced me you wouldn't mind. I hope it's okay?"

He put a hand on her arm, stopping her before they went inside. "You taught her about altruism and selflessness. Whether she realizes it or not, she learned that some people aren't as lucky as she is and may not have the things she has, and she did something to help. I love that. I love you."

She stepped into his arms and kissed his neck, his embrace making her forget what she needed to talk to him about before she went home. "I love you too."

In Mollie's room, the girl handed her a thin picture

book. "Can you read instead of Daddy?"

"Sure thing, Moll." She started to sit in the chair beside her bed.

"No, Daddy can sit there. You have to be next to me so I can see the pictures, okay?" She patted the bed, moving a few stuffed animals to make room. "Here, you can use the turtle pillow."

With her head on the stuffed turtle pillow and an entire pink bunny family propped up by Mollie to hear the story too, Savanna began reading while Aidan listened quietly in the chair beside them. Sometime during the first few pages, the girl snuggled against her and rested her head on her shoulder, small arm flung over Savanna's middle. Mollie's initial soft giggles and comments gave way to steady, even breathing as she fell asleep. Without warning, Savanna was plunged into a glimpse of her beautiful future she was no longer certain would happen.

She followed Aidan out of the room, heart and head filled beyond capacity. She didn't know what she'd expected, simply honoring a little girl's wish for a bedtime story, but this sweet, contented, overpowering love was more than she'd bargained for, maybe more than she was ready for.

Downstairs, he moved through to the kitchen, warming up the dinner she'd saved for him, asking if she wanted a drink and whether Mollie had fed the dog. Aidan closed the refrigerator and froze, staring at her.

"Hey," he whispered, closing the space between them, gently enfolding her in his arms. "Savanna, what is it? Why are you crying?"

Was she? She touched her cheek, surprised. She let out a sound, a laugh, but it came out like a sob. She shook her head, covering her mouth with one hand as she met his gaze. He blurred through her tears.

He drew her over to the couch, sitting her down and holding her. "It's okay. Whatever it is, it's okay." He kissed her temple.

She struggled to find the right words, struggled for any words at all, so he would understand. "I just. I didn't… it's a lot. She's… I love her so much. I'm…" She gave up trying to force coherence into her words. She pressed a hand against her chest, locking eyes with Aidan.

He was quiet, watching her. With one palm against her cheek, he spoke, his voice soft. "She loves you too. We both do. More than I ever imagined was possible. It's overwhelming and intense and wonderful but also scary, I know. Savanna. Don't let it scare you too much. That part stays, it doesn't go away, but it transforms. It's worth it." He gently wiped away her tears.

She circled her fingers around his wrist, holding on loosely. She took a deep breath, steeling herself to say what had to be said. "I think we should wait. It won't matter, changing the date won't matter to us years from now, but it could make all the difference for Mollie and the Becketts and you."

He looked horrified. "No. Listen, no. We're not waiting—" Aidan said, the softness in his tone gone.

"We need to give them time." He started to interrupt, and she stopped him. "We need to, it's the right thing to do.

They've been the caretakers in Mollie's world whenever you couldn't be, even more so since they lost their daughter, and I think me coming into your life now makes them feel like they're losing her all over again. Losing her and Mollie too," she added.

"No." He stared at her. "No, please." He pressed a hand over his eyes, leaving it there. "I don't want this," he said, voice thick. "This isn't just your decision to make. I don't want to wait. They'll calm down. They do need time, you're right, but not at the cost of us not getting married."

Savanna moved his hand from his eyes. She held his face in her hands, her own eyes burning knowing she was responsible for his damp cheeks under her fingertips. "We're getting married. Do you really think I'd let you go? I could never, Aidan. But we can't risk Mollie not having her dad exactly as much as she has you right now. She's more important than a date on a calendar."

He dropped his head, one wide hand pressed against the side of her thigh, holding onto her. He heaved a deep breath and she hugged him tightly. She didn't speak and neither did he. When he did, it was nearly inaudible. "I hate them."

"No, you don't," she whispered.

He shrugged. He lifted his gaze to hers and it broke her apart. "There's another way. There has to be."

She shook her head but didn't contradict him. She didn't see any other way. "I'm going to go. It's late," she said, mindful as always lately of what the Becketts might do if they saw her car at his house at half past ten. "It's late and you need some sleep."

In the driveway, he seemed to be upright on his feet through sheer will alone. She could have chosen her timing better, but the sooner they let the Becketts know they had nothing to worry about, the sooner they could be done fighting over Mollie.

Aidan pulled her to him before she could get in her car. "We aren't finished talking about this," he said, gently forcing her gaze to his, his fingers at her jawline. "Tomorrow morning. When I've had some sleep and my brain is working again."

Chapter Thirteen

SAVANNA ARRIVED IN Lansing to meet with FBI agents early Saturday morning feeling like she'd been hit by a truck. She'd slept fitfully, her body was achy and sluggish, and her mood wasn't much better. Aidan hadn't called yet, but she knew he would; she hoped he'd at least gotten some sleep. She wasn't sure how much he'd really absorbed last night.

"Merry Christmas Eve." Security guard Donald Tate greeted her at the laboratory door.

"Thank you," Savanna said. "Same to you. I'm surprised we're open today. Sorry you have to work."

"I'm not. I never turn down overtime," he said. "Besides, we close at three p.m. today. No big deal." He swiped her in.

A young woman in a sharp black suit stood, approaching her. An FBI badge was hung on the lanyard around her neck. "Savanna Shepherd?"

"Yes." She shook the agent's offered hand.

"Agent Klein. It's just me this morning. My partner's in Detroit. Not sure if you've heard yet, but the Detroit Institute of Arts was broken into late last night."

"Oh no. That's awful. Rob said you guys were predicting that might happen."

"Robert Havemeyer?"

Savanna nodded. "Yes. It's too bad that knowing ahead of time didn't end up helping them prevent it. Did they lose a lot?"

"Let's sit." Agent Klein held out a hand, gesturing. Once seated, she opened a laptop with an official-looking privacy warning on the front and set her phone on the countertop. "Is it all right with you if I record our discussion? It'll help later with coordinating and compiling data for the investigation."

"Sure, that's fine."

"Thank you. We appreciate you making yourself available this morning. Your director, Lawrence Flynn, says you've found something with the defaced paintings."

Savanna powered on the lab's computer. "I did. But I was hoping I could also show you something I found... related to what happened to Rob in Chicago."

Klein nodded. "My Chicago contact let me know you'd left a voicemail for him. I can definitely take a look."

"Oh, that's great. Okay, so first," she said, pulling up the documentation she and Britt had entered yesterday, "I looked at the list of vandalized pieces from us and Chicago and Morton Samuel in L.A. and discovered that they are all from only five artists. All fourteen pieces with graffiti are from just five artists," she clarified.

"Yes, we noted that as well."

"I was sure you would have. You might already know this, too, but at least three of those artists had known forged works that were traced to a gallery in St. Armands, Florida, two years ago. It's a little harder for me to see the full history of the other two artists with my limited access," she said, "but maybe you're looking into them?"

Klein frowned. "That was not on my radar. St. Armands was two years ago?"

"Right here," Savanna said, turning the large, mounted monitor screen toward the agent. She'd reopened the article about the forgeries at the Carson Mansion.

"I remember this. I was still in training for the Art Crimes Team. May I?" She pointed to the mouse.

Savanna slid her rolling stool backwards, moving out of the way. "Absolutely."

"This turned out to be a pretty large breakthrough," she said. "The original forger had works placed internationally through multiple gallerists, most acting legitimately as dealers shopping artwork for private collectors and museums while filtering the forgeries through simultaneously. I wish I'd been in the field already when this broke." She scrolled through the article and clicked a hyperlink, opening another report from a *BBC* news outlet and then another through *Reuters*.

"The local sheriff's detective in Carson—actually, you might have met him here. He works a side job here in security. Nick Jordan. Anyway, I unofficially worked with him on that case, before it became international news. He mentioned to me that the paintings found at the Carson Mansion were just the tip of the iceberg," Savanna said. "I followed the story for a while."

Klein pointed at the screen, enlarging an image of a

mountainous landscape on the *Reuters* site. "The Louvre acquired this Sergei Minkov five years ago for a cool twenty million—except they didn't get a twenty-million-dollar painting. This is the fake discovered because of the Kiernanski name on the provenance. The real Minkov was traced to a private collector in St. Lucia once this one at the Louvre was outed as a fake. You're the reason the team was able to uncover the St. Armands forgery ring in the first place." The FBI agent stared at Savanna. "I saw your name but didn't make the connection. Thank you."

"I'm not... I mean, I noticed some discrepancies in a friend's art collection. She was being taken advantage of by the gallerist buying and selling her artwork for her."

"I examined the small Minkov that I've read was the tipoff for you. *Storm in Sochi*, right? That piece was nearly flawless. You're good."

Savanna smiled. "Thank you. I guess you can take the authenticator out of the fine art world, but you can't take the love of fine art from the authenticator."

Agent Klein took off her glasses. "So, you're installed here now full time, instead of Kenilworth? That was a win on Director Flynn's part."

"No." She shook her head. "I teach art to elementary students in Carson. I just consult here whenever Britt needs me."

The woman was quiet, studying her for so long she grew uncomfortable. Agent Klein took a shiny flat case from her suit coat and handed Savanna her card. "If you ever decide to... level up... call me. You're just as talented as my colleagues—or more so. I'd walk you through what's involved in applying."

She stared at the card, speechless. This was a wild dream, a crazy, out of left offer. There was no space in her future for anything like this. When she raised her gaze to Klein's, the agent gave her one quick nod.

"I mean it."

"Okay." She slid the card into her pocket.

"All right. So. These thefts and acts of vandalism have a significant number of artists and provenance markers in common with forgeries discovered during the St. Armand's bust. Even so, I don't know how likely it is that this new activity is connected."

Savanna spoke. "Here's the other thing." She crossed the lab to the vandalized Francois Laurant and Agent Klein followed. "Britt and I discovered yesterday that the expert who last certified this *Charmante Femme Agée* as legitimate is Ivan Kiernanski. That name was one of the other giveaways in the Carson Mansion pieces. And turns out there is no such art authenticator by that name."

"Ivan Kiernaski versus Ivan Kiernanski," Agent Klein said. "I remember reading about that—the name was misspelled on one of the documents from the Carson Mansion, right? You're ahead of me here. You're saying this Laurant is tied to that fake authenticator?"

"I think so. I don't know how else to explain that name on the provenance. And we do know it's a forgery. I've always loved *Charmante Femme Agée*. This is the chemical composition report for the painting using PIXE." She handed the findings to Klein. "We found titanium white."

"Ah." Agent Klein looked disappointed. "What a disappointment for the museum. It's one of my favorite pieces too. Titanium white wasn't even invented until the early twentieth century, well after Francois Laurant created *Charmante Femme Agée*. Finding that pigment is always a red flag."

Savanna nodded. To an art expert, the knowledge was fairly rudimentary. But it was still one of the most common missteps made by forgers. "At least the real *Charmante Femme Agée* isn't covered in red spray paint. Wherever it is."

The agent moved back to the monitor, peering at Savanna's screen. She leaned in, reading. "So, the vandalized pieces from all three museums are supposed works by Laurant, Minkov, and Rothman, plus Camille Winthrop and Josephine Claire. My partner is still at the museum in Detroit taking statements, I have to find out which works were damaged or stolen from the DIA this morning," she said, almost to herself. "After the St. Armand's bust, the FBI would have done a thorough sweep of any and all paintings coming up with any of the implicated dealers or either one of Kiernanski's two names on the paperwork. I can't explain these—unless provenances were skipped over during acquisition."

Her hackles went up; she didn't like the suggestion that she or Britt might have been lax in their role with examining incoming works. "I'm sure that happens, depending on who's involved in the acquisitions—" She halted abruptly, eyes widening with realization. Helene? Had she been involved in moving forged artwork? She bit her lip, hesitant to say anything that might paint Britt's girlfriend in a bad light. She'd always liked Helene. When she and Britt began dating earlier this year, Savanna had thought they complemented each other nicely. But...

"Do you know the museum's curators? Lansing Museum of Fine Art has three, yes?"

"Yes," she said. Curators were typically an instrumental part of the artwork acquisition process. "Helene Devereaux is the curator who was killed during our break-in. There's, uh, something I noticed when her body was found in the elevator. She had what looked like two cell phones—they were taken by the forensics people. I asked Britt about it. They were dating. I don't think they knew she had two phones, just based on how they acted when I asked." There. It was out there.

Klein's quick nod and lack of change to her expression suggested she wasn't surprised. Her response reminded Savanna of the indifference Lars Anders had shown upon learning Helene was dead.

"Lots of people have a personal phone and a work phone." Savanna nudged the discussion in hopes of the agent commenting. When she didn't, she added, "It just made me realize I didn't really know her too well."

"We're investigating all possible leads. If it helps to know, we're looking at the employee records of several museum staff. Your assistant CEO Ms. Aguilar has been very helpful."

"She doesn't know any of us. If that matters. Director

Flynn might be a better resource," she suggested.

Klein nodded, noncommittal. "Was there anything else, before we wrap this up?"

Savanna handed Agent Klein a sticky note with Rob's username and password for the 360 Dash Cam app. "The last time I spoke with Rob, he said his dashboard camera had caught something the night of the Kenilworth break-in. That's his log in. I checked it out. The clip he's talking about shows a figure being let into the museum through an employee entrance door."

"Really? Rob's phone hasn't been recovered yet, which is slowing down the investigation into his death." Klein quickly downloaded the app and attempted to log in. "Hmm. Hold on, maybe I typed it wrong." She tried again, shaking her head.

"It won't let you in? Ugh—what if whoever has his phone changed the password?"

Agent Klein turned her phone toward Savanna, showing her the screen:

Username not found

Chapter Fourteen

"NOOOO." SHE STARED at the phone. "What does that mean?"

"I'd say it means whoever has his phone deleted his account." Agent Klein picked up her own phone and made a call. "Hey Coop... Good, same to you. I'm going to send you log in info for an app in just a moment. Could you see what you can see? The account's been removed but maybe there's a way to get the data back... Thanks." She hung up.

"I hope so," Savanna said. "Oh! Wait, I have it—the video." She scrolled through and handed her phone to Klein. "When I was showing Britt, I downloaded—" The agent interrupted her.

"Britt Nash?" She was frowning like a disappointed parent. "You shared the recorded footage with him?"

"Them," she corrected automatically.

"Sorry. Them. Besides Britt Nash, who else did you share with?"

For Pete's sake. She wasn't a child. She could've done without the agent's chastising tone. "Just Britt. That's all. They've been my friend and colleague for years. I'm sure it's fine."

"Just to be clear, if you discover any other information

pertaining to these cases, anything that even remotely represents possible evidence, bring it straight to me. And please don't share it with colleagues."

"Got it." Her cheeks burned, in part because she knew the agent had a point. It was common sense and something Detective Jordan had reinforced every time she'd worked alongside him unraveling a case.

Agent Klein handed her phone back. "If you consent to sharing the footage with me, would you go ahead and just hit send please?"

Savanna nodded and complied, sending the downloads to an email address ending in *FBI.gov*. She glanced back up at the agent. "It's the eight second one dated the day of the robbery."

"That's helpful, Savanna, thank you. Let's take a look; can you show me what it is that Mr. Kenilworth saw?"

When she played the short clip, Klein swiped to back up through the frames several times, scrutinizing the dark figure against the building and then the split second of someone from inside pushing open the employee entrance door.

"This is excellent." Savanna raised her eyebrows at Agent Klein; nothing about the dark, fuzzy video seemed excellent to her. But the agent continued. "We'll be able to clean this up and get an image from it, I'm confident. It was quick thinking of you to save the footage in your files."

"Thank you." She might as well share the other thing that had been nagging at her. She couldn't think of anything about it that'd trigger another reprimand—hopefully. "I did have one quick question."

"Shoot," the agent said, pulling on her coat.

"I know you can't share any details about Rob's case—about his murder. I say murder because I'm positive it wasn't an accident. He wasn't clumsy or accident-prone. He was a little obsessive about his nutrition and exercise, so I don't believe he'd have just passed out from like, low blood sugar or blood pressure."

Agent Klein perched on the stool, setting her things down. "Go on."

"Well, you know—or, I don't know it works, maybe the Chicago FBI Art Team agent knows—that he lives in a secure building. Nobody but residents can get in, and even if someone does, you need an apartment key to use the elevator. I don't see how anyone could have entered, killed him somehow, and gotten out of there without it being obvious."

"I see your point."

"I'm just saying, it had to be someone he knew, or else something preplanned, like something slipped into his nightly kombucha that'd affect him once he was in his apartment." What did she have to lose? She'd already screwed up and shown Agent Klein she was a total amateur by sharing evidence. So what if Klein thought the theory was crazy. Maybe Syd was right and she really did watch too much *Columbo*, but the great detective himself would've appreciated the ingenuity of a killer having the forethought to tamper with a set-in-stone portion of the victim's routine in order to execute them with little chance of being caught—said killer would be long gone by the time Rob dropped dead in his bathroom thanks to the kombucha schedule he adhered to religiously.

Klein was scribbling something on a notepad. "Could you repeat that, Savanna, once more for the tape? I just want to make sure my partner doesn't miss anything."

She sensed the agent being overly solicitous and respectful since she'd snapped at her. But she'd been right. She repeated what she'd said as best she could recall. The thought had occurred to her when she'd passed conference room 3A on her way to the lab this morning. He'd been legitimately concerned about getting his health drink when he was here. In the same way he'd always been obsessive about going to the gym, he always had to have his daily kombucha. The man couldn't skip a day, or he'd convince himself he was beginning to feel sick.

At the door to leave, Agent Klein paused and looked back. "I meant what I said. Keep my card. Let me know if you'd ever like to do some consulting for us."

Perhaps the agent hadn't judged her as harshly as she'd thought. She patted her pocket where she'd put the business card. "Thank you so much. I'll keep it in mind."

When she finally turned her phone on in her car after the meeting with Agent Klein, the notifications populated quicker than she could read them. She'd missed a bunch of text messages from Aidan, Sydney in their sister chat, and her parents and uncles in their family chat.

Sydney wanted to know if Savanna had remembered to pick up the joint Christmas gift they'd gotten for their dad. She sent a quick "*yes*."

Her parents and uncles had sent a series of funny GIFs in

the family chat, cousin Ellie chiming in that she couldn't wait to see everyone later tonight.

Aidan's text message was succinct:

"Got some sleep and my brain is back online... we need to talk."

There were also four voicemails waiting for her.

Pulling out of employee parking and heading home, she took a deep breath and ripped off the Band-Aid, dialing into her voicemail. Just the sound of Aidan's voice over Bluetooth filling her car sent hot tears to her eyes.

"When can I see you? Let me know. Soon." That one had come in early this morning around the time she and Agent Klein were shaking hands. His tone was firm with an edge of irritation. The second message was also from him.

"Savanna." He fell quiet. Sighed. She imagined him scrubbing a hand across the top of his head, mussing the unruly black waves he kept cut short. When he spoke again, his voice was soft and sad. "I just came by looking for you. Where are you? It's Christmas Eve. Why aren't you answering or texting back? If this is all part of the plan, if you're trying to push me away or ghost me, just stop. This isn't us. You know that. I'm not okay. Call me. I don't want to do this with you. I don't want to explain to Mollie why we aren't getting married or why it might be weeks or months or longer until she can fall asleep each night under the same roof as the woman we both thought was part of our family. I don't want to wait God knows how long to fall asleep each night beside you either. We need to talk. *Please.*" His voicemail ended abruptly.

She kept going, steeling herself and playing the next message. "I get it," he said. "I understand your reasoning. You love Mollie and just want to do the right thing for her. This isn't it. Please. Talk to me. We're still coming over tonight. I'd like to wait until after Christmas to break my daughter's heart if you're really doing this."

Her own heart was racing by the time he disconnected the call, her eyes blurring the expressway ahead of her. She cleared her throat, blinked quickly, struggling for control.

Savanna summoned her strength for the last voicemail, not knowing how much more she could take of Aidan's guilt-inducing logic. Tiffany Havemeyer's voice came through.

"Savanna, I have some good news, finally. Mother is doing so much better. She's awake, off the machines, and they're moving her to a regular hospital floor. And... arrangements have been made for my brother. I'll send you the details. The funeral is next week."

Savanna hung up. Two funerals the week after Christmas. It seemed unreal that less than twenty-four hours ago, she was certain her wedding would be as well.

She called Aidan back, no clue what she was going to say to him. She hated how distraught he sounded in his voicemails. It was exactly how she felt every time she forgot to keep her focus on the big picture and what was best for Mollie. Relief coursed through her when Aidan's voicemail picked up—and then she panicked and hung up, at a loss for words.

Back in town, she passed her turn and kept going down Main Street toward the lake, turning left onto Caroline

Carson's street. She parked beside Jack's car in the driveway, noting the black and white patrol car out front in the street. It looked like Detective George Taylor was on watch, though she couldn't imagine why he'd gotten stuck on duty instead of one of the deputies. She stopped to say hello and he rolled the window down.

"Merry Christmas!" he said. "Stopping by for one of Caroline's famous Santa cookies?" He held his up, a big bite taken out of the Santa hat decorated withwhite icing and red sprinkles.

"Oh, my goodness! I've missed those! She's still making them? Look at the detail," she said. The plump cheeked, lightly frosted shortbread Santa face bore rosy cheeks, tiny currants for eyes, and a generously iced white beard complete with sparkly white sanding sugar and coconut. "It's almost too cute to eat."

George took another bite and Santa's left cheek and eye disappeared. "Speak for yourself," he said around a mouthful of cookie. "Mmm. She makes the best."

"Did you sign up for this shift just to get Christmas cookies, Detective?" Savanna stood back, arms crossed, frowning at him through the window.

He laughed good-naturedly. "You got me. No, Deputy Harker was assigned but he's home with a sick kid. Rosa and her mom are with ours. I don't mind filling in."

"Very nice of you. I'd better get in there before Jack eats the rest of the cookies. Give Rosa and those tweens a hug from me," she called over her shoulder. "Merry Christmas!"

Inside, Jack led her through to the kitchen where his

grandmother sat at the table with two little boys and a girl, every inch of space covered with parchment paper, icing, sprinkles, and dozens of cookies in various stages of decoration. Her face lit up when she saw Savanna. "What a wonderful surprise! You can help us! We're lucky to have three of my great-grandchildren acting as little elves too," she said, smiling. "Lauren is getting some last-minute shopping done while they're here."

Savanna bent and kissed her cheek, giving her a hug. "Happy Christmas Eve. I feel like I've stepped into a time machine back to my entire childhood around this time of year. We used to have so much fun here with you, decorating and eating our mistakes."

"I remember," Caroline said. "You three made the biggest messes. I'd still find sprinkles and flour weeks later in a crack on one of the floorboards or a dot of icing on the ceiling." She chuckled.

"We were terrible," Savanna said, smiling.

"You were wonderful." She got to her feet, taking her cane from the back of her chair. "I'm taking a break. We're leaving in about an hour for your house," she told her great-grandchildren. "Whatever isn't decorated will just have to be saved to ice and eat next time."

Jack straightened up from taking another baking sheet out of the oven. "Not sure that really qualifies as motivation, Grandmother." He winked at the kids. "Have a cookie, Savanna. She's got a tin with your name on it in the foyer, before you leave, make sure to take it."

Caroline took Savanna's offered elbow. "Let's chat in the

parlor, shall we?"

The Carson Mansion parlor faced west, a wall of two-story windows looking out over Lake Michigan. With Caroline seated in her comfy wingback chair, Savanna moved to the windows, awed by the view. "Wow. Just... wow."

A vast blanket of white covered the rolling dunes and beach, the sheen of today's temperature plunge into the teens making the snow shimmer. Beyond, white caps roiled in the deep blue lake, rolling ever inward toward the shoreline and lightly icing over where the water greeted the land. With nothing on the horizon but bluer, more white-capped, choppy waves, and not a single sail to be seen for the next several months, it took her breath away.

"Beautiful, isn't she?" Caroline spoke at her side, having come to stand with her. "I sometimes forget to notice."

"I don't think I've been here—right here"—she tapped her foot on the lacquered parlor floor—"in the winter since... forever ago. Gorgeous. I'd swear it's an ocean if I didn't know better."

"Yes. It's all in how we choose to see it, isn't it? Maybe it is an ocean, for us, for a moment."

She glanced briefly at the older woman before returning her attention to the view. "What do you mean?"

"Oh, I don't know. Whether I see it as an ocean or my lake, the joy it brings me is the same. Should I list all the reasons it can't be an ocean so I can diminish my appreciation of what I have? Or is it wiser to take it at face value for the happiness it brings me, regardless of how I define it?"

Her throat closed, swelling without warning from un-shed tears. Savanna bit her lip, hard, grappling for control over her emotions. For goodness' sake, they were discussing the lake. Just the lake. She burst into tears, covering her mouth, heart pounding in her ears.

Caroline held onto her and hugged her with one arm around her waist. "Oh, my dear, it's all right. I promise. Let it all go. It'll be okay."

She cried harder, shoulders shaking with near silent sobs, hands covering her face. She was kidding herself thinking she had any control over anything. How did Caroline somehow always know how to say what she needed to hear? How could she face Aidan and Mollie tonight, knowing the wedding had to be postponed or canceled? How would she face her family tomorrow on Christmas? Was she making the worst mistake of her life?

Caroline stood with her, not speaking, simply holding her while her stupid, useless tears flowed. After a while, the woman guided her to the wingback chair opposite hers. Savanna took the offered tissue and pressed it to her face. She drew in a hitching breath. "I'm sorry. Goodness," she said, her tone pushed below a whisper.

"Sorry for what? Here," she said, passing her a few more tissues. "Do you know what brought that on, my dear?"

"I do. I, um. Aidan's in-laws are suing him for partial custody because of me. I told him we have to postpone the wedding until this is all sorted out. Maybe they'll drop the suit if I take a step back." She wiped away the new tears falling against her will.

"And then what?"

"What?"

"Then what?" Caroline repeated. "If their issue truly is with you, it won't get better. Are you going to wait until Mollie graduates high school and leaves for college before marrying Aidan?"

"I... no, I wouldn't think so. That'd be crazy. Right?" She couldn't control the way her nerves pushed her voice into a higher octave at the end.

"It'd be extreme, yes," the older woman agreed. "I don't believe it's about you at all. But it's easier than having no one to blame for their daughter being gone."

"That makes it all sound even more hopeless," she said. "How can I marry him knowing it could cost him Mollie?"

Caroline reached across and took her hand, covering it with her other atop it. "Darling girl, do you really believe you are instrumental enough to separate that man from his child? Don't take that on. It's not yours to carry."

"But it shouldn't be his, either," she protested. "He's an amazing dad. Everyone knows that."

"Yes. Exactly." She gave Savanna's hand a little pat and let go. "Besides, I've already mailed in your wedding's response card and ordered Chef Joe's prime rib."

The unexpected laugh that burst from her lips made her feel suddenly lighter. She sniffled and did a more thorough job of drying her cheeks. She had a whole lot to figure out. Maybe there was some middle ground, something between barreling forward at the risk of making things worse or waiting ten years to marry the man she'd already waited a lifetime for.

Caroline picked up the swatch of yarn connected with knitting needles. "Now. Tell me, are you the reason the police won't let me out of their sight lately? Detectives Jordan and Taylor said something about the recent museum break-ins giving cause for concern about my paintings here. Is this some silly fuss for nothing? Or is it necessary?"

"It's absolutely necessary. Try not to let it worry you, but let's just be glad they're keeping an eye out. The thieves seem to be targeting Impressionist paintings—of which you still have a few, if I remember right."

"I do. I've had the other gallerist Everett and I worked with thin out the remainder of my collection, but I still have that Minkov in the library, the beautiful Monet at the top of the stairs, and I asked Bill Lyle to move the large Matisse painting to the dining room. That wall needed something after the small Minkov was found out to be a fake. So," she said, holding up three fingers, "I have only three left of interest to any potential thief."

"Thank goodness," Savanna said, recalling the first time she'd reconnected with Caroline after being gone so long in Chicago. She'd stopped by as Aidan was leaving after a house call. Whatever Caroline's heart condition was, it seemed to warrant routine visits from her top-notch cardiologist, monitoring equipment she used every morning to check and transmit her vital signs to the clinic, and a little daily pill to regulate her rhythm. With the cops stationed out front for now, there was no reason to alarm her ninety-two-year-old would-be grandmother.

Caroline raised her eyebrows skeptically. "Is that so? You mentioned the value of my Minkov at one point and it was no small sum. If I should be concerned, please tell me. I can move the paintings off site."

"It's not a terrible idea. Detective Jordan asked about that too. The problem is, even if we update the provenance immediately, I'm not sure the thieves will learn the paintings aren't here before they orchestrate some kind of attempt." She pursed her lips. "With all the museums they've robbed, it seems unlikely that they'd come here, but not impossible. Maybe we should move them just in case it helps."

She left Caroline's with a large cookie tin in hand and the plan to move the Impressionist works temporarily to the vault at Carson's National First Bank as soon as businesses reopened after the holiday. She pulled up in her driveway at home and, before she could forget, sent Detective Jordan a brief merry-Christmas-sorry-to-bother-you text, letting him know the plan.

He replied before she could even get out of the car:

"Sounds like a good idea... thanks for the heads-up. Merry Christmas to you and the family."

She'd only been home long enough to let Fonzie loose and drop her things by the door when Aidan's SUV pulled into her driveway. Frozen with anxiety, Savanna stood in the open doorway to the deck and watched him climb from the car. He wasn't supposed to be here until six tonight—he was hours early. Mollie wasn't with him. He reached across to the passenger seat and tucked a thick folder under one arm before heading toward her, his expression somber.

Chapter Fifteen

A IDAN STOPPED AT the top of deck stairs.

"Hi…" she said, her voice sounding small to her own ears. "How did you… I just got home. I was going to call you," she lied. She absolutely was not. She had no idea what to say to him. It occurred to her how much easier it'd be to deal with this tonight, with Mollie here, when they wouldn't be able to really talk. The coward's way.

"I remembered your location is on." He held up his phone. "I saw you were home."

"Should we talk now?"

"Sure." He followed her inside. "Were you planning to just dodge my calls and avoid me until tonight?"

She turned to face him. "I didn't have a plan." He looked so… not tired anymore. Angry? How could he actually be angry with her for trying to put his daughter first?

He dropped into a kitchen chair, setting the nondescript document folder face down on the table. He looked up at her. "I need to ask you a question and I want the truth. Will you tell me the truth, even if it's hard?"

"Of course I will." She sat in the chair beside him. He was scaring her.

"Do you want some time apart?"

Her eyes widened. Her mouth went dry as she tried to speak. Was he breaking up with her?

He asked again. "You're probably still processing the loss of... a man who was important to you once. And you're young. I'm sure you never thought you'd be taking on someone else's child. Maybe some time to step back and think everything through would be a good idea. I'm wondering if that's what you want."

She moved her chair closer to him. "I was just trying to make things easier for Mollie. If you lose time with her because you married me, you'll end up resenting me. Even if you think you won't." She searched his guarded gaze, placing a hand on his cheek. "Aidan, the only thing I want is a future with you and Mollie. You're everything to me."

He didn't speak. Twin lines between his eyebrows punctuated his distress. She realized she hadn't answered his question.

"I don't want to step back, unless you think waiting will smooth things over with Jean and Tom," she clarified. In her mind, they'd become *The In-Laws*, a powerful force trying to tear Mollie from her dad. She resolved to knock that off. Her talk with Caroline had given her a lot to think about. *The In-Laws* weren't villainous or bent on destroying relationships, they were grieving parents afraid of losing the precious, shining light that was Mollie, all they had left of their daughter. "I don't want a break," she repeated.

He slid his hand up her arm and pulled her close and kissed her. When he let go, he pushed the folder over to her. She flipped it over, sucking in her breath. The front bore the gold embossed logo of Carson Community Homes.

"What is this?" It looked exactly like the one she'd received while in the process of buying this house.

He opened it. The first completed form was a listing agreement with his address on it. "It's the signed contract listing my house. You're sure you're sure?"

She grabbed him and kissed him, pushing her chair away to sit in his lap with his arms wrapped around her. "I can't believe you did this!"

"No backing out now. Unless you want me and Mollie out on the street. The real estate agent says it'll sell fast."

Savanna's heartbeat sped up at the thought of him here, with her, every day and night. The house would become theirs, their little family of three, Mollie spending Saturday mornings painting with her or watching cartoons, Aidan choosing that day's suit and tie from his clothes hanging in their closet with hers, Jersey running the dunes with Fonzie.

"I'll deal with Tom and Jean. Whatever happens, they're not taking away time with Mollie. I will not let that happen," he said. "And Savanna. I could never resent you. Sometimes, I..." He hesitated, not finishing the thought.

"Sometimes what?" He'd said it before and stopped. He normally had no trouble saying what he felt.

His gaze dropped to her lips. "It's just..." He met her gaze. "I don't know what I did to deserve you. To feel the way I feel about you. I thought I was done. With this, with love, with all of it. And then there you were. The thought of losing you terrifies me."

Her pulse raced and her cheeks warmed, his words a

beautiful gift. "You won't. I'm not going anywhere." She cupped his stubbly face in her hands, her throat swelling at the knowledge he'd probably heard the sentiment in his marriage, before his wife had gotten sick. She kissed his forehead, his cheek, his lips. She tried for a different take. "I think we're blessed to have found our way to each other. You can't lose me. Just try it—it won't work. I'll pop right back up, in your face, 24/7."

He laughed. "I think I can handle that."

She smiled. "Good. Because you've got me. No matter what."

After he'd left to finish up his holiday tasks and bring Mollie back later for dinner, Savanna walked on a cushion of air through the house, imagining their little family in every space. If they felt cramped and needed more, Harlan had made an expansion sound entirely doable. She finished wrapping presents, put together tomorrow morning's casserole and covered it with foil in the fridge, and popped the lasagna she'd prepared into the oven.

She freshened up with a quick shower, letting her long brown hair air dry into loose waves while she finished getting ready. In the back of her closet, she found a pretty chiffon skirt with subtle sparkles and paired it with delicate gold earrings and necklace and a softer than soft wrap sweater, tying the bow at the side of her waist. "What do you think, Fonz?"

Her little dog was sprawled out on the rug snoring. She slipped a festive red and green sweater over his head, barely finishing the job as the doorbell rang and he was off, sprinting down the steps. Shortly behind him, Savanna ushered in Aidan and Mollie from the snowy deck, big, fluffy snowflakes melting on the little girl's navy-blue peacoat with red wool trim and bows. When she took their coats, she immediately spotted the matching accessory Mollie had chosen for herself and her dad. Mollie's red velvet and organza dress was darling with red and white polka-dot tights and perfectly matched the red and white polka-dot socks Aidan revealed when he and Mollie swapped their winter boots for slippers at the door.

In planning the busy holiday month, she and Aidan had decided Christmas Eve would be just the three of them for dinner, presents, sweets, and warming up by the fireplace. After doing exactly that, stuffed and toasty and basking in the glow of Christmas Eve together, Savanna had to convince herself to venture out into the snowy cold for the second half of their evening. She could've stayed in this cozy cocoon with the two of them forever. But, as promised, they bundled up and arrived at her parents' house at eight p.m.

The Shepherd family had been Christmas caroling on Christmas Eve as long as she could remember. Greetings were exchanged all around, her parents, uncles, Cousin Ellie and her boyfriend from university, Syd and Finn, and Skylar's family all slowly gathering on the sidewalk out front.

Charlotte took the reins, handing out the lyrics to the songs she'd chosen this year. "So, a little information for any of us who are new to caroling. We sing one song at each house, unless they come to the door and ask us to continue. We don't typically ring doorbells or knock, as we don't want to be intrusive. And," she said, smiling at the children in the group, "please join in, even if you don't know the song or aren't sure what you're doing. Just have fun—if you want to add in your own few bars or verse, go for it. Last thing, most folks really get a kick out of carolers but once in a while, we'll meet a Grinch. If anyone is grumpy or rude to us, we try not to be offended. It's not personal... they might be having a sad or upsetting holiday. In those cases, we just move on, knowing we did our best to share a little cheer."

Harlan spoke. "We thought we'd start at the corner house where Bernard Strupp lives. Our pastor mentioned last weekend that he'd like some prayers and positive thoughts while he's recovering from surgery. He lives alone; he might enjoy a little Christmas spirit with our caroling."

"And a plate of Christmas dinner and some sweets; it's tough for him to get out of the house at the moment," Charlotte said, nodding at Uncle Max who carried two large covered containers. Charlotte passed out small caroling bells she'd collected through the years.

Nolan and Mollie whispered back and forth to each other excitedly, jingling their little bells. The little girl reached out and slipped her hand into Savanna's and made her heart grow three times its size with the simple gesture. She couldn't have kept the smile off her lips even if she'd wanted to. She glanced down and found Mollie watching her; Mollie looked away, shy. Savanna gave her hand a squeeze. "Did you see the song we're beginning with?"

Mollie shook her head. "N-no."

"'Rudolph the Red Nosed Reindeer.'"

The girl tugged on her hand. "Yay!"

Savanna bent and buttoned the top button of Mollie's warm wool dress coat, pulling her scarf up around her ears. "Better?"

Mollie nodded. Before Savanna could straighten again, the girl reached up and did the same to the red and white polka-dot winter scarf she'd gifted to Savanna, wrapping it higher around her neck and ears.

"Thank you. Ready?"

All in all, the Christmas caroling was never a lengthy endeavor. Their lakeside town was colder than those farther inland, and Charlotte had a rule that they couldn't carol after nine thirty p.m., when kids would be trying hard to fall asleep so Santa could come. Heading back, Aidan fell into step with her and pulled her close, warming her as they walked. Their group had spread out, Harlan and Charlotte in front talking with Uncle Max and Uncle Freddie, followed by Ellie with the two children. Skylar and Travis pushing Hannah's stroller behind the kids, and Sydney and Finn walked ahead of Savanna and Aidan.

"Look at them," Savanna said softly to Aidan. She tipped her head toward her younger sister, arm in arm with her new husband. They were laughing quietly, zigzagging back and forth together.

"They're perfect together," he agreed.

Savanna glanced up at Aidan. "I keep trying to take mental snapshots," she whispered. "Of the evening, of this, of all of us. Of Nolan and Mollie. Skylar and Trav and the baby. Next year, things will be different. I wish it could always be like this."

"It'll be different," he said, "but maybe even better, in ways we can't imagine yet."

Chapter Sixteen

CHRISTMAS MORNING AT Harlan and Charlotte Shepherd's house was an odd mix of giddy silliness and sentimental sadness. The group was small, with Skylar's family plus Sydney and Savanna for their traditional stocking and gift exchange, breakfast, and lazing around eating too much chocolate. Skylar had given up trying not to talk about their upcoming move; she was clearly excited, and it was catching. As much as Savanna was going to miss her sister, seeing her open gifts of palm-tree decorated coffee mugs and a big beachy tote bag got her thinking about the fun they'd have when her new little family flew to Florida to visit.

Aidan and Mollie were with the Becketts this morning. He'd offered to bring Mollie over to their place, an olive branch, the gesture meant to show them that their role in their granddaughter's life wouldn't evaporate simply due to Aidan getting married. He'd invited Savanna but she'd opted out. It was better if she let them have this, without her involvement. The last thing she wanted was to be viewed as the wicked stepmother or the woman trying to void the memory of Mollie's mom.

Savanna took advantage of Syd being on her own without Finn today and challenged her to an overly competitive, borderline ugly game of Monopoly. Like most healthcare workers, Finn worked rotating holidays and he'd drawn the dayshift spot for Christmas Day; he'd shared with them last night that it was one of the busiest times of the year for paramedics and E.R. staff.

By midafternoon, Charlotte had had enough of the lazing about and board game fights and wrapping paper everywhere and sent them out to Frosty Fest—*"Or anywhere that isn't here for the next two hours."* The festival was technically closed, as no one would be staffing it on Christmas, but the park was open to the public and so was the ice-skating rink.

The Shepherds were hosting Christmas dinner, as they always did, but for some reason, both Savanna's parents were just a tad on edge today. It wasn't about the food— everything was basically done or in the oven. Skylar took her kids home for a much-needed nap, saying she might catch one, too, and Savanna coaxed Sydney into going ice-skating with her.

They took the long way, through the impressive ice sculpture pathway that meandered along the sidewalk to the ice rink. She hadn't seen the whole thing yet in the daylight since Lars had finished the final piece. He'd let her know he'd be heading back home up north over the holiday, but he'd be back next week to do touch-ups. Even without the backdrop of the dark to highlight the colorful lighting, the ice show was breathtaking. Lars and his assistants had outdone themselves with a larger than life Santa Claus and Christmas tree toward the end.

They emerged from the ice sculpture path in front of The Gifting Tree. Savanna stopped, pulling Sydney back with her. "Look. They're all spoken for." She slowly circled the tree, looking for any full hangtags left that she might have missed, but every single one had been torn, the bottom removed, and a bright bow attached to the top half.

"They always are," Sydney said. "I don't know if it's a committee through the town or a local business or what, but someone makes sure that all the unclaimed tags are taken and fulfilled every year. Did you see all the people at the skating rink two days ago, claiming their gifts?"

"No, I was in Lansing all day. There must be at least a hundred or more tags on this tree. So, some secret Santa person is just fairy-godmothering all the wishes left for people? How would anyone have time to do that?"

"Well, to be fair, a lot of the tags get claimed by people in the giving spirit, like you with your Barbie Dreamhouse. But yeah, whatever is left somehow gets fulfilled on December 23rd."

Savanna peered at a few of the wishes. She laughed and held one out that read, *I wish for a pet alligator.* "And how are gifts like this handled?"

Syd smiled. "Last year, Willow's little daughter wished for a unicorn. Nobody had claimed the tag by the last day; I mean, who has a spare unicorn to give away? The gift the fairy-godmothering secret Santa dropped off on her porch was a big, plush unicorn with a picture book called *The Last Unicorn* or something."

"Ah," she said. "Nice idea."

"Savanna!" Yvonne was yelling to her from the skating rink. Her sister and brother-in-law skated past her. "Sydney! Come join us!"

Sydney had her skates on and out on the ice while Savanna was still carefully picking her way along the railing to Yvonne in skates that made her feel like she was in a cartoon, ready to slip and fall any moment with her feet flying over her head. Yvonne took pity on her and met her halfway with a hug.

"Merry Christmas! I'm so surprised," Yvonne said. "I always think you can do anything—but you don't know how to skate?"

Savanna shook her head. "I try... I like it, and I love being outside in this weather," she said, tipping her head back and trying to catch one of the big fluffy snowflakes in the air. "But my balance is terrible. I'm an embarrassment." She laughed. "You should go ahead without me."

Yvonne chuckled and offered her elbow. "You are not an embarrassment. I think I like you even more now that I know there's something I'm better than you at! Come on, take my arm. I'll take you around the rink."

She rolled her eyes. "Fine. It's the only way I'll get off the railing." She let Yvonne lead her, pulling her gently along. She was concentrating so hard on not falling, they were halfway around when she glanced over to find Lars Anders skating alongside them.

"Lars is always full of surprises," Yvonne said, noticing Savanna's own surprised reaction. The adoration in the way she gazed up at Lars was apparent. "I found him in the ice sculptures last night and made him come spend Christmas Eve with us."

"That's great!" Savanna studied Lars's response to Yvonne. He said nothing, but that struck her as his baseline. His eyes crinkled at the corners, but his lower face was hidden by the red beard. "I thought you went back up north for the holiday," she said, unable to stop herself. She had little to no reason not to trust the man, but tiny nagging doubt unsettled her when she thought about him being gone from Mitten Inn the night Rob was killed.

The sculptor shook his head. "No, I had some work to do on the ice."

"Oh. Well, thank you for your dedication! The sculptures are beautiful."

"He's so talented," Yvonne agreed. She slowed, telling Lars to go ahead without them. When he'd gone, she grinned at Savanna. "I really like him. He's quiet but he's very sweet. Maybe you can extend the ice show to keep him around?"

"Um…"

Her friend rolled her eyes and laughed. "I'm kidding. Sort of. I'm going to be so sad when he has to go home."

"I'm glad you two hit it off," Savanna said. "He seems great… but I don't know him very well. Maybe kind of take things slow? I don't want you to get hurt." Emotionally or physically, she thought.

"You worry too much. But thank you." She gave her a quick hug and Savanna reeled backwards, skates skittering and sliding until Yvonne steadied her. "Oops, sorry!"

"No worries. I've plenty of padding, I can handle a fall or two." Savanna smiled, patting her rear and eliciting another laugh from her friend. "So, are you going to your sister's place for Christmas dinner?"

Yvonne nodded, filling Savanna with relief. At least she wouldn't be left alone with Lars.

Sydney slid past them, skating backwards into a looping figure eight. "Hey Yvonne. Happy Christmas!" To Savanna, she said, "Mom wants us home, are you ready?"

She and Sydney were out of the park and on the way back before Savanna remembered that she'd wanted to take a peek at Mollie's wish. She had to have received whatever it was by now, but she was still curious. She'd check next time she was in the park.

Pulling up in their parents' driveway, she found it oddly empty except for her mom's car. "No one's even here yet," Syd said. "I'm going to pick up Finn so we won't have two cars here. He's home from work. Tell Mom I'll be back soon with my granola and yogurt dessert bars."

Savanna wrinkled her nose. "I don't think you should be calling those dessert. No offense. Bring them anyway, Dad said he forgot to buy squirrel food."

"Snot." Sydney shooed her away from the car. "Better get inside. She asked specifically for you. She knows all; what'd you do now?"

"Hush, drama queen," Savanna said. "She probably has an extra gift for me." She blew her little sister an insincere kiss as she backed out of the driveway.

In the kitchen, Charlotte handed her the red and gold

Christmas tablecloth. "I thought you might not mind helping me get ready. And I need to tell you something."

"Okay."

"Sit," Charlotte said at the round kitchen table by the window, nodding to the adjacent chair.

She sat. "What's wrong?"

Her mom put her hands out, holding Savanna's. "I invited Mollie's grandparents to Christmas dinner."

"What—why??" She pulled her hands away. "Why would you do that? Without even asking if I was okay with it? What about Aidan—did you talk to him about this? You know they're suing him. What the hell, Mom?"

Charlotte's eyebrows went up and she sat back, folding her hands in her lap. "I did talk to Aidan. He wasn't sure it was a good idea, but he said it was up to me. I asked him to let me tell you. And—"

"Ugh." Savanna covered her eyes with her hand. "Of course, he did. He's too nice. I can't believe you did this." She stood up, glaring at her mom.

"Savanna," Charlotte said, her voice quieter now, "sit down. Please. Let me talk." This seldom seen side of her mother left no room for argument. When her voice grew quiet and calm, her posture confident and still, was when she flexed her muscles as the ruling force in their little family. Savanna suspected it was also effective in her career as an in-demand consultant for businesses working to trim the fat and improve their bottom line.

"No. I'm not sitting down—I might not be staying. Talk." She crossed her arms over her chest and flinched inwardly as she heard her harsh tone echo back at her in her head.

"The Becketts have no family in Michigan besides Mollie. Jean Beckett's siblings are in the south and Tom has none. Their son lives in Utah or somewhere out west. They're here for Mollie, four years after their daughter died."

"That's their choice."

Charlotte remained still, but she scowled at Savanna. "Really, that's your response? I thought I raised an empathetic daughter."

"Mom."

"Savanna."

"Ugh! Fine." She dropped in the chair. "How do you think this is going to work? You invite them for Christmas dinner, and they show up and decide to drop the suit? I bet Aidan's lawyer would think this is a really bad idea."

Charlotte lifted one shoulder, a careless shrug. "Jillian Black can think whatever she wants. I talked to Jean and she was grateful to be included. Would you set aside your righteousness and anger for a moment and think about it from their point of view? Before Olivia died, they were an integral part of Mollie's life, especially on holidays. After she died but before Aidan met you, that didn't really change. The time they get with their granddaughter now has diminished, and it's no one's fault. It's life. They have every reason to think it's going to continue dwindling. So, they didn't handle that fear in the best way. We'll all be family six days from now. Tell me, Savanna, what harm can come from including both sets of Mollie's grandparents for Christmas dinner? Explain it to me."

She bit her lower lip. Her mother held a blackbelt in the art of persuasion… but she was right. "When you put it like that, I guess no harm can come of it," she admitted.

"Thank you." Charlotte stood, inclining her head toward the stack of good dishes on the counter. "Grab those and help me set the table. And, in case it hasn't yet occurred to you, people tend to be quite pliable with full bellies and a sip of good wine. You'd mentioned being frustrated you weren't able to speak with the Becketts." She left the room without another word.

Savanna stood, heavy stack of fine china in her hands, staring after her mom. If she ever decided to get out of teaching and fine art and try her hand at mind manipulation, she knew where to find a top tier tutor. She couldn't even fault anything she'd said. Now it was on her to come up with the right words to let the Becketts know she valued their role in Mollie's life and would never do anything to interfere with that relationship.

In the end, she told them exactly that. After far too much delicious food and more gifts exchanged, followed by a table filled with pies, cakes, and Syd's disgusting granola concoction, Savanna took advantage of a quiet moment in the dining room after most of the family had retired to the living room for a game of charades. She reached around Aidan at the kitchen sink, scrubbing a pan, and turned off the faucet. "Come here please," she said, pulling on his shirt. He grabbed a dish towel, drying his hands, and followed her to the far end of the dining room where Tom and Jean Beckett were chatting with Uncle Freddie about organic farming.

"Well," Uncle Freddie said, standing, "I'm going to get myself in trouble if I don't bring that second piece of pie to my husband. I do want those red cabbage seeds, though, we like to start them in the house first—I'll call you."

Savanna watched him go, catching in her peripheral vision the Becketts starting to stand. Her nerves threatened to take over, but this might be her only chance. "Wait," she said, meeting Jean Beckett's gaze. "Could we—is it okay if we chat for a moment? May I join you?"

The older woman nodded, sitting back down. "Of course." Her eyes flitted to Aidan and then to her husband next to her.

Savanna's heart beat in her ears. "I want you to know I'd never do anything to come between you and Mollie," she said. "I know how hard... no, I mean, I imagine the last few years have been incredibly difficult. I am so, so sorry about your daughter. I know I can't fathom that kind of pain. I know she should be here with you and Mollie and Aidan." Her cheeks burned. The words hurt to say, but it had to be how the Becketts felt. How could she expect them to listen to a word from her if she didn't acknowledge how they'd all gotten here?

Jean's hand pressed against her throat and Savanna could see her fighting tears. "She—" Jean cleared her throat and started again. "She was such a bright light. A wonderful daughter and mother."

"She was," Aidan said. His hand closed over Savanna's tightly balled fist clutching the arm of her chair. "She was a wonderful wife. Mollie has that brilliance, that same ability to light up any room she's in. She got that from Olivia."

"She really did," Jean agreed.

"I believed I'd never find someone as special to spend the rest of my life with," Aidan said. "I wasn't looking; I didn't plan to get married again. But then I met Savanna. She brought hope and laughter and love back into my life—and Mollie's."

Savanna spoke. "Mollie is the way she is because of all of you, because she's known only love from her parents and grandparents. I see that. She needs you, all three of you. I promise you, Jean, Tom, I will never, ever get in the way of your time or relationship with her. I'm not her mom," she said softly. "I know that. I'd never try to be a replacement. Mollie doesn't need me; she has plenty of love in her life. But maybe I can add a little more. That's all I hope to do."

Jean Beckett leaned forward, resting her clasped hands on the table. "I believe you, Savanna. We know you're a good person, none of this was ever about us questioning that."

Her husband spoke for the first time. "Things change. You see it in the news and on television shows, a man remarries and things start to change, priorities shift, people switch jobs, move away, and one day we'll realize we hardly get to see our granddaughter anymore because Aidan's new family has moved on without us."

"Tom." Aidan shook his head, sighing. "I think you know me better than that after all these years. Why do you think I'm still here? Why haven't I moved back to New York or at least to an actual city to expand my practice? Until my brother showed up, I had no family here but Mollie."

"And us," Jean said. She met her husband's eyes, something wordless passing between them, before she looked at Aidan. "We've been your family for over ten years. I like to think we still are."

"You are. But if you feel that way, if you think of me as part of your family," Aidan said, "then you have to know I'm in it for the duration. I can't leave Carson. I cannot, would not, take Mollie away from you. She already lost Liv. You know when that happened that I committed to raising Mollie here. Tom. You know that."

The older man met Aidan's eyes. "I know," he said. "Except there are no guarantees. Life changes. If we have a legal agreement covering our rights as grandparents, then no matter what happens, we won't lose Oliv—Mollie."

The room fell silent. Tom Beckett pressed a weathered thumb and forefinger roughly against his eyelids. Savanna ached for them, for the heartbreak and grief afflicting them like an open wound.

Abruptly, Tom shoved his chair back and stood. "I've gotta go—"

"No." Jean gripped his forearm, gently pulling him back. "Sit. Please, honey. Just… stay with me here. We have to work through this. Please."

He sat, scowling at the table.

Aidan began to speak just as Savanna did. He hesitated, nodding at her, his own brow furrowed nearly as deeply as Tom's. He looked lost.

"Maybe a legal agreement is a good idea," Savanna said. She took a deep breath. "Not a change of custody, but what would it hurt to have something in writing saying that Aidan agrees to have Mollie spend a certain amount of days and overnights and summer vacation time with her grandparents? You could make it flexible enough to accommodate little changes like trips or sports camp or whatever might lie ahead."

"I like the sound of that," Jean said.

"It's not a bad idea," Aidan said, staring at Savanna. His gaze moved to Tom.

The older man's shoulders slumped. "The lawyers could draw something up, I suppose. You think it's good enough?" he asked his wife beside him.

Jean nodded. "I think so. I do think you're wrong about something you said, Savanna. Mollie does need you. She's attached to you; she talks about you all the time. Aidan is truly..." She broke off, reaching across the table and gripping Aidan's outstretched hand. "You are a great father. I'm sorry Aidan, we were never trying to hurt you. We're so thankful Mollie has you. But she'll be blessed to have you as her stepmom, Savanna. She does need you," Jean reiterated.

"Thank you." Savanna felt as if the weight of the world had been lifted from her shoulders; she sensed Aidan's relief as well. He told Tom and Jean he'd change his meeting with Jillian tomorrow morning to include the Becketts and their attorney, to talk everything through and start the paperwork.

WITH THE CHRISTMAS party winding down, Savanna saw them out while Aidan was occupied coloring with Mollie. Jean put a hand on her arm at the front door. "I really appreciate you and your family including us today. You have no idea what it meant to us, seeing Mollie so happy and comfortable here. We'll have you and your parents over soon."

Savanna impulsively hugged the woman. "Thank you. For everything."

Jean hugged her back. "Will you come to tomorrow's meeting? You should be part of the discussion."

Savanna warmed to her even more. The invitation was a good sign. "Thank you. I'll be there."

The rest of the evening zipped by much too quickly. Sydney taught them a card game called Spoons, a playing card version of musical chairs that became more cutthroat the longer they played. When Uncle Max surprised them by accumulating the most points quickest and winning, he requested six dice and reacquainted the family with the game Farkle, winning again. A little past eleven, Skylar and Travis gathered their sleepy kids and said their farewells. Savanna realized they'd all been hanging out, delaying the inevitable—wrapping up the family's last Christmas together while they still all lived within a few miles of each other.

Aidan carried Mollie outside to the car, as the little girl was asleep on her feet. He deposited her in her booster seat and Savanna leaned into the dimly lit car, fumbling with getting the seat belt buckled. She felt the click, but before she could move away, Mollie reached up and hugged her, both their puffy winter coats rustling. Savanna's breath caught in her throat and she hugged her back. Savanna kissed her forehead. "Merry Christmas, honey. Love you," she whispered, not wanting to break the spell.

"Love you more," Mollie murmured. She'd already fallen back to sleep by the time Savanna got in the front seat with Aidan.

He pulled a small card from his pocket, his eyes shining with unshed tears. "Her mom used to say that to her. I didn't know she remembered." He handed her the card without any explanation.

In her hand was the lower half of Mollie's hangtag from The Gifting Tree—written in purple ink in the eight-year-old's careful handwriting were the words, *I wish for a mama.*

Savanna pressed it to her chest, unable to speak. Good God. She rolled her head on the headrest to look at Aidan. She smiled, the abundant sweetness of the moment pinching at the back of her throat in the best way, flooding her with exhilaration and love and a precarious vulnerability all at once.

He drew her to him, holding her, chin resting lightly atop her head. After a while, he asked, "You okay?"

She nodded, letting go of him and getting buckled. "Yeah. I think I get it. Even though…." She glimpsed Mollie behind her, head tipped back and mouth open, deep in sleep. She lowered her voice. "Even though she isn't actually mine. It feels like wearing your heart on the outside of your body," she said, picking up a conversation they'd had two months ago as if they'd just discussed it—when Aidan had tried to put into words for her the often intense experience of being a parent.

"You get it. And she is yours."

Behind them, the caravan that was Skylar's car, the uncles with Ellie, and Finn's truck backed out of the driveway. Aidan followed suit. They didn't talk on the drive back to her house, so he could drop her off. The quiet in the car was light and comfortable, in the same way time spent with her dad could be. He turned left onto Main Street and was about to turn right toward her house when she stopped him.

"Wait. Do you see that?" She was turned almost all the way around, looking out the rear window. The faint, rhythmic flash of red and blue lights reflected off the storefront windows at the end of Main Street.

"See what?" He slowed to a stop; the snowy road deserted at the late hour. He adjusted his mirror, peering in it, and then turned around to look. "It's just Christmas lights. Probably from one of the houses on Shoreline Drive."

"I don't think so. Can you go back? To double check?"

He nodded, making a U-turn. "Caroline's house is down there. Let's make sure…"

Dread washed over her when Aidan reached the intersection and turned on Shoreline Drive. Just around the bend, three police cruisers and an ambulance in front of the Carson Mansion lit up the night with their flashing red and blue lights.

Chapter Seventeen

"OH NO." SAVANNA gripped the dashboard, peering through the windshield. It had stopped snowing, but with the position of the first responder vehicles, she could see nothing. "We have to—" She stopped abruptly, reality snapping her back to the fact that a child was in the back seat sound asleep.

Aidan tore his gaze from the scene to meet Savanna's. His own expression reflected the worry she felt. "I can't." He made another U-turn, leaving Caroline's house in the rearview mirror as he headed back toward Main Street.

"I know," she said. "It's okay." Her mind raced. Was she... what if something had happened to her? Was this even related to the Minkov, or something much worse? Her phone in hand, she tapped Detective Jordan's name, about to text him, but she hesitated. She shook her head, trying to shake off the unwanted thoughts of how he might be involved. Why, every single time she shared some bit of information with him, did something terrible happen right after?

Aidan's car rolled to a stop at Sydney and Finn's house, behind Fancy Tails and Treats. "If something happened to Caroline I need to be there," he said. "Let's go see if they can watch Mollie."

Finn was already on his way out of the house in pajama pants, pulling a tee shirt over his head. Syd was close behind. They met in the driveway. "I was about to call you," he told Aidan. "I just turned my scanner on. Dispatch sent EMS to assist the sheriff's department at Caroline Carson's. I'm waiting for my buddy Ace to update me on why; he's on tonight."

In moments, she and Aidan were back in his SUV while Finn carried a still sleeping Mollie up the steps to the porch. Syd held the door open for him, telling him to settle her on the couch, and then sprinted back over to Savanna. She leaned in the car window. "Be careful. You have no clue what's happening over there. We'll sleep in the living room with Mollie, so she won't wake up confused. Just come get her in the morning, okay?" She gave Savanna a quick hug.

"Thank you," she and Aidan said in unison.

"Wait. Here," he said, grabbing Mollie's stuffed bunny from the back seat and passing it to Sydney. "If Finn hears anything else have him text me."

They were back around the corner at Caroline's in two minutes flat. Savanna's heart sank like a stone in the pit of her stomach. In the short time they'd been gone, the ambulance had left. She dimly remembered Finn once saying something about a lights-only trip in their small town meaning low urgency. Syd's house was close enough that they should have heard sirens as the ambulance headed back to the hospital. So, was it low urgency because it was empty? Or no one was hurt? Or because... someone was hurt beyond hope?

Detective Jordan met them at the door. "Uh—Savanna? Dr. Gallager." He frowned, clearly trying to make sense of their presence. "Did one of the family call you?"

"We saw the lights," Savanna said. "What happened? Is Caroline okay?"

He looked from her to Aidan and back. "All right. Step inside. It's freezing out. We might actually need your services," he told Savanna. He pulled blue shoe covers from his coat pocket. "Put these on. Follow me and don't touch anything."

"Hey, is she okay? Was the ambulance for her?"

"Sorry—I should've said. She's not here. We asked for the ambulance before we knew that. She's at her grand-daughter's house for the holiday."

"Oh, thank God," she breathed. She put the shoe covers on.

Jordan led them through to the library, where a pair of evidence techs and a deputy were huddled in a circle with Detective Taylor looking up at the empty space where the Carsons' cherished Sergei Minkov painting used to reside. The deputy was young, probably very new, and looked as if he was about to cry. "I swear, I didn't see or hear anything," he said to Detective Taylor. "I've been stationed out front since seven p.m."

Below the void left by the Minkov, at eye level, the familiar, bloodred devil's face was spray-painted on the wall. As cautious as she thought they'd been and had planned to be, she really hadn't expected the thieves to come after the

Minkov.

"You've seen what was here? The missing painting?" Detective Taylor asked her.

"Of course." She pulled up the famous piece on her phone, turning the screen toward them.

"Nine point two million?" Aidan asked, staring at the painting's description on the fine art website. "She had a nine million-dollar painting here, at her house?"

"It was my grandfather's favorite," Jack Carson said from the doorway. "We wanted her to sell it or loan it out someplace, but she couldn't part with it. It's her painting in her house. She should have been able to keep anything of any value she wants to here."

"Yes," Aidan said. "For sure. I'm just surprised a painting would be worth that much. I clearly don't know anything about art, sorry Jack."

He nodded, joining the small group in the room. "She's heartbroken. Lauren broke it to her. But she's thankful she wasn't here." Caroline's poodle must have heard Jack's voice. Duke emerged from under the couch, circling Jack's legs, whining. He picked him up, looking around. "Where's Princess? Has anyone seen her?"

"I'm pretty sure I saw her. She's here somewhere," Detective Taylor said. "Probably just scared."

Jack circled the room, calling her. "They're never apart. If she was here, we'd see her."

The stone was back in Savanna's stomach. The temperature on Aidan's dash tonight had read 28 degrees Fahrenheit.

Jack said the obvious. "I need help finding her. I can't

tell Grandmother Princess is gone." He left the room, calling out for her, and Savanna and Aidan followed.

Detective Jordan hurried after them. "We have to preserve evidence," he said. "I'll—"

Savanna looked back at him. "Can you just help? Please? Be more human, Nick."

He stared at her. "Sorry. I'll go check outside."

She couldn't bear the idea of the tiny poodle shivering in the cold. But the break-in must've been terrifying for the dogs. What if Princess had gotten scared and ran, instead of hiding like Duke? She and Aidan left Jack and the deputy now on their way upstairs and followed Jordan outside. He headed around the porch toward the back on the lake side.

"Check the front and maybe the neighbors' yards," he ordered.

George Taylor came out, flashlight in hand sweeping over white snow in all directions. Princess with her fluffy white fur would be virtually invisible in this weather unless she heard them and was able to bark.

Using their phone flashlights, and aided by the half-moon overhead reflecting against the blanket of snow, she and Aidan followed the lattice board deck siding around the house, stooping over and calling out, "Princess..." She made the kissy noises Caroline did when she wanted the dogs to come to her. Aidan left her, running toward the SUV, and for a moment she thought he'd found the dog. He returned with a crinkly bag of dog treats from Fancy Tails, rustling and shaking it.

Nearing the back of the house, she straightened up, shining her light out toward the beach and the Carson cabana. The cell phone's flashlight was too weak. She carefully walked through the snow, making sure she was stepping into fresh, untouched waves of white and not what appeared to be a zigzagging path of footprints. She stopped and Aidan bumped into her. "Look." Now she was close enough. The flashlight illuminated the clear shape of a footprint, two sections of tread—what looked to be the heel and toe of a boot sole.

"I see it. We should try to mark it somehow." He used his phone to take a couple pictures.

"There are more. See? Those are already covering over with blowing snow, but I see another one up there. Princess," she called again. Aidan rustled the treat bag. When they were only a few feet from the cabana, she heard a high-pitched bark. She grabbed Aidan's arm and ran around to the front.

The cabana was roughly the size of a three-car garage. In warm weather, the thin front panels were kept wide open, sheer netting keeping out bugs. At the base of one side was an inset doggie door with a flap. "Smart puppers," she said. "Hang on, Princess."

"One sec," Aidan said, sprinting away from her again toward one of the many patches of big, now leafless, scrubby bushes sprouting from the dunes. He kicked the snow around and grabbed a stick to use as a pry bar, forcing one of the doors open enough for them to get inside. Cushy chaise lounges, a table and chairs, mini fridge, TV screen, and tall cabinets filled with necessities—sunscreen, life jackets, plenty of beach towels—were all stored away now for winter. From atop the skeleton of a stacked lounge chair, Princess yipped at them.

"Oh my gosh, poor baby! Come here," Savanna said, expecting the energetic little dog to hop down and run over to her, but she didn't; she stayed where she was, shivering. Savanna scooped the poodle up, hugging her tightly. Princess's small frame shook violently, and she shoved her face into the neck of her winter parka.

"Hold on," Aidan said. He unbuttoned the first three buttons of his thick wool coat and tucked the poodle inside, pulling the lapels together. Savanna buttoned Princess up in the coat.

"Is she freezing you?" she asked, pressing one hand on the wool. The dog's shaking seemed to be slowing.

"It's okay," he said. "I can take it. I'm not sure about her, let's get her inside."

Savanna took the stick used as a pry bar with them as they trekked back to the house. She shone the flashlight on each footprint along the way until they disappeared beneath the swirling snow, choosing the one she thought was most clear. She jabbed the stick into the foot or so of snow to mark the spot, but all of this would be covered over soon if she didn't get one of the detectives out here quick to take a look.

"We found her!" Inside the Carson Mansion foyer, Aidan carefully unbuttoned his coat. The poodle had stopped shaking but didn't move—until she spotted Jack with Duke under one arm. She lunged toward Jack. He caught her easily, hugging both dogs.

"Thank you so much. You're lifesavers," he said. "Where was she?"

"She's tough. She made it all the way to the cabana. I need one of you," Savanna said to both detectives who'd just come in. "And an evidence tech."

With some effort, she and Aidan were able to locate the stick they'd left. Most of the footprint was still visible in the damp, dense snow. The evidence technician exclaimed excitedly upon seeing it. She stuck her bottle of water in the snow and opened her plastic case. She set up a short tripod with a light on top and snapped several photos from a variety of angles. "It's so rare to find a full print in snow. This is amazing." She rummaged around in her kit and sprayed something onto the footprint.

"What is that for?" Savanna asked.

"We spray a layer of Snow Print Wax to make the footprint set, so the snow won't melt from the casting material. We give it a few minutes to set." After a bit, the tech used a graduated plastic beaker to measure out cold water from her water bottle in the snow, took a plastic pouch of powder from her kit, and tore the top off with her teeth, both hands full. She poured the water into the pouch and mixed the concoction well, glancing up at Savanna. "It's dental stone, used for casting impressions."

"Fascinating," she murmured. "It's the same stuff my dentist used to make a crown for my molar?"

"Yep, pretty much. Now to wait for it to set."

"Thanks for the explanation. Very cool. So crazy that

little dog made it out to the cabana in the cold."

"She must've been spooked," Aidan said. "And one of the thieves chased after her."

"Weird. That's weird though, isn't it?" Savanna asked. "You'd think they'd have just let her go."

"We don't know that this is a footprint from the thief," Detective Jordan said. "Where are the dogs footprints?"

"The dog's feet are practically toothpick-sized, you'd never see them in all this snow," Savanna said. An exaggeration, yes, but Nick Jordan was being extra irritating tonight. Was it because he was involved? She couldn't imagine a much easier robbery than stealing from a citizen under protective surveillance, especially with Caroline's house empty over the holiday weekend. The rotating officers were privy to the keypad code; they had to be, in case of an emergency inside. The idea of Jordan doing anything like this turned her stomach.

"We're also close to the public beach during Frosty Fest. The footprints could be anyone's, and the dog just took the path of least resistance, where the snow had already been tamped down by someone," Jordan pointed out.

"Someone who was on the edge of Caroline's property?" Savanna asked.

"Anyone. Teenagers sneaking out to drink or party. We'll need a better look at the area in daylight."

It was the first thing he'd said out here that made sense. She and Aidan left them to do their thing; she was freezing from running around in the snow. Back in the warm house, she stood back, studying the graffiti on the library wall while the other evidence tech took photos and searched for finger-print oils and any other clues throughout the room. She opened her social media app and found the post from last week with the graffiti tag on the dummy account. The image had gone viral. Aidan looked over her shoulder at it.

"Over four hundred thousand likes?" he asked, pointing. "Why did the FBI leave this up?"

"Rob mentioned that they hadn't had luck finding the account or getting it taken down. But by now, maybe they've left it up on purpose for some reason, to watch the engage-ment activity, who knows." She held it at arm's length while facing the graffiti on the wall. "The thieves left this image on a wall at each museum and also on paintings they defaced with it..." She was about to add that at least some of the vandalized paintings were fakes but stopped herself.

She hated this feeling of not knowing who to trust. She considered Nick Jordan a friend and a good detective, but did that mean he was impervious to corruption? He'd mentioned working security at the museum for extra income, but how much extra money did he need? And for what? She tried to push her doubt from her mind, but that was a mistake. Hadn't she learned by now that people could be more than one thing? More than they appeared? Jordan could be a friend and a good detective and also in so much financial trouble that he might compromise his integrity. Not wanting to believe it didn't make it impossible.

"The FBI Art Crimes Team is viewing the graffiti as a calling card," Detective Taylor said. "I don't know if they've figured out why some paintings were tagged, but this image is left at every Impressionist robbery site, including the Detroit Institute of Art break-in two nights ago."

"And now they've got the Minkov. Poor Caroline."

Aidan spoke. "She must've had insurance for it, right? Even if it's not found, it won't be a total loss for her."

Savanna nodded. "I'm sure she does. But it's not about the money for her." She tipped her head, frowning at the crude, horned devil's face. It appeared to be just like the others, but again and again, staring at it, her gaze was drawn back to the Xs that were its eyes. She changed her angle, moving closer but at a diagonal, hoping to catch whatever it was that seemed off.

"I've got something," Detective Taylor shouted from the opposite side of the large library. He waved them over. "Check this out."

At the set of windows on the only outside wall, Taylor used a gloved hand to slide the window up a little farther. He poked the bottom edge of the screen and it flapped outward; it'd been sliced from side to side along the track and up one side, the undone corner plenty big enough for a person to climb through. "We know the thieves left through the kitchen door; it was standing open when we arrived. But the kitchen dead bolt and keypad are intact. We weren't sure how they broke in. This explains it—the security screen is cut."

"Wouldn't that have set off her alarm?" Savanna asked.

"Not if the entire circuit was shut off." Jack spoke from the doorway. "I just checked and her fuse box—or breaker panel, since she had it updated—must've been tampered with. The circuit breaker for this quadrant of the security system is off. The system default doesn't trigger an emergency response alert unless half the panel goes down at once… it's a failsafe so the system can be serviced."

"Show me," Detective Taylor said, taking the tech with him and following Jack out toward the basement stairs.

Stomping boots sounded from the foyer, the sheriff's department team coming in from the snow. A dry set of blue shoe covers back on, Detective Jordan crossed to look at the screen and directed the other tech to catalog it. He stood in the center of the library, staring up at the void left by the Minkov. "So, what do you think?"

Savanna glanced at him. "About the graffiti?"

"Yes. Or about the scene. You always have a sharp eye… anything seem off?"

Under any other circumstances, during any of Jordan's other cases she'd been involved in, it would have been a completely normal question. Expected, even. Now she felt as if he was testing her. The graffiti was "off." He'd used the word, but she'd thought it first. Something about it was inconsistent.

"Nope. Not really. We should probably get back to Mollie," she said to Aidan. On their way through the foyer, she stopped to pet Princess and Duke. "I'm so glad you guys are okay. Caroline would be a mess if anything happened to you." The poodle turned in a circle to lie back down and Savanna caught a glimpse of bright red. She gasped, picking up the little dog carefully but now not seeing it.

"What's wrong?" Jordan asked.

"Is she hurt? I saw blood…" She turned the poodle over on her back like a baby. On the underside of her chest, embedded in the fluffy white fur, were two bright red stripes. They were tacky to the touch. Savanna sniffed the marks. "It's paint."

Chapter Eighteen

MONDAY MORNING FOUND Savanna back at Caroline's house bright and early, waiting in her warm car for Jack. He'd taken the poodles home with him last night after the evidence tech took photos of the paint on Princess. To her, the two red marks looked finger shaped. She hadn't seen any red paint on anyone at the crime scene, and she'd made sure to get a look at Detective Jordan's hands, but whoever left the graffiti tag had probably worn gloves.

Jack pulled into the driveway beside her. The emergency vehicles had all cleared out, and yellow crime scene tape decorated the front door.

Jack plucked at it, then unlocked the front door. He took the heavy case she carried, setting it inside the door, and then held the plastic strips out of the way for Savanna to enter. "Are we allowed to be here?" he asked.

"You're family. She can't come home until the investigation is finished, and she asked you to fetch some things she needs. Right?"

Jack smirked. "Yes, she did. I'll get right on that."

"Hey, is Princess okay? I can't stop thinking about the poodles, about Princess, since last night."

"She seems to be. She's extra clingy right now. Grandmother is beating herself up for leaving them home for Christmas, but they're getting older, and she was worried about having them around so many people at Lauren's house."

"I wondered why they were home without her."

"She was supposed to come home last night after dinner, but the grandkids convinced her to stay over. She sent me to get Princess and Duke—I was already on my way there when I got the alert that the back-door lock had been opened."

"Caroline shouldn't feel bad... she was trying to keep the dogs safe. She couldn't have known what would happen. Every time I think about finding Princess freezing and scared in the cabana, it makes me furious. And that paint on her fur... she and Duke must have been barking at whoever broke in and they grabbed her, and she got away. What kind of monster goes after a tiny little dog? What were they going to do if they caught her?" She winced, frowning.

"Oh, believe me, I'm right there with you. I'd like to get my hands on whoever almost killed Grandmother's dog. She loves Princess and Duke like her own children." He took off his snowy boots. "So, what's up? Why are we here?"

"I need another look at the graffiti tag. I thought I saw something about it last night, but I... didn't want to say anything unless I was sure."

"What do you think you saw?" He led her through to the library, where she took a few photos of the spray-painted devil's face, moving from side to side for different angles.

"The sheen on this paint seems different than the others. The arc of the face isn't quite the same either, it's a little shaky, the paint too thick, like it was done by an amateur. And the eyes…" She stared at the image, about twenty feet away from her. The Xs were not the same as in the other images. She stared long enough to allow her eyes to blur, the edges of the red bleeding outward. "That's it!" She rushed over to the painting, scrutinizing the blank wall between the devil's left eye and the outline of its face, but the wall wasn't blank.

Jack moved closer, squinting and trying to see what she saw.

Savanna opened the case that held her mobile art authentication tools. She plugged her handheld Firefly microscope into her laptop and scanned the faint hint of paint overspray she'd spotted beside the X depicting the eye. She tapped a few keys and began another scan, this time of the upper quarter of the devil's face. Unplugging the Firefly, she set up her newest piece of equipment, the MVP of her case so far. She'd gotten it at auction this summer for a fraction of its $15,000 price tag when she and Britt had attended an art specialists conference.

"What is that?" Jack asked. He picked up her laptop from the floor and set it on a folding table for her, pushing a chair over from the reading area.

"This little rockstar is called a 4300 Handheld FTIR spectrometer, which stands for Fourier Transform Infra-Red, from Agilent Technologies." She held it up proudly. "I haven't had a chance to use it yet outside the lab. It's a spectroscopy system that analyzes chemical composition and molecular structure of materials without breaking them down."

Jack blinked at her. "All right, in English now please?"

"It's a way to sort of dissect exactly what something is made of, all the different compounds, without damaging the subject. So, without it, I'd want to scrape a decent sized chip of the spray paint off the wall and take it to a lab for analysis of the molecular makeup… but as you can imagine, in fine art, that's a difficult proposition when you're trying to keep a piece intact. Or if you're not near a lab and need to know what something is made of."

"Okay, I think I'm getting it. But spray paint is spray paint, right? What are you trying to find out?"

"Spray paint isn't all the same. The spray paint used in all the museum robberies has been a very specific type, BBG brand in the shade Violent Red. So, this paint should match, if your grandmother's painting was really stolen by the same art thief ring. But I don't think it was. Look." She turned her laptop and moved the mouse over the scans taken by the Firefly. "The overspray here is going in the wrong direction. The Xs for eyes were painted first, and then the outline of the face was added around the eyes. In the museum tags, the circle of the face and horns were painted and then the Xs added last. You can tell by the overspray and also by looking at the angle of the arc," she said, motioning in a wide semicircle in front of her as if she was holding a paint can.

He frowned at her. "But… I know I don't know much about art, but it's a creative process, right? Even graffiti? So why wouldn't there be variances in the way an artist paints from one day to the next?"

She was quiet, trying to think of a good analogy. "Well,

first, think about the masters. The famous artists everyone knows. Van Gogh. Rembrandt. Picasso. They each obviously had their own style, but more than that, they have specific techniques that are recognizable across their body of work. Brushstroke patterns can reveal a lot about the work, sometimes even more so than types of paints and pigments used. Those habits and techniques apply to spray-painted artwork as well. An artist will vary their subject, their use of color and shading, but we all have ingrained, muscle memory ways of doing things. Like… putting on your left shoe first every time."

He laughed. "That's not a thing."

"It is. You put on your left shoe or boot first. Try it the other way. It won't feel natural. We all have our own versions of individual brushstrokes. I've noticed mine when I paint, but I bet Aidan has a specific manner of holding a scalpel when he's operating. You probably always start with the same corner of paper when you make your origami animals." Jack's librarian desk at school bore a continually rotating parade of small origami animals students could earn with completed assignments.

Jack moved to the foyer, bent down and picked up his right boot. He stood on one foot to put it on and nearly fell over laughing. "Yeah, that feels weird."

Savanna went to work with the FITR spectrometer, examining the dried red paint at a few different spots. She reviewed the analysis and downloaded it to her laptop, then searched through her work email inbox for the spray paint reports from Director Flynn last week. When she had the reports set up side by side for comparison, she was rewarded with the thrill of discovering a crucial detail she'd hoped to find. She showed Jack.

"This is the OSHA report from the spray paint we analyzed in the lab last week—we used a different method than the FITR, with the goal of needing to remove the graffiti from the artwork. And this is the environmental health and safety engineer's analysis of the molecular structure, identifying the paint brand and color. And this one is today's report of your grandmother's graffiti. It's a different brand of paint from all the other robberies."

"Are you thinking this break-in wasn't done by the same thief or thieves?"

"Yes," she said. "It seems like someone wanted it to look related, but I don't think it is. I have to talk to Agent Klein." She picked up her phone and saw the time. "Oh jeez. I've got to run. Give Caroline a hug for me!"

She packed up and hustled out the door, parking out in front of Skylar's law firm two minutes before the meeting with attorneys, Aidan, and the Becketts was set to start. Jean Beckett inviting her was a huge gesture of goodwill and she wasn't about to screw it up. She checked her lipstick and headed inside.

The meeting took less than an hour. It wasn't an official mediation, but with Aidan and the Becketts being on the same page about time spent with Mollie, Jillian Black had a simple agreement drafted that all parties signed. The contract was focused on minimum time frames that Tom and Jean Beckett would have Mollie, similar to what had been suggested in the first place, with the stipulation that they could always request more. She and Aidan promised to allow Mollie as much time as possible with her grandparents. They no longer had to worry about the Becketts.

Outside, after Aidan had gone back to work, Savanna checked her phone to see if Agent Klein had returned her call yet. Savanna had left her a voicemail on the way here, saying she'd found something new and wanted to share. The only call she'd missed was from Britt.

She could easily walk right over to the sheriff's department office and update the detectives on her findings about Caroline's graffiti. Skylar's law office sat in front of Carson's government offices, each connected with a sidewalk and tied together with a small courtyard in the middle. She could head in to see the detectives, or she could wait for Agent Klein to call her back. She decided to wait.

She instead took the sidewalk that led to the Parks and Recreation offices and poked her head in to say hello to Yvonne. "Hey there bestie! Feel like a coffee break?"

"Perfect timing," Yvonne said. She grabbed her coat. "I'm not actually working today; the village offices are still closed until tomorrow. I was just trying to catch up."

"You're so dedicated. They're lucky to have you," Savanna said. They headed across the street to Holy Grounds. "Hey, do you know if Lars is still in town? I have his final payment for the ice sculpture show."

Yvonne blushed, her cheeks flooding with color. She gave Savanna a sideways glance. "He's in town."

"Hmm. Interesting," Savanna said. She leaned closer to

her friend. "Is this getting serious?"

Yvonne grinned. "Maybe."

"I'm happy for you!" She held the coffee shop door open for her. "Do you want to come by Mitten Inn with me, so I can drop of his check?" They got in line, Savanna giving Griffin Alexander behind the counter a little wave.

Yvonne pursed her lips, not answering.

"No pressure," she said, a little confused. Her friend seemed totally smitten but what was the issue?

"He might not be at Mitten Inn," Yvonne whispered. She couldn't keep from smiling. "He stayed with me last night. I like him so much, Savanna."

"*Girl.*" Savanna stared at her, wide eyed. She started to ask more but it was their turn.

They stepped up to the counter. Griffin smiled and greeted them to take their order. She was so glad to see him happy and seemingly doing well. She'd gotten to know him and his family well a couple months ago when her dad and his had disappeared during a sailing regatta. "How's the art going, Griffin? Oh, I've got both our drinks," she told him, stepping aside for Yvonne to order.

"Going great," he said. "My dad's been giving me lessons. I think he finally gets that I'm not him, my work is different than his. If I ever get another art show set up, I'll let you know."

"Please do. I'd love to see what you're working on. I haven't painted lately, and I really miss it." She paid, and at the end of the counter, the assistant barista presented them with two steaming cups of coffee, the frothy foam topping decorated by Griffin. "So pretty! This is some mystical magic, I have no idea how you do this," she told him, admiring the lovely leaf designs on each of their cappuccinos.

"It's not hard," he said, "you just—"

She held up a hand. "Nope. Don't ruin the magic for me. Thanks, Griffin." She and Yvonne found a table near the front window. "Okay. You have to tell me. What is happening with Lars?"

Yvonne's cheeks flushed again. "I don't really know… but he's so sweet to me. He came over last night because he said there was some problem with his card to swipe into the Mitten Inn parking lot and he didn't want to wake Mia or Remy."

The back of Savanna's neck prickled. "That's weird, maybe there was some glitch with the system," she agreed. "But Mia's run that place forever. She wouldn't have minded him calling. I'm sure it wasn't super late." She was fumbling her way through, hoping for enough information to know for sure whether to burst Yvonne's love bubble with Lars.

"It was pretty late, almost midnight, by the time he came over. I didn't mind, trust me. I wish he didn't live so far away," Yvonne said, making a sad face.

Caroline's break-in was around eleven or eleven thirty last night. And why was Lars even still in town after he'd planned to go home for the holiday? And where was he the night Rob was killed and why did he act so strange upon hearing of Helene's death? She took a deep breath. "Yvonne, I kind of need to tell you something. I think." Her good friend hadn't had a decent boyfriend in years. She wanted to keep her safe, but she hated to do this.

"Okay…" Her eyebrows went up in worry, making her look even younger than her pale-yellow curls and fair, unlined complexion already did. She'd always been a little naïve.

"About Lars…" Savanna hesitated. Was she really entertaining the idea of Lars either being part of the elite art theft team that had successfully robbed four high-profile museums, or single-handedly breaking in and stealing Caroline Carson's Minkov? To what end? The artist drove a forty-year-old hippie camper and presumably lived in a similarly nonmaterialistic house up north. The pieces wouldn't fit, no matter how she tried to force them. "Do you know much about his past?"

"A little. He's been married before. He moved to the U.P. after their divorce."

"I didn't know that. I guess I wouldn't have, it's not the kind of thing that goes in an artist bio. Were you two together late last night until he went back to Mitten Inn and had trouble with the parking lot gate? That'd make sense," she said, to herself more than to Yvonne. It would take him out of any possible break-in equation at Caroline's at least.

She shook her head. "We ate pretty early. He left around eight. He has an old friend in Lansing he'd promised to stop by and see."

She made up her mind. "We've been friends a long time, right? Since high school. You trust me?"

Yvonne covered her heart with her hand. "I trust you with my life," she said dramatically. She smiled at Savanna. "Why?"

"Come with me to give him his check. Can you text and see if he's at Mitten Inn or still at your place? I need to ask him about something, and I think you should be there."

"What do you need to ask him? Please don't tell me I got another bad one. I really like him, Savanna." She texted Lars and watched her phone, waiting. Her phone dinged. "He's back at Mitten Inn. He says he felt weird sitting at my house without me."

"Okay, let's go see him. I'll explain on the way."

On the two-mile drive to Mitten Inn, Savanna gave Yvonne the simplest summary possible of her concerns. She really had nothing concrete. But she was glad Lars was in a public place and not at her friend's rather isolated, rural home.

"Look," Yvonne said, pointing. Lars's camper van was parked behind a row of other cars, lined up out in front of Mitten Inn. The parking lot was almost empty and there was a bright orange, handwritten OUT OF ORDER sign taped to the parking arm at the entrance.

"Oh wow! Sheesh, that's inconvenient," she said.

"He's in room twelve. If you park all the way at the end, we'll be closer than at this end," Yvonne said.

Lars opened the door a moment after Yvonne knocked. He wore a lined, red, flannel shirt over a blue hoodie and a black winter hat. "Hello. Come in," he said, holding the door. "Hi," he said separately to Yvonne, his voice soft.

Savanna could see how conflicted her friend was. She'd started toward him and then backed off, taking a seat at the small round table.

"Would you like to sit?" he asked Savanna, holding out a hand toward the other chair. "Yvonne said you have a check for me. I didn't expect that until the end of the week."

She gave him the envelope with the remainder of his fee in it. "I received it the other day. I didn't feel right holding onto it; you've done such a wonderful job with the ice show." She could feel Yvonne staring at her. She sat across the table from her and dove in. "Lars, I apologize in advance, but I need to ask you a couple things. I've known Yvonne for almost fifteen years. She's the nicest person I know." She glanced at Yvonne.

Lars pulled the armchair on the other side of the TV over and sat with them. "I agree with that."

"So, I'm just looking out for her. You know about the robbery at the museum where I work—where Helene worked. There have been several high value thefts, including one last night in town. Police haven't made any arrests yet. Were you... Yvonne says you weren't in town last night?"

The big man exhaled, leaning forward with elbows on knees. He rubbed the palm of one hand on the side of his beard. "Last night, I went to Helene's house."

"What?" Savanna and Yvonne both spoke at once. "She's... why?" Savanna asked.

"She was blackmailing me. After we divorced—"

Yvonne stood up. "What?" She stared bug eyed at him. "The curator who put us in touch with you for Frosty Fest? You and Helene were married?"

Lars was almost eye level with her even though she was standing. He reached for her hand. "I was nineteen when I married her. Young and dumb. I stayed too long. We divorced five years ago. While I was trying to get my sculptures seen, she was climbing the ranks at Musée National des Beaux-Arts du Québec and then started—what's the word?—flying to other museums to—"

"Consult?" Savanna offered.

"Yes. I remind you," he said, the slight accent coming through, "I was dumb, and I trusted her."

Yvonne sat back down and touched his knee. "Don't say dumb. Maybe you were ignorant? About certain things?"

Lars stared down at her hand and then up at her, relief apparent in his tough-to-read face. "Thank you. She promised to get my work seen with her connections, but first she needed me to create copies of some of the most well-known sculptures... she said it would demonstrate my talent, and then I'd start selling my own. She told me the copies were commissioned by art lovers who didn't mind having a—it's like a print of a Van Gogh. Yes? You know it's not the original but still hang it on the wall."

"I understand," Savanna said.

"But it wasn't true. Helene used my copies as replacements of the real sculptures. I don't know where or how she connected with these people. I made three, thinking she was helping me. I kept photos of all of them. But so did she. By the time I knew what she'd done, I'd broken the law. Many laws, I think. Again, I was dumb. Ignorant." He took a deep breath, sitting up a little straighter. "I gave her everything in the divorce. I still pay her... I agreed, I had to, or she would tell the police. I made the copies. I have no proof of her connections or what she did with the copies—the fakes. I should use the right word. I made fakes that Helene used to steal works of art worth a fortune."

"But… you didn't kill her," Yvonne said it as a statement, not a question.

He recoiled, shaking his head vigorously. "No. I could never hurt anyone."

"So, why did she put us in touch with you for the ice show?" Savanna asked.

"She wanted me to do one more sculpture—a copy of Giovanni DiBeppo's *Man In Flight*."

Savanna gasped. "We have that one. It's at my museum—that piece is on loan from DiBeppo's estate. It was valued at twenty-two million six months ago when Helene… acquired it." Her eyes widened with realization. Helene had acquired it on loan in order to orchestrate its theft and replacement. "Did you… please tell me you didn't do it."

"I did not. When Helene called me about your ice show, she was nice. She knew I needed the money. But then she tried to convince me to make the *Man In Flight* copy and I refused. I had a feeling she would try something like that; I recorded our conversation. When I wouldn't help her this time, she said I was finished. I'd go to prison. I was afraid to go back home, where police are looking for me… but they will find me here, too, I know."

"Holy cats." She didn't know what else to say. His words about Helene, she's not a friend, made sense now.

"I will turn myself in. I can give police the photos I have of the three fakes I made, but I don't know what Helene, or her group did with the real sculptures."

"That's why you went to her house," Savanna guessed. "Hoping to find some sort of proof or record of what she did."

He nodded. "I drove there last week, too, but I saw your friend through the window—the skinny blond man who was dating Helene. So, I had to wait."

"Britt was in Helene's house last week? What night was that?"

He counted on the fingers of one hand. "Last Wednesday. The first night of your Frosty Fest."

That answered her other question, assuming Lars was being honest. He hadn't been in Chicago that night, poisoning Rob somehow. "When you went back last night, did you find anything?"

"No. I don't even know what to look for. Maybe there's something on her computer… the police could look, if they knew what she did. I have to tell them."

Savanna exchanged a glance with Yvonne. "You do need to tell them," she agreed. "It will probably help solve some of what happened the night of our museum robbery too. But I think I can try to help with how to do this."

Chapter Nineteen

S AVANNA STOOD. "I'M sorry. I owe you both an apology," she said. "Yvonne, I really was worried about your safety. I hated thinking I might have accidentally set you up to date a dangerous man. And Lars, I'm so sorry I suspected you of being dangerous. Everything you've said makes perfect sense. I'm sorry you've been through what you have because of Helene. Will you drive Yvonne home when she's ready? I need to go yell at someone who actually deserves it."

Yvonne hugged her goodbye at the door. "Don't be too hard on Britt. They probably have a good reason for being in Helene's house after she died. You know Britt loves you."

"I thought I knew that. I'm not sure how well I know them at all now. Lars, I'll be in touch as soon as I can chat with the Art Crimes Team agent and get some guidance."

She checked her phone as she walked out to the road to her car. It was noon. She'd called Agent Klein two hours ago… judging from the last time, it might be tonight or tomorrow before the agent called her back. She'd have to be patient. But the last time she'd slept on a piece of important information, it'd nearly disappeared. She was lucky she'd saved Rob's app footage on her phone. Was it fair to the sheriff's department investigating the Carson Mansion robbery not to notify them of what she'd found?

She made a detour on her way to the expressway. She kept going on Shoreline Drive past Main Street instead of turning, gratified to see a police cruiser in front of Caroline's house. The crime scene tape this morning meant the investigation was still underway. Now she had to hope the detective she wanted to talk to was there.

She rang the bell, and this time Caroline herself answered the door after several minutes. "Savanna! Come in!" Caroline greeted her with a hug and a kiss on the cheek. "What would I do without you? Jack told me you rescued Princess from freezing to death last night. I had to bring them home; they're so out of sorts, poor babies. Come." The poodles flanked the older woman so closely, Savanna worried she might trip, but every time she took a step they scooted out of the way.

Savanna followed Caroline and the dogs past the library toward the parlor. She craned her neck, hoping to get a glimpse of which law enforcement office was here, but spotted no one. "Does Detective Jordan still have protective surveillance on you?"

"No, that'd be silly," the woman said. "I can't go in there," she added, seeing Savanna looking. "It's going to take some time for me to grow accustomed to the library without Everett's Minkov."

"I'm sure it will," Savanna said. "I'm sorry this happened."

She took a seat in her wingback chair and patted the armrest of the other one. "I appreciate that. You tried to warn me two years ago, when I insisted on keeping high-value pieces on display. It's my own, stubborn fault. I just wish they hadn't taken that one."

"This wasn't your fault, Caroline. I'm um, still hopeful we might be able to get your painting back. You never know."

"Always the optimist."

Lauren poked her head into the room. "Hi Savanna. How about some tea? Grandmother?"

"We'd love some," Caroline answered.

Savanna hadn't planned on a lengthy visit… she'd hoped to update Detective Taylor and then go find Britt. But she couldn't leave yet; she'd never be rude to Caroline. "Have you talked with Jack today?"

"Just a bit. He mentioned your… findings this morning."

She raised her eyebrows. "Really?"

Caroline mimicked zipping a zipper across her lips. "No one will hear a peep from me. It's your show, dear. You know I'd trust you with my life. And the lives of both of my poodles."

"She seems to be doing all right," Savanna said. "I hope they're both not too traumatized. I'm sure it was scary for them."

"Lauren helped me get them checked at the veterinarian's this morning. Everything seems to be all right, except for a touch of frostbite on Princess's back paw pad. Your sister's picking her up soon for a little trim to get rid of this nasty red paint." Caroline kept a hand protectively on the little dog beside her.

"She has frostbite? Poor puppers."

"The doctor said it could have been much worse, with last night's temperatures. You really did save her life."

She smiled. "It was my pleasure."

When Lauren brought in the tray of tea and cookies, Savanna held her cup in both hands, letting it warm her. Somehow, Caroline's black tea always tasted better than anywhere else. The doorbell rang again, and Lauren brought Sydney into the parlor. "I'll bring you a cup," Lauren said.

Syd opened her mouth to protest, but too late. There was no declining Carson hospitality. Savanna left her sister to chat with Caroline, excusing herself to use the restroom. She had to try to catch Detective Taylor away from the sheriff's station. She was still second-guessing her suspicion of Jordan, but she wasn't taking any chances after the last bit of privileged information she'd shared with him. In the library, she spotted the evidence tech from last night who'd explained casting a footprint in the snow, on the upper level near the railing where the Minkov had hung.

"Hi there," she said. "Savanna, from last night?" She placed a hand on her chest. "I'm wondering if one of the detectives is here with you?"

The girl nodded. "Yes—outside, walking the grounds along the dunes to make sure nothing was missed."

"Thank you!" Savanna grabbed her coat from the hook in the foyer and stepped out onto the porch, hurrying around toward the lake side. She didn't want Caroline to think she'd left without saying goodbye or send Lauren looking for her. On impulse, she typed and sent a quick text to Sydney, a feeling of déjà vu washing over her from the last time shady events happened here and she'd sent secret, urgent texts to her sister.

"Can you kill a little time with her? Don't leave yet. I'll explain later."

In the distance, she spotted Detective Taylor... and Detective Jordan. They walked about fifty yards apart in the blowing, blustery cold, surveying the snow. She backed up around the corner of the porch before either of them saw her. She'd have to find another way.

Back inside, she leaned down to hug Caroline goodbye, her cold cheek touching the woman's toasty warm one. "Oh! You're an icicle!" Caroline shivered, pressing a hand to her cheek. "Remind me to knit you a new scarf, will you? Were you out looking for the good detectives?"

"I was, but they're pretty busy. Plus, it's way too cold out there," she said. "I'll walk out with you," she told Sydney. Her sister held Princess in her arms, bundled up in a fluffy pink blanket with only her tiny face showing.

"We'll get them warmed up with some nice tea when they come in," Caroline said. "Would you like me to let them know you were looking for them?"

"Oh, no, that's okay. Really. I'll see you Saturday at the wedding!"

Outside in Caroline's driveway, Sydney grilled Savanna until she admitted she'd been trying to get Detective Taylor alone to share what she'd found this morning. "I'm just not sure about Jordan right now."

"What do you mean? You know him, Savanna. The guy

wouldn't jaywalk if his life depended on it."

"I know, I've always thought that too. But he was literally the only person who knew we were going to move the Minkov to the bank vault right after Christmas. So, it gets stolen Christmas night? That's weird. He was also the only one I told about Rob's 360 Dash Cam footage, and then Rob turns up dead."

"Okay, I see how you'd put two and two together," Syd said. "But it's Jordan. I dated him forever ago, he's a massively grumpy nerd who would never dream of going on a crime spree."

"Maybe you're right. I don't know." Savanna tipped her head at Princess, making a sad face. "Poor baby. I'll let you get your poodle burrito to the salon. I can't believe she almost died because of some jerk art thief's carelessness."

"I know. Anyone who could hurt an animal should be locked up. I hope they catch whoever did it."

She debated calling Britt on the way to Lansing and decided against it. She'd check at the museum first, and then their house if needed. Her mind spun in circles all the way there. Helene blackmailing Lars explained a lot, but not everything. The curator had to have been working with the group responsible for the Impressionist thefts. But had one of them killed her? Why?

Once at the museum, Savanna bypassed the lab and headed for the block of administrative offices on the other end of the hall. She reached Helene's office door before Britt's. The gold plate on the door still bore Helene's name; she'd only been gone a little over a week. Her funeral was tomorrow. There was no way she'd go now. Savanna tried the door handle and found it unlocked. She slipped into the office, shutting the door behind her.

The office was a mess—not at all what she'd expected. But the space wasn't simply untidy. The end table beside the leather couch was turned on its side. The couch cushions were upended, two desk drawers were pulled half open, a loose pile of paper and folders was scattered over the floor near the open closet door. The scent of Helene's perfume still hung in the room. Had she been interrupted just prior to heading down the hall to Britt's office? Savanna sat at her desk, slowly spinning around in the swivel chair. She opened the desk drawers that were still closed, rifling through them and coming up with mint gum, lipsticks, a dozen pens, but not much else. The laptop that normally occupied her desk was missing, presumably taken into evidence by the Art Crimes Team. Turning in a full circle again, her attention caught on something hanging on the back of the bathroom door. Helene's robe or a towel, perhaps?

In the full en suite bathroom only the offices of the lead curator and the museum director were fortunate to have, Savanna closed the door and plucked the white men's shirt off the hook. The tag read 44L. The owner of the shirt was most definitely not Britt, who she knew wore a 34L, equally as long as this one but much, much smaller. On the counter opposite the stall shower, along with more of Helene's makeup, a perfume bottle, and other items for a mid-day or after-work spruce up, was a small jar of men's hair pomade, a can of shaving cream, and two toothbrushes. If she was noticing these items, the FBI must have cataloged them too.

She left the bathroom and reassembled the disheveled couch cushions. Had the FBI done this, searching the room? It seemed a bit aggressive. They'd likely found the office this way. She sat down on the leather couch across from the desk. She lay down, then turned around and lay down on the other end of the couch. The underside of the desks center drawer was a different shade of finished wood. She slid onto the floor and saw it clearly, noting a small screw in each corner. She returned to the desk and pushed the chair out of her way. It rolled until it hit the wall with a clatter. She sat cross-legged under Helene's desk with a letter opener found in the drawer and, one by one, unscrewed the panel. She was working on the last screw when money began falling out, several crisp hundred-dollar bills. Removing the last screw, Savanna gasped as a windfall of money and two official-looking documents dropped into her lap.

The doorknob rattled and Britt peered inside. "Hello? Savanna? What on earth?" Britt entered and shut and locked the door behind them.

She stood up quickly, gaping at the money and then Britt, speechless.

Britt was at her side, making her sit. "I thought I heard someone in here. Are you okay? What in the world…"

She nodded. "I'm fine. I need to talk to you."

Britt gathered the money, some in loose bills, some in thin stacks, and dumped it on the desktop in front of Savanna. She helped sort it into piles, losing track after she passed $50,000. "How did you know she had money stashed here?" Britt asked, still counting.

"I didn't. Did you know Helene was married before?"

Britt's face responded louder than any words.

"You knew? Did you know she was married to Lars Anders? And he says Helene was involved in an art forgery ring?"

Britt sighed. "I—"

"Seriously?" She was incredulous. "What is going on? You're keeping these things from me? Are you part of it?"

"Oh my God, no!"

"The night of the gala, did you kill Helene and then race down to the lobby to tell us you couldn't find her?" Savanna surprised herself—she hadn't realized that was there, filed away in some compartment of her mind, waiting to be voiced.

"Oh cheese and rice Savanna, are you kidding me?" Britt dropped onto the leather couch. "I loved her. Before I really knew her. All of this came out in the open the day before she died, when we were back at her place after meeting with you and the sculptor in Carson. We had a *huge* fight about it… her history with Lars, the way he forced her to swap out real sculptures for the fakes he made, even her past association that she ended with the art dealer Felix Thiebold."

"Her *what*? Good grief. We have to get ahold of Agent Klein." She sent the agent a quick text, saying she had information to share. She looked back up at Britt. "Helene told you Lars was the mastermind, pushing her to make the swaps?"

Britt nodded, a trace of doubt clouding their features.

"Okay, first of all, Lars had no idea what he was making sculptures for. Helene duped him into thinking it was just to showcase his talent. He's a bit naïve... I believe he really bought into what she told him. Think about it. Any connection she had to Felix Thiebold is incredibly incriminating. To my knowledge, he's still in prison along with a bunch of the people the FBI connected him to." She studied her friend's face as they considered that. "Lars saw you inside Helene's house last week after she died."

"I had to get my things. And... I was snooping, trying to see if I was right about something." They glanced toward the restroom. "You went in there?"

She nodded.

"Helene was seeing someone else. The night of the gala, I waited in my office to give her gown to her, but she never came. I checked hers and swore I heard her in here, but the door was locked. When I came back the next day, after she was murdered, it was unlocked, and everything was messed up in here like this. Agent Klein and her partner interviewed me right after Helene was killed. I told them everything I know."

"Oh jeez. I'm sorry you learned all of this about Helene."

"Thanks. I kind of already knew she had secrets. She was so vague about her past relationships or how she was so well off. I guess... I shouldn't be surprised she was seeing someone else behind my back." Savanna gave them a hug. Britt sighed. "So, you think her arrangement with Lars for the forged sculptures wasn't what she told me? It was the other way around—Helene was using him, and then using what he did as leverage?"

"I really do," she said. "So, when Helene told you she knew Felix, what did she say?"

"She said she did some jobs for him and only realized the extent of what he was up to when the St. Armands case broke wide open, thanks to you," Britt said. "She'd already gotten out a few years earlier."

"She got out of the St. Armands art thief ring, but she didn't keep her hands clean. I believe she might have moved into a different circle. I have an idea of what's going on with the Impressionist thefts and the vandalized fakes, but I want to run it by Agent Klein first to see what she thinks. Anyway, Helene set Lars up with the Carson ice sculpture show to try to coerce him into making one last sculpture, a copy of DiBeppo's *Man In Flight*. Helene acquired the twenty-two-million-dollar piece for our museum so she could orchestrate its theft, using Lars's copy to swap it out. He recorded her threatening him. He just didn't know how to share any of this without ending up behind bars himself."

"Have you told Detective Jordan about this yet?" Britt asked.

"Not yet. I kind of can't. Britt, look at this. Tell me if you see what I see." She opened her gallery and zoomed in on the screenshot she'd taken from that crucial 360 Dash Cam recording. She kept thinking she was seeing some sort of badge or emblem on the arm of whoever had opened that employee entrance at Kenilworth. With increased resolution and some tweaks to the saturation and sharpness, she'd proven herself right. The cuff of the men's dress shirt bore the Kenilworth security logo.

"It's a museum guard. This is from that dashcam footage? A guard let them into Kenilworth? Are you thinking that's the case for all the robberies?"

She nodded. "It makes sense. Everything about the break-ins has been organized and regimented, the same methods used in all four so far, if we don't include Caroline's break-in—and we shouldn't. Security also would've had the required access and clearance to take specific alarm and camera grids offline."

"If I know you at all," Britt said, "you've already narrowed down the potential guards."

"Based on who was on-site the night of the gala and some of the shady behavior we've seen since then, yes. Donald Tate. George Taylor. Or Nick Jordan. It has to be one of them."

Chapter Twenty

"SO, HYPOTHETICALLY," BRITT said, eyeing the neat stacks of cash on Helene's desk, "if one stumbled upon, say, $232,500 that no one knows exists, is it wrong to keep it?"

Savanna laughed. "I mean, that would pay a whole lot of our bills plus cover an extended vacation in the south of France…"

Britt nodded. "We could see it as a victimless crime? One of those 'if a tree falls in the woods but no one is there to hear it' things. Who would know?"

"Um. Dangerous killers and thieves in an art crime ring, maybe."

"Yeah, yeah. There's that. I was only kidding."

"For real, though," Savanna said, "what do we do with this? We can't just leave it here. Someone else with less scruples than us could find it. But we can't just take it. That'd look really bad."

Britt frowned. "Do we put it back and tell Agent Klein where to find it?"

"Seems risky. But you have a good idea." Savanna held her phone over the desk and snapped a photo. Then another one from a side view. She typed a text message to Agent

Klein and showed it to Britt before hitting send:

"Found $232,500 in a hidden compartment in Helene Devereaux's desk. What should we do with it until you can get it?"

Britt seemed uncertain. "Could you not say we? I'm sorry, I just worry that it already looks bad that Helene and I fought right before she died, and she was seeing some random dude, and I didn't tell the authorities when I found out she'd worked with Felix Thiebold. I'd rather the FBI think you found the money on your own. Unless you're not okay with that."

"That's what happened. It's totally fine." She changed *we* to *I* and sent the photos. "Why didn't you at least tell me about her connection to Felix?"

"Because love makes me stupid. I'm sorry."

"I'm sorry, too, for your loss. You deserve someone as wonderful as you, Britt." Her phone rang. "Hello, Agent Klein," she said, putting the call on speaker.

"Hello Ms. Shepherd. You found $232,500 in Helene's desk drawer? We searched her desk."

"Underneath the center drawer. There's a compartment the size of the drawer under the false bottom. You can only get to it from the outside, which is impossible to notice unless you're lying on the floor."

"Which you were doing in Helene Devereaux's office just now for what purpose?"

Britt watched her, silent and wide eyed.

"I stopped by her office to see if I had missed something. The way she died has been on my mind a lot. And I ended up getting a new piece of information about her past from an artist doing a show in Carson right now, which made me want to know more about her. She admitted to working in some capacity for the St. Armand's art thief group. I was going to explain better tomorrow when I saw you."

"Our team has been through her office," Klein said. "Your find is helpful and pretty impressive, to be honest. Out of curiosity... you were lying on the floor to... try to learn more about her?"

Savanna smiled at Britt. "Not exactly. I sat at her desk and on the couch and laid down as she might have done... did you see the man's items in her bathroom?"

"Yes, we did. We got a hit on the toothbrush DNA."

Britt's brows rose in surprise.

"Are you able to share any information about who?" Savanna asked.

"I'm not at liberty to discuss that. For now, I need you to stay right where you are until I can find a field agent close enough to come take possession of those funds... it might take a few hours to get someone there. If you can't wait, are you okay taking the money off-site? It obviously can't be left there."

She and Britt exchanged glances. "Um. I'm not super comfortable staying here waiting. I'm not sure who might have seen me here today. I don't really feel very safe just sitting here like this. But—you want me to just walk out of here with it? It's a lot of money, Agent."

"It is and it isn't. Think of it more as petty cash. It may be Helene's collection of skimmed funds from some of her... endeavors. I agree it's not the best idea for you to be there. Find something inconspicuous to pack it up in."

"And then you'll come get it from me tonight?" Being responsible for this much cash made her nervous.

"Tonight or tomorrow. It'll be fine."

The perfect solution appeared in Savanna's mind—the large storage safe at Skylar's law firm. She'd seen it once last year and it looked formidable. "My sister is an attorney in Carson. Her firm has a secure, locking safe for clients' items when needed. There are cameras at both entrances and an alarm system. Could I store the money there until then? I'd be a nervous wreck having it at my house."

"I understand. That sounds like a great idea," Agent Klein agreed. "I'll be in touch as soon as I have a plan."

The call ended, Savanna agreeing to phone Klein once she was with Skylar at her office. She hoped the plan would be okay with her sister; it had to be. Britt found a zippered gym bag in the closet and emptied it out. They held the bag at desk level and swept all the bills into it. She and Britt stared into the bag before closing it.

"It's kind of beautiful," Britt said.

"Klein called it petty cash," she marveled.

Britt laughed.

They walked out to the employee parking lot.

"You're sure you're fine?" Britt asked. "Do you want me to follow you to Carson?"

She shook her head. "I'll be fine. Look," she said, holding up her phone, "I have the FBI on speed dial."

"All right. I'll see you tomorrow after work... after I get off work," they said. "Some of us don't have holiday weeks off. I have an appointment at your village clerk's office to show proof of my ordination so everything's all set for your ceremony."

"Tomorrow's Helene's funeral," Savanna said. "I don't plan to go, unless you're still going and want me there. Up to you, my friend."

"I'd rather not. I already let her sister know I wouldn't be there. I don't think I really knew her at all," Britt said.

"You knew the version of her she wanted you to see. Maybe that's a little bit true of all of us, at least at first. You were an amazing partner to her, Britt. Stay for dinner tomorrow and I'll show you what Lars created—it's beautiful at night."

An hour later, Skylar closed the heavy, automatic locking steel door while Savanna and Agent Klein via video call watched. The duffel bag would be safe and secure at Black, Jones, and Sydowski until tomorrow when Klein could get to Carson to pick it up.

Home at last, Savanna flounced onto her cushy couch feeling like she'd run a marathon. Toting around a quarter of a million dollars was exhausting. Even though she'd be seeing him this evening, she called Aidan. "You will never believe what just happened," she began.

Aidan's deep voice came through the phone, warming her. "Try me."

She skipped right over any steamy, sassy retort she might've dreamed up under normal circumstances. "I just got rid of $232,500."

"What?" His tone was incredulous. "You mean you were rich this whole time but I'm marrying you for love?"

She burst out laughing. "I was rich for about forty-seven minutes. And of course, you're marrying me for love, not money, silly. Anyway, it wasn't my money." Savanna recounted the wild events of this afternoon.

He was quiet—too quiet—when she finished.

"Aidan?"

"Sorry. You really said two hundred something thousand? A good six figures in cash? What was Britt's girlfriend doing with that kind of money? And you *took it with you?*"

"Crazy, right? It was all stuffed into this hidden space under Helene's desk drawer."

He shook his head. "And the FBI agent knows about it, she's coming to get it tomorrow? The whole thing is crazy."

"I didn't want to be anywhere near that money," Savanna said. "I don't know how or why Helene had it. I'm just glad it's locked up at Skylar's office and out of my hands."

"I am too. That was smart," he said. "I can't stand thinking about you being in danger; I'm glad you thought to keep it there for the night."

"Me too." She'd felt instantly lighter once that duffel was locked away in the safe. Now she felt lighter still after sharing the whole story with Aidan. "I can't wait to see you," she said.

"See you soon, my love," he replied.

THAT EVENING, SAVANNA and Aidan were scheduled to meet with Uncle Max at In Bloom to see the floral arrangements he'd planned for their wedding. Max had bought the flower shop last spring after the previous owner had passed away. Uncle Max and Uncle Freddie's Corgi, Lady Bella, had settled nicely into her shop dog role at In Bloom, spending quality time with Max while he worked.

Savanna stopped across the street at Fancy Tails and Treats to pick up Fonzie. "I feel like I should pay you for dog sitting," she told Sydney, moving to the bakery counter to choose some goodies for Lady Bella and Fonz, who sat down on her foot and stared up at her expectantly.

"No way," Syd said. "You more than pay me back whenever you fill in for Willow. What can I get you? Are these for Jersey or Lady Bella or our little friend on your feet?"

"All three please. I just realized Fonzie will have a live-in playmate soon. It's a good thing Jersey's so easygoing. I don't know what I would've done if he was a spaz like this guy," she said, patting the top of the Boston terrier's head.

"I'm so excited for you," Sydney said, bouncing a little behind the counter.

"I'm excited but nervous for Saturday," Savanna said.

Syd shook her head. "Your wedding is going to be amazing, but that's not what I meant. I'm so excited for you and Aidan and Mollie to start your life together. You deserve every bit of happiness coming to you."

"Thank you!" She tipped her head at her sister. "See, you can be nice when you try."

"Whatever. I have to show you something. Do you have a minute?"

"Sure. Uncle Max said for us to come after closing so he

can show us the flower arrangements he's planning. I have a little time."

Sydney boxed up the favorite treats of each dog, handing Savanna three small white bakery boxes tied with string and labeled *Fonzie, Jersey, Lady Bella*. "Come here." She disappeared through the door to the baking kitchen, which connected to the bathing and grooming area.

Savanna followed her through, curious. "What's up?" She lowered her voice. "Are you okay?"

Sydney handed her half a hangtag, torn from The Gifting Tree.

She read it and held it out to Syd, confused. "It says this kid wants a *Star Wars* Lego set. But the deadline for these was days ago, Syd, were you supposed to grant this wish?"

"No. I found it in Finn's glove compartment. Along with these." She produced several more from her winter parka on the coatrack. "Look. There's like twenty of them or something."

Stunned, Savanna set them on the counter, spreading them out. "There's so many. Finn granted all of these wishes?"

"I think so! I can't be sure, but this one," she said as she picked up a card, "is Kate's son's wish—a stuffed animal, he wanted a frog or a toad. That's their address. When I went to yoga this morning, I asked Kate what Gabe got for Christmas and she said someone left a plush green stuffed frog toy in a wrapped package on their porch before Christmas. So, if Finn fulfilled that one, I think he probably did all of these."

Savanna beamed. "I'm not even surprised. He's such a

sweet guy; he just doesn't want everyone to know it.'"

Syd laughed. "Well, that's true. But look. Some wishes are small, like this one—*chocolate*. But others are expensive, see—*a new chair for Grandma*. Finn doesn't have the kind of money needed to fulfill all these wishes."

"The Gifting Tree's been a thing for several years," Savanna said. "Finn's only really been around the last couple. What if..."

"What if Aidan started it," Sydney said.

"And then Finn joined in? That would make sense," Savanna said.

"I don't know how many they'd have to do. I know a lot of the tags get torn and claimed throughout December, but somehow in the end, all the leftover wishes always get granted. It would take a team to pull off doing something like this each year, with the time and money involved."

"I'm going to find out. Can I borrow one of these?" Savanna asked.

"Go ahead. If we're right, we keep this between us, right? Everyone loves the mystery of it... it should stay that way."

She nodded. "Yes, I agree a 100 percent. If we're right, they just gave us even more reasons to love them—which I would've said five minutes ago was impossible. Sneaky brothers!"

She crossed the street with Fonzie and the bakery boxes, spotting Aidan already inside, chatting with Uncle Max. The Gifting Tree question would have to wait until later. The bell over the In Bloom door rang as she entered, sending Lady Bella over to greet her. Savanna stooped down to give the stout, fluffy pooch plenty of pets and belly rubs. She straightened up, stepping in Aidan's welcomed arms for a hug.

"Hi," she said, smiling up at him.

"Hi there." He gave her a quick kiss and let go so she could say hello to Uncle Max.

Max wore his standard white button-down, shirt sleeves rolled up, a gray, paisley patterned waistcoat complementing his neat, silver hair. He grinned widely at them both, clapping his hands together. "I can hardly wait to show you what we've done." He locked the shop door and flipped the sign to CLOSED. "All right, bride and groom, follow me." He led them through to the staging area at the back of In Bloom.

Bride and groom. The thrilling words echoing in her head, Savanna looked up at Aidan and he took her hand, following Max.

A wide wedding arch overhead and multiple displays surrounded them, a fragrant, gorgeous garden of bouquets of roses, buttercups, and peonies in jewel-toned reds, from ruby to wine to burgundy, set off with ivory and sage green. Hand tied ribbons of ivory, maroon, and a splash of deep blue—her something blue—held the bouquet blooms in place. Uncle Max had also created mockups of Aidan's boutonniere, the centerpieces for each banquet table, and the floral spray that would adorn the front of the bridal party's table.

Savanna touched her throat, not sure how to thank him. "They're perfect," she whispered. "Oh, my goodness." She caught Aidan's expression—he felt the same awe she did.

"Thank you, Max." Aidan shook Uncle Max's hand,

then pulled her into him, kissing her temple. "I don't know what I expected. I don't know much about flowers. But this—I'm blown away."

Uncle Max beamed. "You're both very welcome. It's completely my pleasure." He carefully picked up the bridal bouquet and handed it to Savanna, pressing his hand to his chest. "Oh, love. Look at you." He gently turned her by the shoulders to the mirror on the back of the door.

Savanna gasped, a quiet laugh escaping her. "Look at me." She couldn't stop smiling. She'd never once imagined herself holding such a breathtaking wedding bouquet. Her puffy winter coat, faded jeans, and ugly snow boots did nothing to detract from Uncle Max's creation.

"Obviously, these are samples. Yours will be fresher and fuller. Any modifications?"

"None," she said. She glanced at Aidan.

"No notes. You're a magician, Max. Her smile says it all," Aidan said, meeting her eyes in the mirror.

"Thank you, Uncle Max. You're the best."

Savanna turned to Aidan outside, before they parted for their separate cars. "Do you have any gum?" She knew he did. He kept it in his console for Mollie.

"I think so. Let me check—"

"I'll get it," she said, leaning into his car and popping open the glove box first. It was empty except for the vehicle manufacturer book and his oil change receipts.

"If I have any, it should be in the console," he said, looking at his phone.

Inside the console, she found gum, but no Gifting Tree

tags. Where would he have put them? She got out and shut the door.

"No gum?" he asked. "I don't have Mollie tonight. Are you free to get dinner? I was thinking Guiseppe's unless you have—"

Savanna pulled the tag from her pocket and showed it to him. "Is it you?"

He leaned in, reading, "'*I wish for my Dad to get better.*' Oh man. That's a tough one."

"Sydney found a pile of these in Finn's truck. We think you two are The Gifting Tree fairy godfathers. Are you?"

He stared blankly at her, his expression unchanged, not moving.

She stood on tiptoe and put her hand on his chest. "Aidan. Did I make you glitch? Are you in there? Did you do this?"

He nodded slowly. "Yes." He rolled his eyes. "We did. Leave it to Finn to keep the tags."

"You don't keep yours? When did you start doing this? And why? When did Finn get involved? How do you even find the time—and how do you even handle wishes like this one?"

He opened the SUV car door for her. "Get in. I don't want to talk out here."

Savanna glanced around at the mostly empty parking lot. "Okay… but I think we're fine."

When he'd gone around to the driver's side and joined her, he started the car and got the heat going. "I started the tree five years ago. I had two pediatric cardiac cases in a row that just... they kind of wrecked me for a while. I started the tree to try and make myself feel better... and it helped. I love doing it, even when it means I'm stretched way too thin the couple days before Christmas. Mollie helps me sometimes with the shopping. She thinks we're buying gifts for patients, less fortunate kids and others at the hospital who need things. It's a small lie... all she knows is the gifts we get are for people in need.

"I never keep the tags after the wishes are granted," he said, answering another of her questions. "I got Finn to help me the first Christmas after he moved here. The concept is almost too big to handle now, especially for just me. Even with Finn pitching in last year, I'm not sure how much longer we'll do it. This year was better though..."

"Why? Were there fewer unclaimed tags this year?"

"No. Your dad caught me collecting them last week. So now he's part of it too."

"My *dad*?"

"During December I go to the park around six in the morning twice a week to clear out the unclaimed wishes I know no one will take on. Like that one." He eyed the one she still held. "Your dad was walking Daisy in the park last week on the last day, while I was hurrying to collect the rest. When did he start walking the dog so early?" Aidan asked, laughing. "I didn't expect to see anyone."

"He's in partial retirement now and Mom says he gets bored. He's never been a good sleeper. It's probably a miracle he hasn't caught you before now."

"It turned out to be a good thing. Finn and I were in

over our heads. Your dad took a solid third and as far as I know, got through them without any issue. He seemed happy to do it."

"I'm sure you made his Christmas this year, involving him."

"I'm glad. As for this kind of wish," he said, taking the card from her hand, "these are the hardest. You never really know how dire the situation is that made someone, usually a kid, make a wish like this. Or an even tougher one."

She nodded, watching him. This size of this man's heart was immeasurable. "I saw a couple of those."

"For this one," he continued, "Finn and I put together a big basket that was part care package, with hot cocoa, fuzzy socks, markers and coloring books and snacks, and part community resources... a few restaurant and grocery store gift cards, an Uber gift card, phone numbers for free services through the town and county. That kind of thing. I've thought about including a card with some nice thoughts or prayers in it, but, if it was me in that situation, I wouldn't want to hear platitudes or specific religious wishes that might not be in line with my own beliefs. I'd just want to know someone cares."

How many times today had she been left speechless? She'd lost count. Her throat felt swollen with tears or an overabundance of love, or maybe it was the same thing.

Aidan's warm hand closed over her knee. "Did I make you glitch?" he teased, his voice soft.

She shook her head. Swallowed hard. Drank him in. "Good God, man," she whispered, remembering his version of that on her deck. "You are even hotter now than you were twenty minutes ago. I don't know what to do with you."

His lips curved into that half smile that always weakened her knees and quickened her pulse. "I have some ideas."

Chapter Twenty-One

"OKAY, YOU'RE OFFICIALLY creeping me out," Skylar told her. "Isn't there a better way to do this?"

"I can't think of one." Savanna was perched on the edge of her seat, peering through the blinds on Skylar's office window. For the second time in less than twenty-four hours, she was thankful her older sister worked at this law firm. From here, she had a clear view across the courtyard in the center of the village offices to the sheriff's department front entrance. "There's nowhere else I'll be able to watch from in order to catch him leaving."

"And you can't just call or text Detective Taylor because... why?"

"First of all, because I don't have his cell phone number. Second, if I call the station, they'll just give me Jordan. Third, why are you so bothered? Am I inconveniencing you, sitting quietly in my chair not disrupting your work?"

Skylar rolled her eyes. "No, you aren't. I don't have much work. Jillian's cut my caseload back since I'll be leaving soon."

"Are you excited?" Savanna asked.

"Very. We all are. I'm excited for you to visit—the house and view are incredible."

"Just tell us when you're ready and we'll come. I—"

"There he is." Skylar pointed. "Now's your chance! Stealth mode, activate. Need a disguise?" She plucked her oversized sunglasses from her desk and waved them at her.

"You're such a brat. Thank you for the use of your window—and your safe. I'll be back later on with the FBI agent." She had her coat on and was out the door in seconds. She caught up with him as he neared his car. "Detective Taylor."

"Hey Savanna, what's up?" He opened the car door, putting his lunch cooler and gloves on the passenger seat.

"I was hoping to update you on something, but it's a little sensitive. I don't really want to do it in there." She inclined her head toward the sheriff's station.

"Uh, sure. Yes. Where's good?"

"It might be easiest to show you. Do you have time to run to the Carson Mansion with me, or were you on your way somewhere?" She glanced uneasily at the building behind him, willing Nick Jordan to stay inside.

"That's fine. I'll follow you."

Jack opened the front door at Caroline's. "Good morning, come in! How are you, Detective? Hey Savanna. Grandmother's actually not here right now. Lauren took her to the dentist."

"We needed another quick look at the graffiti in the library, if you don't mind," Savanna said.

"Not at all. You know the way. I'm painting the sunroom off the kitchen; I'll be just through there if you need me."

In the library, Savanna powered on her laptop and pulled up the spectrometry reports. "I analyzed the paint in the graffiti. I thought you should see the report." She turned the laptop toward Taylor.

He narrowed his eyes at the columns and rows of numbers and chemical compounds on the side-by-side reports. "I thought you'd said nothing seemed off to you when we were here right after the robbery?"

"I didn't want to say anything without being sure. But the handheld spectrometry system I used gives a breakdown of the chemical and molecular structure of a substance, in this case, this particular red paint. It's a different brand than the one used in all four museum robberies. You can see that through these compounds, here," she said, pointing at the screen.

"Hmm. So... maybe they ran out and couldn't get more of the same brand of paint?"

"That's possible. But I'd say it's not likely. Every aspect of the museum thefts has been so carefully orchestrated. And then the thieves just run out of their trademark paint?"

"Maybe, maybe not. I'm not sure it'd be admissible, if the FBI is ever able to build a case."

"Well, this devil face also was not painted by the same hand as the museum robberies."

Taylor frowned. "What makes you say that?"

"Overspray pattern, heavy-handedness, the arc of the head and horns. The order in which the features were painted."

He smiled at her, and for the first time, she read condescension in his face. "I don't see how you can tell any of that looking at this graffiti tag. The paint was dry when we discovered it, and besides, it's not like we're talking about the high-end paintings you normally work with. It's just spray paint."

"Art forgery cases have been tried and won based on less. Every artist has some type of undeniable habit or trait that shows through in the physical process of creating, even if they aren't aware of it."

"That seems farfetched. You're saying you think this graffiti was not done by the art theft group that hit the museums?"

"Exactly."

"And... this chemistry stuff here backs that up? In addition to the things you said about overspray and sequence?"

She nodded. "Yes. You get it."

He stood back, gazing at the image, his expression pensive. "All right. It's worth considering. You did the right thing in coming to me. Have you had a chance to review your findings on this with anyone else yet?"

"No, not yet. I thought it was important to keep this a little quiet, so it could be handled properly. I'm concerned that this might have nothing to do with the museum thefts. It could be an individual, someone who knew about Caroline's Minkov capitalizing on the string of Impressionist thefts." Like Jordan or any of the deputies assigned to protective surveillance or you, she thought. George Taylor had always struck her as Nick Jordan's more congenial counterpart. She felt a stab of uncertainty now.

"I'll contact the FBI Art Crimes Team today and go over all of this with them. This is good work, Savanna. For now, it'd be a good idea to continue keeping it to ourselves. We don't want to compromise the case."

She nodded. She still planned to get into her findings today with Agent Klein. "Of course. Do you want—" She bit back what she'd been about to say: *do you want the FBI agent's contact info?* It'd be much better if Detective Taylor wasn't aware she'd been talking with the FBI team.

"What's that?" he asked.

"Do you want me to email you the spectrometry reports?"

"Let's… put a pin in that for now. As soon as I update the FBI on these findings, I'll get in touch with you and have you send everything. Sound like a good plan?"

"Yep," she said agreeably.

On their way out, Taylor stopped, a few paces ahead of her. He turned, scratching his head briefly. "By the way. I almost forgot to ask you. What made you decide to come to me instead of Jordan with this?"

The tiny hairs on the back of Savanna's neck stood up. George Taylor was trying to Columbo a hardcore *Columbo* fan. She'd seen every episode. Twice, at least. She'd bet her wedding gown that he'd been waiting for the right moment to ask that question. It was anything but an afterthought. She played along.

"Y'know, I almost called him. Nick's been so stressed and busy lately, I just hated to bother him with one more thing. But then I ran into you and it all worked out."

"Sure, definitely. I feel for him. The in vitro costs are killing him lately. I'm glad you caught me instead."

Savanna did everything she could to channel Nick Jordan's expert level poker face. Don't react, don't move your eyebrows, don't comment on it. He thinks you already knew, so you already knew. She climbed into her car, putting the window down to wave goodbye. "Thanks for your help, Detective Taylor!"

Nick and June Jordan were trying to have a baby—how exciting! When she'd lived in Chicago, a good friend had gone through three rounds of fertility treatments without success. She and her husband had ultimately decided to adopt instead; Savanna had just mailed their daughter's birthday card last month. The in vitro fertilization process could be heartbreaking, unless it wasn't. She really, really hoped all went well for the Jordans. And no wonder he was moonlighting for extra income. Her Chicago friend had taken out a second mortgage while trying to start a family.

Knowing the reason for Jordan working security didn't change anything she'd been suspicious about, but the interaction she'd just had with Taylor made her even more anxious to meet with Agent Klein. And it wasn't completely true that she'd kept her findings and theory on Caroline's break-in to herself. Jack had watched her whole examination process. She'd also talked it through with Aidan and Britt. It made her feel a little better knowing she wasn't the sole owner of her findings.

Even so, the first thing she did after greeting Fonzie back at home was to make sure her doorbell camera was charged and working and then email the FITR report to Agent Klein along with the other composition results for the museum graffiti that Director Flynn had sent her.

She was anxious and on edge the rest of the day, waiting for Britt and Agent Klein. She positioned herself in her living room at the coffee table, assembling wedding favors where she could see both directions on the road to her house. Savanna still hoped she was off base and just feeling paranoid about George Taylor, but her gut instinct knew better.

Britt was ten minutes earlier than they'd planned, which was actually right on time for them. "You're lucky I love you," Savanna said, holding her door open. "Chronically early people make me feel like I'm always running late."

Britt removed their beret and scarf and hung them up with their elegant white wool coat. "That's because you are. It's all right, we balance each other out."

She smiled. "True. Coffee? Wine? Vodka?"

Britt's eyebrows rose. "Is it going to be that sort of meeting?"

"I honestly don't know what to expect."

"Look, I'm officially registered as your ordained minister." They handed her the official, notarized document from the clerk's office.

"I hope it wasn't a pain. I'm so glad you'll be marrying us," she said.

"It was easy, no worries. I'm honored you asked me!"

She'd just set out coffee and tea when Agent Klein arrived. Fonzie sat at Savanna's command, vibrating with the urge to leap and bark but holding it in at the moment. "Do you mind dogs?" Savanna asked when she'd stepped inside. "He's sweet but... energetic."

At the table, Britt's laughter came out as a snort.

Agent Klein dropped to her knees. "Why would I mind this cutie patootie? Look at you! You want to be friends with everyone, don't you?" Fonzie took the baby talk as his release word and sprinted over to Klein, entire body wagging and wiggling while the FBI agent petted him.

Savanna exchanged a look with Britt. She'd warned him the agent was very somber and serious, a little like Jordan. Klein finally stood, joining them at the table. "I love your dog. I miss mine. So... let's talk. Then we'll go retrieve the money. I'll have to thank your sister for storing it. Our new vehicles have a built-in evidence safe for transport to the field office."

"Nice. I've been a little nervous today," Savanna admitted. "I talked with Detective George Taylor this morning about the Carson Mansion break-in."

"I saw your email. I agree with you—her Minkov wasn't stolen by our Impressionist thieves. It's a completely different modus operandi. You suspect George Taylor? I thought you mentioned being concerned about Nick Jordan," Klein said.

"I did. I think I was wrong about Jordan. Nothing about Detective Taylor's behavior today was natural. He was hyper focused on who I'd shared my findings with. And he didn't want me to email him the spectroscopy reports. I'm guessing he never called you or your partner today?"

"He did not. I'll have my partner delve deeper into Taylor's activity, see what comes up. We may find something we can use to bring him in for questioning."

"Thank you. I've been watching the news for any updates on the museum robberies but haven't heard anything. What happened with the Kiernaski find, did the vandalized paintings at the other museums turn out to be forgeries as well?"

Agent Klein nodded. "That was one of the reasons I wanted to meet. The FBI Art Crimes Team owes you our gratitude, Ms. Shepherd—"

"Just Savanna. Please."

Klein nodded. "Savanna. Every single defaced painting involved is a forgery that originated out of the St. Armands gallery. Those pieces are more widespread than we suspected. With this new information, our tech team has re-coded the criteria for the search and discovery software we use to track pieces like this down. We've already discovered another two St. Armands forgeries overseas in Japan, thanks to you breaking this case open for us."

Britt beamed at her. "Total rockstar. Tell our director you require a raise if he wants to keep you. I mean it."

"Not a bad idea," Savanna said. "About the St. Armands forgeries… and the probability that Helene wasn't working for that particular crime ring anymore, but a different one. I've been wondering, is it possible that the Impressionist thieves are choosing these forgeries to vandalize out of rivalry? Rather than steal pieces that are known fakes among art criminals, or leave them on display, which our art thieves minds might seem like a win for the competition, vandalizing them makes a statement to the St. Armands forgery ring. Kind of an in-your-face, we won, you lose, message. Or… maybe I'm overthinking it."

Agent Klein stared at her. "Well. Let me say, you are not overthinking any of this. Our Midwest team leader, a senior agent on the Art Crimes Team, voiced this theory as well. It was not a popular take. But we follow up on every lead, and he didn't bring his theory to the table without good cause. I can't elaborate while the investigation is ongoing, but preliminary findings have proven him—and you—correct."

Britt sat back, crossed their legs, and watched the back-and-forth volley smiling.

"So," Agent Klein said, when they'd finished discussing next steps, "I'd like to reiterate that offer. I think you'd find consulting work for us very interesting, Savanna. Will you give it some thought?"

Savanna felt her friend's gaze on her; she'd neglected to mention the offer to Britt. She hadn't really taken it seriously that day. She did now. "I'll think about it. Thank you." She and Britt walked outside with Klein.

"You're planning on visiting the ice sculpture exhibit at what time tonight?" Klein asked. "I want to make sure I'm on-site, just in case. And I don't know if you've noticed, but that black Ford parked near the mailbox down the road will have eyes on you until we can bring George Taylor and Nick Jordan in for questioning. That should happen before morning."

"We can't thank you enough, Agent Klein," Savanna said. "We'll be heading to the park around seven, after dinner."

"Perfect," she said. "Now, you lead the way into town. Let's go thank your sister and retrieve that bundle of cash."

Chapter Twenty-Two

"ALL RIGHT," BRITT admitted later that night, "this is just fantastic. I don't think I've ever been to an ice sculpture show this extensive. You should get Lars Anders down here to do this every Christmas. He lives up to the hype."

Savanna held out the cone of cinnamon toasted almonds and Britt took a few more. "Yvonne is smitten with him," she said. "I think it's mutual, though he is impossible to read. They're here together somewhere; we might see them. Yvonne said they're going to the bonfire on the beach later tonight."

"From what you've told me about him and Helene, it seems like he dodged a bullet getting out of that marriage," Britt said. "I'm glad he and your friend are happy together. He's clearly talented. Look at this reindeer family he created," they said, stopping.

"Mollie loves the big Santa toward the end, but this is Nolan's favorite sculpture."

"How did he carve these antlers? That must be crazy difficult. I really love the glowing red nose on Rudolph, it's a nice creative detail," they said, pointing to the smaller of the ice reindeers. Lars had carved a slot underneath the deer's snout to insert a red LED light, one of the many special touches he'd incorporated. Britt glanced behind them. "Are you scared, walking around out in the open? Should we be?"

"I can't hide out in my house day and night," she said. "I'm still hoping I'm way off base. Jordan has been a good friend the last couple of years, and now he might have a baby on the way. And I teach with George Taylor's wife, Rosa. He has a nice family. I hope I'm wrong."

"I hate to tell you this," Britt said, "but you aren't wrong about much."

"Hush," she said, laughing softly. They went around the curve on the path and headed under an ice archway into a cluster of larger-than-life holiday sweets carved from ice: candy canes, sugar plums, gingerbread men, and gumdrops all lit up in a rainbow of colors.

Britt stopped to admire the detailed work on the gingerbread men. In her peripheral vision, Savanna caught movement behind the sculptures at the curve in the path ahead. Eyes wide and pulse speeding up, she craned her neck to see, but it was just a couple of teenagers in a snowball fight. She couldn't let her imagination get the best of her.

As they continued, a figure came up alongside her and she jumped a mile. "Savanna, goodness!" Her mother gave her a squeeze around the shoulders. "Hello Britt, how are you?"

"What do you guys think? Is this your first time walking through?" Savanna asked.

"No," Charlotte said, "we've been a couple times. Your dad brings Daisy in the mornings too."

She smirked up at her dad. "I heard about that."

He cocked an eyebrow at her. "Did you now." Harlan put his head close to hers, keeping his voice low. "Is everything okay? You're jumpy. Can I do something to help?"

Her phone buzzed, a text message from Agent Klein.

"Quick update… my partner has Nick Jordan, interviewing him now. Will pick up Taylor as soon as we locate him."

"I'm okay, Dad. But thank you." She watched her parents stroll on ahead holding hands.

"When I grow up, I want to be like them," Britt said.

"Same. They know how blessed they are. My sisters and I do too." Her phone buzzed again in her pocket, reminding her to update Britt. "Hey, Agent Klein says they're talking to Jordan now, and they'll have Taylor soon."

"Agent Klein thinks she's your new bestie," Britt said as her phone buzzed yet again in her pocket. "Is there hot cocoa at the end of this thing? I'm dying for some."

Savanna fumbled her phone from her pocket, and it skittered across the snow at her feet. As she bent to grab it, the loud crack of a gunshot rang out and she was yanked to the ground by her arm linked through Britt's as her friend collapsed. Screams penetrated the night air. Someone ran by them carrying a crying child. She leaned over Britt. Where were they hit? She could see no injury. She shouted Britt's name, hands on their cheeks, but they were passed out or— she shook her head hard, couldn't think it. On the bed of snow and ice feeling like an open target, she frantically grabbed Britt's still form and dragged them with her behind the nearest ice sculpture, putting her ear near their face and flooded with momentary relief hearing her friend breathe.

From behind the oversized ice gingerbread man, she peered up and down the deserted ice show path, mind racing.

Beside her, Britt came to, groaning. On the right side of their chest, bright red bloomed through onto the white wool coat. Her friend struggled to sit up, disoriented.

"No, stay down." She clamped her hand over their chest beneath the fabric, pressing on the wound and forcing Britt back on the snow. "You're okay. We'll be okay," she whispered, ducking her head around the ice to peer out again. Her phone lay ten feet away on the path amidst several diluted drops of blood soaking into the snow.

Britt gripped her wrist and she looked at them, taking in her friend's enormous eyes in their pale face. She followed Britt's gaze, felt the heave of their rib cage as they gasped. "I'm shot? Is it bad?"

She shook her head. "It's nothing. You were grazed," she lied. "I need your phone," she said, patting the pockets of the coat with one hand, finding it and holding it up in front of Britt's face. No one knew they were here, hiding; no one knew Britt had been shot—except the shooter. She set the phone down to call 911, still one-handed, maintaining the pressure with her other hand. The iPhone's error message flashed on the screen—her friend was unrecognizable in their panic. "No no no no," she muttered, trying again and again getting the error.

"Help's coming?" Britt asked, dazed. "Why doesn't it hurt?"

Savanna's heart lurched. With a shaking hand she found settings and the prompt for a passcode. "Help is coming.

What's your passcode?"

"Twenty-two seventy-two three... no four... I think... I never use it." The sound of sirens drifted to them, faint but growing louder. "Just go get help, I'm fine... you said I'm fine."

Savanna shook her head, typing in her fourth passcode attempt. "I'm not leaving you." Police were coming, she just had to wait. Someone would point them this way. She fought the urge to yell for help. There'd only been one gunshot, she hadn't heard any more, but the stretch of walkway they were on was flanked on each side by open space in the park. For all she knew, the shooter—Taylor? Lars? One of the art thieves?—could be watching them right now, waiting to get a better shot.

Her dad's voice shouted for her, then for both of them, from nearby. She was first relieved and then terrified at the thought of her father rushing back through the ice sculptures, searching for them. This couldn't be happening. She didn't answer at first; she needed his help but wanted him to get to safety, to stop heading this way. But her dad wouldn't stop—she knew that.

"Dad! Over here!" She held her breath, peering around the gingerbread man's leg and then behind them. What if she'd just given their location away to whoever wanted them dead? Realization dawned on her. They weren't trying to kill Britt. That bullet had been meant for her.

Britt's eyes were drifting closed again. Savanna lifted the collar of the white coat, afraid to look under it but looking anyway. She was slowing but not stopping the bleeding. She pressed a little more firmly, eliciting a cry from Britt, their eyes wide open now, her stomach flipping queasily over at the wet, sticky feel under her palm.

A shadow crossed the icy path beyond the gingerbread man, and she shrieked, trying to shove backwards while keeping her hold on Britt as a large figure ran toward them. There was nowhere to hide. Her heart pounded in her ears. The man loomed over them, backlit by the ice show flood-lights and then dropped to his knees closing the gap—it was Aidan.

He wrapped his arms tightly around her, stifling the happy sob that burst from her throat, and then moved to Britt, moving the coat aside to look. "Don't move your hand," he ordered.

She shook her head, tears streaming down her face. "I won't." He had his phone to his ear, telling someone where they were.

In the distance, shouts interspersed the now loud siren noise, several voices yelling at once. Aidan hung up and put his fingers to the side of Britt's neck. He bent forward, resting his head on Britt's chest, clearly listening. Frowning, he picked up their hand, pressing on a fingernail and then another one. He carefully slid a hand around to her friend's back and then checked it for blood. "No exit. And there's no other wound?"

"No. We heard just one shot," she said.

Finn appeared in uniform, huge red bag slung over one shoulder. He dropped it on the ground, quickly and effi-ciently pulling supplies out. "Hey there. Hi Britt. We'll get you fixed up." To Aidan, he said, "Kelly and Ace are coming with the stretcher. Can you flag them down?"

Aidan got to his feet and stepped out onto the path, making Savanna nervous.

"It's not safe. Finn, thank you, but he's not safe, whoever shot—"

"The park is crawling with police," Finn said calmly, opening several packages of bandages on a large square of paper he'd laid out on the snow. "It'll be okay. I'm positive."

She took a deep breath, trying to believe him.

"Savanna." Finn locked eyes with her. "On my count, when I reach three, you're going to let go. All right?"

"I—how do I—are you sure? Just let go? They're still bleeding." Her heartbeat galloped at an alarming pace in her throat.

"I'm sure. This is a pressure dressing." He tipped his head at the supplies. "We're gonna use it to keep doing exactly what you've been doing and get the bleeding the stop. Ready? One, two, three." As she removed her hand, Finn seamlessly covered the bullet wound with the thick, rubber-backed bandage and secured it.

Savanna gripped Britt's hand with both her own. Their eyelids were dropping again. She leaned close. "It's okay. Britt, I promise, you're going to be okay. Finn's got you."

"It just grazed me," Britt murmured.

"Over here!" Aidan called, and she heard footsteps crunching quickly toward them over the icy path.

She kissed Britt's cheek, their eyes now closed. "Yes, you're right," she said, tears falling again. "It barely got you.

Nothing you can't handle. I'll be here when you wake up."

His colleagues joined him carrying a long red board. In quick succession, an oxygen mask was placed over Britt's mouth and nose, a plastic device clipped to one finger, an IV line secured in their left arm, and Savanna's friend was smoothly transferred onto the board and secured with straps. Amidst the flurry of activity, Finn gave a rushed, clipped report, most of it sounding like some scary unknown language to her ears. "Gunshot to the right lateral chest, third intercostal space, pressure dressing applied, sats 86 and dropping, BP 90 over 50, pulse thready at 130." Finn halted, looking up at Aidan before finishing. "Breathing's tachypneic. Suspected hemothorax. Aspirate or chest tube, here or en route, your call."

The other two paramedics, Kelly and Ace, stared up at Aidan along with Finn, silent, somehow making the whole situation even more terrifying as Savanna watched.

Aidan dropped to his knees, took Finn's stethoscope, and put his head down, listening, as he moved the bell around on Britt's chest and side. He checked the plastic oxygen meter clipped to their finger and Savanna saw a red flashing 84 on the small screen. Aidan exhaled forcefully. "Sats are dropping too fast and they're already in distress. We'll aspirate here and they might not need the thoracostomy."

Finn changed his gloves and peeled open another package, passing something to Aidan and rustling through the bag again. Savanna backed out of the way as the other two paramedics moved around to Britt's left side, obscuring her view. She slowly got to her feet and was surprised to find her parents, hovering close and quiet.

Harlan gathered her into a hug and Charlotte embraced them both, the three of them not moving for a long minute. "They got him," Harlan said when Savanna let go. "They arrested George Taylor and took him away."

Savanna covered her mouth, eyes wide. She wasn't surprised—not that it was Taylor. But she was stunned he'd actually tried to kill her.

"This is insanity. I just don't understand," her mother said. "Are you okay?"

Savanna nodded. "I'm fine. Britt isn't. It's my fault. Detective Taylor was aiming for me. What if…" She saw her parents exchange a look, one she recognized to mean there'd definitely be more discussion about this at another time.

Her mom rubbed her back. "Honey, Britt's in the best possible hands."

A few feet away, Aidan uncapped the largest needle and syringe Savanna had ever seen.

In minutes, the three paramedics easily lifted Britt on the red board and headed for the parking lot. Aidan joined her standing with her parents.

"Was Britt shot in the lung? Will they be okay?" Savanna asked.

"The gunshot caused blood to collect in the space around Britt's lung, collapsing part of it and making it hard to breathe. We drained most of the blood, and oxygen saturation came up almost right away," he explained. "How are you? Do you need to sit down?"

She shook her head, hugging him and pressing her face

into his neck. "Thank you." He hadn't answered the rest of her question.

"I need to run. I'm scrubbing in for Britt's surgery. But I don't want you to be at home alone."

"We'll take her," Harlan said.

"No. I need to be there for Britt. When they wake up after surgery. I promised. I'm going with you to the hospital," she informed Aidan.

In the parking lot, she hugged her mom and then her dad. "I love you both so much. I'm..." She was about to say they shouldn't have risked their lives to come after her, but there was no sense in wasting her breath. She understood. She couldn't fault them. She'd do the same for them or Aidan or Mollie or any of her family. "Thank you."

At Anderson Memorial, Aidan ushered her to his consultation office to wait. He shed his suit jacket and tie, grabbing his long white lab coat before sprinting from the office, phone to his ear. Savanna was still standing in the center of the room near his desk when he came back a minute later, breathless.

"What did you forget?" she asked.

He crossed to her, pulling her into him with one firm arm around her waist. "This." He tipped her chin up and kissed her, his fingers sliding along her neck and curling around the back, into her hair, tenderness and urgency mingling as she kissed him back, melting into him. She was trembling when he loosened his hold on her. "I thought it was you. I heard that shot from Main Street and I thought it was you. I thought I'd lost you."

She opened her hand wide on his chest, trying to slow her breathing and calm her heart. "Thank you for coming for me."

"Always."

She pulled him back as he turned to go. "Aidan, will Britt get through this? I know their brother and parents are coming, but... I'm not sure what to tell them."

Aidan hesitated, the muscle in his jaw pulsing. "Tell them Britt will be okay. I'll send someone to get you when they're safely through surgery."

She collapsed into a chair when he'd made his second exit, pulling out her phone to finally read the messages she'd missed. Agent Klein had tried to reach her several times, both before and after the incident. Savanna was suddenly thoroughly and completely wiped out. She sent a reply message:

"Thank you for the info... I'm okay, Britt's in surgery. Is tomorrow all right?"

Her phone notification buzzed less than a minute later with Klein's reply:

"That's fine. We're working from the sheriff's station, come by when you can. Oh, and my team made an arrest in the murder of Rob Havemeyer. I'll share more when I see you."

Chapter Twenty-Three

NICK JORDAN MET Savanna outside the sheriff's department building early Wednesday morning with a hot coffee from Holy Grounds down the street. "Are you all right? I heard Britt is stable now, right? Dr. Gallager said they were able to remove the bullet."

"Yes. Thank goodness. That was so awful. When I left the hospital around two a.m., Britt had been moved to surgical ICU. Aidan said Britt did well in surgery and their vital signs were much better. I wasn't allowed in the ICU, immediate family only, but their twin arrived from Detroit; he said he'd be staying with them." During the hours she'd spent in Aidan's office waiting for updates on Britt, she'd scoured the internet for devilish faces, cartoons, photos, drawings, anything. She was excited to show Agent Klein what she'd found. Warming her hands around the steaming cup, she told Jordan sheepishly, "I should be buying you coffee."

"Why's that?" The detective crossed his arms in front of his chest but made no move yet to head inside.

"I think you know why. I'm sorry, Jordan. I owe you an apology. I never should have doubted you."

"No, you shouldn't have," he agreed. "But between the

timing of the Carson Minkov being stolen as well as what happened to Rob shortly after you filled me in on the dashcam clip, I'd have suspected me too. I give you credit for not letting our friendship get in the way of logic."

His words warmed her. "I still should have known you wouldn't have been involved. I can't figure out how someone got the information about the dashcam video Rob had, unless... do you think Detective Taylor overheard me telling you about it the night before I flew to Chicago?"

"It's possible. But the FBI Art Crimes people found more involved parties at the Kenilworth end of things too. They'll fill us in." He held the door open for her.

Agent Klein looked up from her laptop as Jordan led Savanna into his office and shut the door. Beside Klein was a young man dressed in a black suit nearly identical to Klein's, FBI badge on a lanyard around his neck. "Savanna, this is my partner, Agent Peele. Peele, this is the art authenticator I told you about, Savanna Shepherd."

Once greetings were out of the way, Savanna and Nick Jordan joined the two agents at the table in the detective's office. "Let me catch us all up," Agent Klein said.

"We were just talking outside about the dashcam footage," Jordan said. "Might be a good jumping off point."

Klein nodded. "We located Robert Havemeyer's phone. His personal driver Alec Green was in possession of it. He admitted to deleting Rob's dashcam account. He says he was wiping the phone to sell it, since Rob left it in his car just before he died."

"But... factory resetting a phone wouldn't have deleted

his account, just the app from the phone," Savanna said. "He's lying."

"Yes. He's in custody," Klein said.

"For the theft? So how would he have learned about the app or the footage Rob caught the night of the Kenilworth robbery? Or even that Rob added a dashcam to his BMW? The Havemeyer's drivers always use cars from the family garage."

"Rob's girlfriend Effie Thompson knew about the 360 Dash Cam and the video capture. During her interview as a person of interest in Rob's murder, she gave up Alec Green. She confessed she'd shared the dashcam information with Rob's driver."

"So, I didn't kill him," Savanna murmured. She'd been carrying around the weight of Rob's murder. "I thought someone in Chicago found out about the app footage because of me."

"Not likely. The two people involved in his death have that on their conscience," Agent Klein said. "Effie and the driver also both knew he never wavered from his nightly kombucha drink." She stared pointedly at Savanna.

"Are you serious? I was right?" Savanna asked, incredulous.

Jordan frowned, watching the exchange. "Right about what?"

Klein explained Savanna's early theory. "You were afraid it seemed farfetched, but it's really the only way anyone could've killed him from a distance while he was alone in his apartment. High levels of cyanide were discovered on Rob's toxicology report and in the remnants of the empty kombucha cup he discarded in his kitchen. Cyanide in that form would take around one to four hours to be lethal—he had plenty of time to get home before it hit him. Forensics found a supply of sodium cyanide in Alec Green's tool shed, and the driver's fingerprints are on the empty kombucha cup along with Rob's. Both those points are circumstantial, but that combined with Green having the phone is enough probable cause."

Peele added, "Rob's personal driver is in custody awaiting arraignment. The girlfriend Effie Thompson may still be charged, as she's still a person of interest in the theft investigation. But we have traffic cam video confirming Alec Green made a stop at Rob's usual kombucha place a few hours before he died."

"What about Faye Havemeyer, Rob's mother? Was Green involved in the Kenilworth robbery—did he attack her as well?"

"Green denies it. But the image on the dashcam clip is a partial match for his face, and once Mrs. Havemeyer was well enough to speak to us, she ID'd him," Agent Klein said.

Detective Jordan spoke. "And you've narrowed down which Kenilworth guard provided access to the thieves?"

"We have. He was a new hire at that museum about four months ago, quite similar to you, Detective," Peele said.

Jordan didn't look offended. "Luckily for the Impressionist thieves, Lansing Museum of Fine Art already had a crooked guard on staff—who happens to have a deep hatred of Felix Thiebold and the St. Armand's forgery ring."

"What do you mean?" Savanna asked.

"First," Agent Klein said, "our team backed up everything you found at the Carson Mansion proving that Minkov wasn't stolen by our Impressionist thieves. It was a solo operation. We didn't have clear differentiation on whether it was George Taylor, Nick Jordan—no offense—or the deputy assigned on duty when it happened. At least, we didn't, until this morning when the results came back from the footprint in the snow our tech took the cast of. Do you want to do the honors, Detective?" She pushed a thin manila folder across the Jordan.

He flipped it open. "The cast came back definitive for a 5.11 brand boot—police issue, Taclite 2.0. Allegan County Sheriff's Department uses the 5.11 brand exclusively, and Taclite 2.0 style boots were issued to the entire department last year. The cast puts the boot at a size 12.5 E. George Taylor is one of only two officers in the county with that size. The other is out on medical for a knee replacement last week."

"I can't say I'm surprised. I'm just glad you got him. Especially after last night."

"Our surveillance spotted him checking out your house, but he must've seen us as well and figured he might have a better chance of getting you in public, without a constant eye on you. It almost worked," Agent Klein said. "When we grabbed him, he was in plainclothes and made it to the parking lot, running away like everyone else scared off by the gun shot. He'd gotten desperate, trying to stop you from exposing his theft of the Minkov."

"Were there witnesses to him shooting Britt?" she asked, curious. "Or did he confess?"

"No, and no," Jordan said. "But the bullet Dr. Gallager took out of Britt is a match for the personal handgun Taylor owns. And... guess where the agents found that 9.5 million dollar Minkov painting stashed?"

Savanna stared wide eyed from Jordan to Klein to Peele. "You found it already? That's amazing; Caroline must be thrilled!"

"It's early; we still have to tell her," Jordan said. "We removed the Minkov from Rosa Taylor's craft room around six this morning."

Savanna clapped a hand over her mouth, stunned. When she'd recovered from her shock, she asked, "Rosa knew? Did she know what it was and where it came from? She—"

Agent Klein smiled. "We don't think she knew. George had told her he'd bought it as a Christmas gift for her from some estate sale he'd gone to. Rosa thought it was ugly and planned to donate it somewhere after she'd left it hanging on the wall for long enough to make him happy."

"Oh jeez," Savanna said, laughing. "Can you imagine stopping in at our local Goodwill and finding a priceless painting? If only!"

A sharp knock at the door startled her. The desk sergeant poked her head in. "Taylor's lawyer's here."

Agent Klein pushed her chair back and stood. "That's our cue. He declined to speak with us without a lawyer. We'll have to finish—" The agent interrupted herself, looking first at Peele, then at Savanna. "This will actually wrap things up, either way, I feel certain. Would you like to observe with Jordan?"

"Yes! Please."

"Perfect. It'll give you more insight into what our team does. Ready?" Klein asked, turning to Peele.

In the darkened room opposite the interrogation room where George Taylor sat with his lawyer, Savanna peered through the two-way mirror, careful to keep her distance from the glass. She glanced at Jordan. "I know how this works, but it's always seemed wild to me that they can't see us."

He nodded. "But they know they're being observed. So, why do you need insight into what the FBI Art Crimes Team does?"

"Caught that, huh? Agent Klein mentioned I should consider doing some consulting work for them."

"Savanna. That's quite a compliment. So, you're thinking about it?"

"I'm... not not thinking about it," she said, her tone tentative. "I'm not sure what to think. Between teaching and my occasional work at the Lansing museum, I'm not sure where it'd fit. Something would have to go."

He nodded. "Sure. But... it's a rare thing to make an income doing something you love that you're also uniquely gifted in. Why wouldn't you do it?"

She pressed her lips together, staring at him. "I don't... I don't have a good answer for that," she said honestly. "I'll think about it. Thanks, Nick. That's really nice of you to say."

"It's not nice. It's true."

The two agents entered the room on the other side of the glass.

After some back and forth, without admitting anything outright, Detective Taylor leaned over and whispered something to his attorney, a stern-looking middle-aged woman in a navy suit. She shook her head. He said something else to her and she sighed and addressed the agents.

"My client would like to know about any leniency that might be granted were he to offer information helpful to your case against these..." She reviewed the papers in front of her. "Impressionist thieves."

"It would depend entirely on the value of the information shared by your client. Mr. Taylor, I want to make sure you understand the charges and the evidence we have concerning your actions last night as well as the missing Carson Minkov painting and the thefts and acts of vandalism at the museum the night of December 17. Any questions about the prosecutor's case against you?"

George Taylor swallowed hard. "For the museum charges, if—" He stopped, looking down at the attorney's fingertips on his arm, a warning gesture.

She put her head near his, speaking quietly, but not too quiet for Savanna to hear. "You'll incriminate yourself. Keep quiet."

Taylor moved his arm away from her, looking earnestly at Agent Klein. "If I were to tell you I witnessed the murder of Helene Devereaux, if I could describe in detail what I saw, how would that affect the charges against me?"

"In what capacity were you working at the museum, Mr. Taylor, when you witnessed that? A guard, or an accomplice?"

"Not an accomplice to her murder," he blurted, looking offended. "All I did was let them in and take the grids offline. That's it. I didn't know what was going to happen to Helene."

The attorney looked to the ceiling, shaking her head. She closed the leather folder on the table and sat back, crossing her legs, demeanor now disinterested.

"What happened to Helene?" Agent Klein asked. "You telling us what you saw can only help toward proving you didn't kill her."

"I wouldn't kill anyone. I mean… I didn't want to hurt Savanna, but I had no other way to stop her. I've never killed anyone," he said, tone firm.

Klein remained quiet, giving him a nod.

"Tate used our two-way radio to signal me they'd left the Impressionist area and were on their way back. I got the grid back online just as he and his team made it to the third floor with the paintings. On my screen, I saw Curator Devereaux pull Tate into her office. He wouldn't answer on the two-way. There's no visibility in the admin offices and no audio in security footage and we had a time constraint to get Tate's team out the south exit and Tate and me back to the gala to be seen and avoid suspicion. He'd been clear on that. I ran around the corner from the control room to admin to get him—they were fighting, Tate was shouting something about Helene lying and costing them a job? I know it doesn't make sense, I'm sorry. His team heard it all too."

"Do you recall exactly what you heard him shout at Helene?" Peele asked.

Taylor frowned. "Something like, you promised he'd do it. Why did you lie? You cost—or lost—us a job," he said. "Anyway, it got quiet, they came out, and it looked like they'd made up, everything seemed fine. I ran back to the control room, I had to take out the lobby's grid next. On screen in the admin hallway, I saw Tate and Helene get in the north elevator. He grabbed her—I thought he was kissing her. But when he let go of her, there was blood all over her neck and chest and she tried to grab him as he stepped out, but the doors closed. Tate wiped off whatever kind of knife he'd used to stab her on the admin hallway curtain."

Peele was furiously typing notes into a laptop while Klein maintained her position, her face somehow reflecting calm. "A lovers' quarrel or a fight over whatever Helene's role was in the Impressionist robberies; maybe both," she commented, completely ignoring the thousand other questions Savanna would've asked before that one.

"They'd been seeing each other, off and on—off while she was dating Britt at first, but this month I saw Tate leave her office a few times looking, uh, less than professional."

"Good to know. I wonder if the men Tate used for the Lansing museum job were the same guys with him in Chicago," Klein mused conversationally to Peele.

"They probably were," Taylor said, slipping unaware into cop mode. "Tate and those three were tight, each step of the plan seemed like… business as usual to them. I'd never seen them before that night. They all wore ski masks except for Tate. He was smooth—until about a week before the heist, I had no idea he was planning this."

"Interesting. So, he seems to have planted himself in his role well ahead of the planned rash of Impressionist robberies. But Tate had access to the museum and a high level of security clearance as team lead. Why did he need you?" she asked Taylor.

"It's his operation. I assume he needed me to let them in so his keycard wouldn't flag as swiped before the robbery, and he couldn't have dealt with the grids while also being in the Impressionist room. I was his right hand." The pride in Taylor's tone was unmistakable.

Savanna shuddered. "He enjoyed it. The whole ordeal."

"Sure sounds like it," Jordan agreed.

"Except, maybe, when Helene was killed. Hopefully."

THE INTERVIEW CONTINUED for another hour, George Taylor covering the more minute details with Agents Klein and Peele. When Klein came and fetched Savanna and Nick Jordan afterward, she searched Savanna's face. "Helpful?"

"Very," she said. "I just can hardly believe… do you know how many times I've crossed paths with Donald Tate, said good morning, sat in meetings with him? I had no idea. And Britt had no idea who Helene was screwing around with on the side."

"I'm sure it'll come out," Klein said. "You may want to tell Britt before that happens."

"I will," Savanna said. Klein walked with her while Jordan stepped into the interview room with Taylor. At the exit, Savanna gasped, pulling out her phone, remembering the thing she'd wanted to tell Agent Klein. She opened her camera roll to the two side by side screenshots she'd saved. "Look what I found. Your team has probably already figured this out, but I was excited to make the connection," she said, turning her phone so Klein could see it.

Klein's eyes widened, brows lifting. "Get. Out. No way," she breathed.

Savanna zoomed in on the first image. "This is our museum's vandalized *Taiga Desolation* by Sergei Minkov, determined to be a forgery. You see the red outline of the devil's face, the horns, and the Xs for eyes. And this one," she swiped, "is the calling card the St. Armand's art crime ring used at nearly every robbery in their first few years. They'd tag a wall, a door, the front steps, wherever they felt like painting it before leaving the scene."

"How did I miss that?" Klein said, shaking her head.

The image was a red outline of a devil's face, horns atop the head, and circles for eyes. "It's simple. I knew about this, I remember seeing it sometime in school, but it didn't occur to me either. Probably because it's too simple. We felt like the graffiti in the current case sent such a disrespectful message, the criminals thumbing their nose at us by ruining priceless artwork. We were half right. It is a message of disrespect, but it's not aimed at us. It's the Impressionist thieves running their victory lap around the St. Armand's group, painting the dead version of that stupid devil's face onto every St. Armand's forgery left in circulation while getting away with hundreds of millions in stolen art."

Chapter Twenty-Four

THE CARSON BALLROOM was dressed up for New Year's Eve. Savanna had never seen it look so lovely. Red brick and polished wooden flooring was set off with soft white light strands suspended from the vaulted ceiling, lush green foliage and Uncle Max's flower arrangements against white linen covered tables and chairs, and thousands of tiny white fairy lights that seemed to subtly dot every surface.

At one end, where the dance floor would be after dinner, Jack Carson had helped Uncle Max and Uncle Freddie set up the flower covered wedding arbor where a recovering Britt would officiate. Savanna flitted around the ballroom in jeans and sweatshirt an hour before it was all set to start, straightening place cards, taste-testing Chef Joe's delicious concoctions, and making sure the band had everything they needed. Skylar finally took her by the arm, forcing her to the dressing room where Charlotte helped her into her gorgeous silk and chiffon wedding gown, she'd discovered at the first bridal shop they'd gone to. With delicate spaghetti straps, a scoop back, and a sweetheart bodice that narrowed to her waist, the gown flowed into a full skirt that fell like sparkling snow drifts to the floor, elegant and timeless.

Sydney put the finishing touches on her hair and

makeup, and then Savanna used the corner of a baby wipe from Skylar to gently scrub off half the eye shadow and liner until she looked more like herself, but fancier. She peeked out into the ballroom and caught a glimpse of little miss fancy herself, Mollie, dancing in a giggling circle with Nolan and a teetering baby Hannah. The ballroom was glowing with joy and laughter as guests filtered in, the room spacious even with the sixty-something guests she and Aidan had invited.

Yvonne slipped in and shut the dressing room door behind her. "Oh, my stars, Savanna." She hugged her. "I'm so happy for you. Are you ready?"

"I'm so ready." She watched as, one by one, Sydney, Skylar, Ellie, and Yvonne each took their turn walking down the red-carpet aisle through the middle of friends and family she cherished. Her father stood beside her and she slipped her hand through his elbow. She looked up at him, waiting for him to begin, and was met with her dad's tear-filled gaze. He took a deep breath, and she did the same. Harlan covered her hand on his arm with his own and they walked.

In the eternity it took to reach Aidan, her future husband never took his eyes off her. He met her and her dad at the head of the aisle as they approached. Harlan put out a hand, bringing Aidan toward him as they shook. She didn't hear what her dad said, but Aidan nodded, once, face somber. Harlan hugged him, saying something else, and Aidan smiled. "Always," he said.

Under the wedding arbor, Britt spoke of love and commitment, starting over and second chances, and all the different incarnations of family. "The bride and groom have prepared their own vows," Britt said.

Savanna smiled at Aidan, any nervousness she'd had an hour ago, five minutes ago, disappearing in his gaze. "I wasn't sure how to write my vows," she began, trying and failing to brush away a loose strand of hair tickling her face.

Aidan's fingertips grazed her temple as he carefully caught and moved the tendril. His hand lingered before dropping, as if he'd forgotten they were surrounded by dozens of people.

Thank you," she whispered, making him smile. She started again. "Two years ago, when I tried to lasso you with poodle leashes the first time we met, I never imagined myself here, in this spot, marrying you. But today, I realized that we were here, in this spot, two years ago when I fell in love with you. I still remember how I felt sitting on the piano bench with you, your shoulder touching mine," she said, briefly touching her shoulder. Her tone grew softer. "I asked you to play something for me, and you did. I never told you that I sang the words to "Falling Slowly" out loud and in my head, over and over for a week afterward. I love you and Mollie so much. I promise to spend an eternity making sure you feel as loved and cherished as you've made me feel ever since that day."

Aidan gave her hand, in his, a squeeze. He tipped his head down, swallowing hard, before raising his gaze back to hers. She slid his ring onto his hand, holding onto it. She was happy to spend the next sixty years counting the flecks of gold in his lake-blue eyes.

He spoke. "Savanna. That day, when you tried to lasso me with poodle leashes, you brought light back into my life. After a very dark time, when I'd forgotten what hope felt like, you reminded me. When I played "Falling Slowly" for you, I was lying to myself. I'd already fallen, quickly and completely. So," he said, letting go of her hand and fetching Mollie from the first row with her grandparents, "these vows have two parts. Mollie?" He handed her a note card. Savanna saw that it was printed in the eight-year-old girl's handwriting with purple pen.

"I p-promise to hug you every day," she began in her soft, high voice. "I promise to always make us be matchy. I promise to always be good. And I promise to be your daughter. Daddy said my mommy in heaven would want me to have a second mama."

Savanna bent down, close to Mollie. "I think he's right. I promise to be your second mama, Mollie, and sometimes you might not always feel like being good, but guess what? That's okay. I promise I will always love you no matter what."

The girl wrapped her small arms around Savanna, hugging her. "Thank you," she whispered. "Mama," she added, trying it out.

Savanna smiled, the sweetness of this girl, this moment, this overwhelming love forcing sudden tears to her eyes. "That sounds perfect," she whispered.

Mollie returned to her grandparents, smiling at Savanna and swinging her legs once she sat down.

"Now mine," Aidan said, flashing a grin at her. "I promise to make you laugh. I promise to play your requests on piano. I promise to work on my first-mate sailing skills. I promise to be present, and when I can't, I promise to make it up to you. I promise you exotic vacations and sunset sails and family camping under the stars. I promise you my heart. I promise you will never doubt how much you are loved. I promise you forever, Savanna." He placed the ring on her finger, his warm hands around hers the only thing keeping her from floating on her little cloud of happiness right up to the ceiling.

Britt cleared their throat, wincing and pressing one hand to their left side. "Ow." Britt produced a tissue and dabbed at the tears on their cheeks. "All righty then," they said, "by the power vested in me by the state of Michigan, I pronounce you husband and wife. You may now commence the kissing part." Britt gave a quick thumbs-up to Mollie. She'd come along with Savanna two days ago to help Britt get settled back at home, and she'd created in Britt another *Princess Bride* fan after watching the movie twice in a row.

Aidan caught Savanna mid-laugh, sweeping her into his arms and kissing her deeply. When she drifted back to earth, she murmured, "The kissing part's my favorite."

Before the reception got into full swing, Aidan stole her away briefly, leading her out into the vestibule. Big, fluffy white snowflakes fell in gusts outside, making the glow inside the ballroom even cozier. He drew two plain white envelopes from his tux jacket pocket. "I know we've talked about a honeymoon, but I really think we should have two." He handed her the first envelope.

Inside was a travel itinerary for a family trip to Hawaii, the front of the resort brochure a beachy photo with the bluest ocean she'd ever seen. "Oh! This looks amazing! Thank you, Aidan. Does Mollie know yet? We'll have the best time!" He was amazing.

"Mollie helped me choose Hawaii and that particular resort for mid-winter break from school. She won't be interested in the second one." He grinned, handing her the second envelope. "This one's just for us."

She gasped. She had to reread the ten-day travel plan before it really sunk in—he'd planned a tour of the best art museums in and around Europe, starting in with the Louvre, from Paris to London to Rome, and then south to coastal Mondello for three days. She stared at him. "You're too much. This is too much."

He laughed. "Nothing's too much for you. For us."

She wrapped her arms around him, overcome. Marriage, instant motherhood, double honeymoons, an expanded home for her new family, a potential new venture with the FBI... everything was about to change. With Aidan by her side, anything was possible.

The End

Acknowledgements

Thank you, dear reader, for taking this journey with the Shepherd sisters and their community. I have enjoyed every moment I've spent in their world. So many of the characters in this series feel like old friends to me. I am forever grateful for the opportunity to greet these imaginary friends who appear without warning in my mind, to get to know them, to learn about their hopes and dreams and worries and goals while discovering the stories they have to tell. You're the reason I get to do this.

When I stop writing, in the middle or at the end of a book, to step away for whatever reason, I always feel like I've left my characters—my friends who've grown to trust me—standing in the middle of the road, peering into the distance and waiting for me to come back and finish their story. So, I am eternally grateful to Tule Publishing for bringing this series into the world. Jane Porter, Meghan Farrell, Kelly Hunter, Julie Sturgeon, Lee Hyat, Mia Gleason, Cyndi Parent, Jaiden Colling, and indeed the entire Tule team have been phenomenal in championing these books. Editor Kelly Hunter homed in on fine details and major scenes alike, providing me with invaluable insights and notes to help shape this manuscript into the story it was always meant to be. Thank you so much.

A world of thanks to my superhero literary agent, Frances Black, who has believed in my writing since I began my journey with her way back in 2012. Fran, you are amazing and I'm so grateful to have you in my corner!

Long before I started writing with a mind toward publishing, I was a shy, awkward thirteen-year-old in Mrs. Nancy Stoner's advanced placement seventh-grade English class. Mrs. Stoner is a brilliant woman with shining blonde hair, a kind smile, and the unique ability to make an introvert like me want to be heard. In her class, I learned about the magic to be found in books. I learned that I enjoyed the act of putting one word after another after another until they began to flow like a melody. I discovered the transportive effect of losing myself in words, whether reading or writing them—any reader (or writer) knows that feeling. You are no longer interpreting words on a page or extracting them from your brain to tell the story; you're in the story, experiencing it all happening around you. My seventh-grade English teacher changed my life. Thank you, Mrs. Stoner, for giving me the lifelong love of books. You created a writer.

Talented London artist Charlotte Lonsdale of CL Designs Studio Art created the absolutely adorable town map of Carson, Michigan, in the front of this book (and each one in the series). It's prettier than I could've imagined. I can picture the characters there!

My life has been shaped by my family. My husband Joe is everything I wished for when I was that shy, awkward teenager dreaming of my future husband. Thank you, Joe, for always cheering me on throughout my writing journey.

Thank you, Katy, Joey, and Halle, for not thinking Mom's crazy when she's on deadline... or maybe just for your love and kindness despite my frantic race to the finish line, no matter how lengthy a time I had to get there.

Big thanks to my beloved circle of family and friends, including my mom Joni Gardner, my little sister Julie Velentzas, my always-first readers Ann Sullivan and Rocsana Oana, and so many wonderful, supportive author friends and book community friends who make me feel like most of my writerly angst is perfectly normal. You guys rock.

Much love and gratitude to you, wonderful reader. I hope you find something of yourself in the sisters and their world. Enjoy!

Skylar's Ham and Split Pea Soup

Ingredients

- ¼ cup unsalted butter
- 1 & ½ cups chopped onion
- 1 cup diced carrot
- 1 & ½ cup diced celery
- ½ to 1 teaspoon salt, to taste
- ½ teaspoon pepper
- 1 & ½ teaspoons minced garlic
- 1 pound dried split peas, rinsed and sorted
- 1 pound ham, any combination of diced and ham from ham hock, ham bone
- 2 small bay leaves
- 2 teaspoons fresh chopped thyme leaves
- 6 cups chicken stock
- 2 cups water
- Oyster crackers

Instructions

In a large pot, melt butter over medium heat. Add onion, carrot, celery, ¼ teaspoon salt and ½ teaspoon pepper. Cook until vegetables are softened, 5-8 minutes.

Add garlic and cook for 1 minute, until aromatic. Stir in split peas.

Add chicken stock and water. Then add ham bone, fresh thyme, and bay leaves.

Bring to a boil, reduce heat, and simmer uncovered for about 90 minutes, stirring occasionally, or until split peas are cooked down and soup is thickened to desired consistency.

Stir often, as the soup begins to thicken. During the last 15 minutes of cooking, add diced ham.

Additional stock or water can be added if soup becomes too thick or on day 2 of serving (when soup flavor is typically even better).

When ready to serve, remove and discard ham bone and bay leaf. Season to taste with salt if needed. Serve hot with or without oyster crackers. Serve with garlic bread if preferred.

If you enjoyed *A Brush with Murder*,
check out the other books in the

The Shepherd Sisters Mysteries series

Book 1: *Death by Deception*

Book 2: *Murder on Display*

Book 3: *Still Life and Death*

Book 4: *A Brush with Murder*

Book 5: *A Stroke of Murder*

Available now at your favorite online retailer!

About the Author

Tracy Gardner is an Edgar Award nominated author of two cozy mystery series, one recent novel earning a spot on New York Public Library's Best 100 Books list. Tracy also writes book club fiction with heart and grit under pen name Jess Sinclair. A Detroit native with one foot in the sand of Florida's Gulf Coast, Tracy is a mother of three, the daughter of two teachers, and works as a nurse when not writing. She lives with her husband and a menagerie of spoiled rescue dogs and cats who inspire every fictional pet she writes.

Thank you for reading

A Stroke of Murder

If you enjoyed this book, you can find more from all our great authors at TulePublishing.com, or from your favorite online retailer.

TULE
PUBLISHING